Death Gems

Book One

"Soul Stealers"

JACK O'DONNELL

Visit www.jack-odonnell.com to see more works written by this author.

Visit www.landoffright.com to learn more about Jack O'Donnell's Land of Fright™ series of weird tales.

Visit www.odonnell-books.com to see more works published by ODONNELL BOOKS.

CHAPTER ONE

Junto Kral studied the portrait of the man. It was a rough sketch done in charcoal on a torn piece of parchment, but the drawing still revealed the dark cruelty in the man's face, the blatant threat of menace in his eyes. The man's name was Ulster VoGrat. And he was a bad man. Plain and simple. A violent killer.

And Junto had to stop him.

Junto looked at the death gems on Ulster's face. There were four gems buried in his forehead in a straight row, each gem about two inches in diameter, each somewhat circular in shape, each with faceted surfaces that helped give them their name. Death gems. Another two gems dotted his left cheek, positioned vertically, and one more gem was visible on his right cheek, positioned a few inches down from his right eye and off to the right of his nose. Sometimes these killers kept their death gems hidden on their backs or chests, or beneath their clothing on their arms or legs, but not Ulster. He proudly displayed them across his whole damn face.

Ulster was a soul stealer and he wanted everyone to know it.

Junto looked over to the slender woman sitting across from him. The burning candle on the table cast a pleasant glow on Sekanna's features, caressing her skin with flickering touches of orange or yellow light, blending corn silk color with a pastel orange hue, then throwing in splashes of amber light. Sekanna was a good half a foot shorter than Junto's six-foot frame, with a muscular sleekness to her exposed arms that was similar to Junto's muscular arms but in a much more feminine way. "Where did you see him last?" Junto asked.

Sekanna looked up from her mug. She was a platinum blonde with searing blue eyes, in stark contrast to Junto's black hair and deep chestnut eyes. "Near the whore camp," she said. She was a strikingly beautiful woman, who could be both charming and abrasive, with a mix of Northern gentility and Southern crudity that had clearly been bestowed upon her by her mixed parents; her barbed-tongue Southern mother had given her the streak of abrasiveness, of that Junto was certain. Her skin remained a pale white no matter how much exposure to the sun she received; again another stark contrast to Junto's deeply tanned bronze skin.

Junto tilted his head to the side and raised an eyebrow.

"I was just checking on someone," Sekanna said and frowned. She looked away and sat back in her chair.

Junto waited for her to continue, prodding her with a slight cock of his head, but she did not elaborate. He waited a moment longer, but she still said nothing more.

He glanced up, looking away from her. They were in the trophy room of their manor home. At least that's what Sekanna had nicknamed the room. Junto didn't like the name, but it had stuck. Two of the walls were plastered with charcoal portraits of other soul stealers. Each portrait only made it onto the wall if they had captured the soul stealer, or if they could confirm the soul stealer was now dead. The portrait had a large red circle around the subject if they were captured, with the number of the cell they occupied scrawled beneath their face. Any portrait of a known dead soul stealer was crossed out with a very unsubtle large red X. One wall was completely full of portraits, about thirty in all, while a second wall was nearly a quarter filled. Only a few of the portraits were marked with any red circle, and even fewer with a red X.

A small shelving unit made of wood, comprised of numerous square slots, was positioned near a third wall. Dozens of rolled-up parchments filled many of the slots, each of them containing a drawing of a suspected or known soul stealer, or scribbled notes that contained clues to the whereabouts of a soul stealer; some were maps of villages where suspected or known soul stealers were rumored to live.

Looking at the portraits, staring at the dozens of unmarked faces of the soul stealers still running wild in the world, often sent a wave of exhaustion flooding over Junto; they had a lot of work ahead of them. He looked back to Sekanna. "Any idea what he was doing there?" Junto asked.

Sekanna shook her head. She took a drink from

her mug, then added, "Well, there's one thing he might be doing in a whore's camp."

"Besides the obvious, I mean."

Sekanna again shook her head.

"And you are sure it was him?" Junto asked.

She motioned towards the parchment he held in his hand with a flick of her head. "Look at him. He's pretty hard to miss, don't you think? I think he had at least one more death gem on his face that's not in his portrait, another one on his right cheek."

Junto laid the parchment down on the table, staring at Ulster's portrait. "Cell five is ready. We can put him in there."

"Is that the deep one?"

Junto nodded. "Takes a thirty foot ladder to reach the bottom and the walls are as smooth as glass."

Sekanna nodded. She was quiet for a moment and a sour expression twisted her sensual mouth into a puckered grimace. "I wish we could just kill these bastards and be done with them."

Junto had heard her mutter that wish a hundred times over the last few years, but now it came out of her lips more as a habit than with any true conviction. He knew that she understood well enough why they couldn't do that. Not now and not ever.

"Maybe Zerin will do it," she mused.

Junto shook his head. "Zerin is trying to atone for what he has done. Not add to his collection."

She said nothing. "I still think we should use him like the animal he is." She made no attempt to hide the contempt in her voice. "Who says he even deserves a chance at redemption."

"Everyone but you," Junto muttered.

"He had seven death gems on his body. Seven! Not one or two. Seven!"

"All the more reason to keep Zerin as an ally and not as an enemy."

"He'll never be an ally of mine," Sekanna said, her voice firm. "You just don't atone for what he did."

Junto let it go. It was an argument he feared he would never win with Sekanna. She seemed calm in appearance most of the time, a layer of grace her Northern father had bestowed upon her, but Junto knew she had a boiling pot of emotion constantly bubbling beneath the surface, one that could erupt at any moment. Besides, Zerin was tracking a lead in Yoknari and he might be gone for several more weeks, if not months, so his participation on this particular mission was not even an option.

Junto rolled up the parchment portrait of Ulster and slid a silver metal ring over it to keep it tightly rolled. "You think he's still there?"

Sekanna shrugged. "He certainly seemed like he was going to be awhile. He had three women with him. All whores by the looks of them."

Junto raised an eyebrow, but made no comment on that. "I'll bring Irchly with us," Junto said. "No sense in getting too close to a man with that many death gems." Irchly was their best archer, as well as the best with the throwing daggers. The man had an uncanny accuracy with projectiles of all kinds. Irchly was constantly in the weapons hall practicing, so his skills were finely honed by the ruthless rituals he put himself through to keep his form sharp. Junto sometimes pined for the skills Irchly had, but he knew he didn't have the tolerance, or the patience, for the amount of practice Irchly put in to keep his skills at such an extremely high level.

"Ulster is big," Sekanna said. "I'd say use a double dose of blackout. And even that might not be enough to knock him out."

Junto nodded. "Did he have anybody else with him?"

Sekanna shook her head. "No one that I saw beside those three whores, but that doesn't mean anything. I didn't really get that good of a look at them." She shrugged. "There could be others there I just didn't see." She took another drink from her mug.

Junto sat quietly for a moment. He raised the rolled parchment and gave it a quick shake. "You ready to catch a soul stealer?"

CHAPTER TWO

Ulster thought of killing the blonde woman after he finished with her. She was a lifeless slug, just lying on the bed as he pumped into her. She made no sound, not even a fake moan of pleasure. As whores go, she was the worst he had ever had. She had closed her eyes the moment he mounted her and hadn't opened them since. Did she really expect him to pay her? He looked over to one of the other whores waiting her turn. "What is wrong with her?" he asked, looking down at the blonde woman beneath him, then over to the purple-haired whore sitting in the chair near the bed. A third whore, a slender raven-haired woman with pale skin, was asleep on the floor, curled up on a thick sheepskin rug; an empty, overturned mug rested near her.

"She's afraid of you," the whore in the chair said. "She don't like all them death gems on your body." Ulster vaguely remembered this purple-haired whore's name was Tallie.

"You know what they are?" Ulster asked her.

Tallie nodded. "Sure. Everyone round here does." Tallie pointed to the death gems on his face. "Means you killed them people and ate their souls."

Ulster laughed. His voice was deep and hearty,

his mirth genuine. He was a big man, about six and a half feet tall, with a large, squarish face and a square jaw. His brown hair was cut short, tightly cropped to his large skull. His skin was a dark brown, deeply tanned by prolonged exposure to the sun, his flesh having a slight leathery look to it, but still supple and smooth. "I ate their souls? Never heard it put that way before." He paused and laughed again. "But I kind of like it."

The blonde whore beneath Ulster kept her eyes closed and her mouth shut as he continued to move in and out of her.

Tallie rose up out of the chair and cautiously moved over to the bed. She was dressed in a lavender-hued sheer negligee that left little to the imagination. Her large breasts shifted slightly as she approached him, her nipples pointed and erect, pushing against the fabric. Her pubic hair was dyed a vibrant purple. She reached up towards a death gem that was sunk into the flesh on Ulster's right shoulder, moving her vibrantly colored purple nails closer to him. The gem seemed to glow ever so slightly with a reddish tint. Her fingers hesitated before touching the crystalline surface of the gem. "They really in you?" Tallie asked. The death gem was warm to the touch.

Ulster glanced at Tallie, continuing to thrust into the blonde whore lying listlessly beneath him. He looked down at the death gem in his shoulder where Tallie was touching him. "That one was some fool who looked at me the wrong way. I stuck a sword in his gut and pulled his intestines out with it." He looked at Tallie. "You know what happened after that?"

She didn't answer.

"He stopped looking at me the wrong way." Ulster laughed a hearty laugh.

Tallie withdrew her fingers, lowering her hand to her side.

Ulster grinned at the distraught look on Tallie's face. "Don't worry. I don't have any whores in me." He paused. "Not yet at least." He laughed again. He continued to thrust into the blonde whore, giving his thrusts a little more vigorous momentum. The blonde whore clenched her eyes closed even tighter.

Tallie didn't find his comment amusing at all. She was quiet for a moment, staring at the death gem on Ulster's shoulder. The small jewel-like object shimmered in the candlelight, continuing to give off a very faint glow. "So where is he? Is he trapped in the death gem?"

Ulster stopped thrusting and pulled out of the whore on the bed. He was disgusted by her lack of reaction to him. She wasn't even wet and his member was starting to chafe in her dryness, which only served to fuel his aggravation. "You ask a lot of questions." He moved to sit on the edge of the bed. He grabbed a chalice from a nearby side table, drained it completely of its contents, and tossed the empty chalice to the floor.

"I'm just curious," Tallie said. "I never been with a soul eater before." She looked at him. "So is he trapped in there?" She pointed at the death gem on Ulster's shoulder.

"Yes. I suppose you could say he's trapped. Or at least his life-force is. But that's all that's left of him anyway so, yes, you could say he's trapped."

"You... talk to him?" Tallie asked.

Ulster squinted an ugly squint at her. "What?"

"Do you... talk to him?"

Ulster shook his head. "No. It doesn't work that way. I don't talk to any of them."

"So what do you do with them?"

"They give me life."

"They give you life?" Tallie frowned curiously.

Ulster pointed to several blackened gems that dotted the back of his left shoulder. "See those? They used to be alive. Now they are dead. I used their life-force."

"You used their life?" She reached out and touched one of the blackened gems. None of these dark gems had any hint of the subtle shimmering glow, making them stand out from the other gems because of their deep blackness. The black death gem was icy cold to the touch. She quickly pulled her hand away.

He nodded. "When I needed to. So I can keep living."

Tallie was quiet for a moment, thinking. "Like when you get stabbed or something?" she asked.

"Yes. Or shot with an arrow. Or poisoned. Or slashed with an axe. They keep me from taking that final trip to Hell's Wood."

"You got a lot of black gems on you," she commented.

He laughed. "I've got a lot of people trying to make me stop breathing."

Tallie looked at the glistening death gems on his face, then glanced at a few others adorning his body. "I see like ten of the shiny ones. That mean you got ten lives left?"

"Don't matter. I don't plan on ever running out." He reached for the blonde whore's throat, clutching at her neck with a deathly grip, yanking her to a sitting position. She finally opened her eyes and stared at Ulster with wide blue orbs. She grabbed at his big hand with both of her hands, gagging under his vicious squeeze.

"Now she wants to talk," Ulster said derisively. He looked over at Tallie, keeping his grip firm and deathly tight around the blonde whore's throat. "Want to watch how it's done?"

Tallie just stared as he started to strangle the blonde whore with an ever tightening grip.

"She ain't a friend of yours, is she?" Ulster asked.

Tallie said nothing.

The raven-haired whore sleeping on the floor didn't move during the attack. She just continued to snore softly.

The blonde whore fought back, slapping and grabbing at Ulster, but he was far too strong for her to fend off. Ulster put both of his big hands around her throat, continuing to squeeze, his grip tightening. After a few moments, when the whore's eyes were open and glassy, Ulster took his hands from her throat and let her body fall back onto the bed.

"Now comes the fun part," Ulster said. "You only get a few minutes before the life-force leaks away. That's when you need to steal it." He looked at Tallie. "Or eat it, if that's how you prefer to describe it." Ulster reached into a leather bag that rested on a small side table near the bed and pulled out a small wooden box. He opened the box and reached inside. He gingerly removed a death beetle, making certain to grip the creature on the back, clutching at the edges of its shell, making certain not to let any of the creature's tendril-like legs touch his own flesh.

The death beetle was a small creature about two inches long and an inch wide. Its back was a hard shell that looked like a gem; this particular death beetle had a dusty brown coloring to its shell. Numerous weaving tendril-legs wiggled in the air beneath the death beetle's body, giving it somewhat the appearance of a cross between a beetle and a tiny jellyfish.

Ulster lowered the death beetle towards one of the dead whore's bare breasts. The creatures long, slender legs acted much more like tendrils than legs now, wiggling excitedly as they neared her flesh. He set the creature down on the dead blonde whore and sat back. The death beetle immediately sank its tendril-legs deep into the whore's chest.

Tallie watched, rapt with fascination and utter fear.

The creature pulsed and throbbed, its hard shell starting to take on a vibrant red color. The death beetle flared for just a brief second, glowing brightly hot.

"There," Ulster said, pointing to the glow, making no attempt to hide his excited enthusiasm. "It's absorbing the life-force right out of her."

After a few moments, the pulsing beat of light

waned and the creature was still.

Ulster grabbed at the now scintillating red shell of the death beetle and tugged sharply, pulling at the creature. He had to pull hard to rip the tendrils from the whore's dead flesh. The tendrils came free with a sharp ripping sound. Some blood dripped down from the wriggling tendrils as Ulster raised the death beetle up. Ulster held the creature pinched between his fingers, the blood-stained tendrils wriggling wildly. He looked at Tallie. "Where do you think I should put it?"

"How about on your cock?"

Ulster frowned at her. "I ain't that crazy." He glanced down at the back of his left hand. The skin was bare. He lowered the creature down towards his hand. The tendrils seemed to sense they were getting close to his flesh because they started to wriggle wildly with great intensity. He continued to lower the creature until the tendrils reached his hand. He gritted his teeth as the tendrils sunk into his flesh. He let go of the creature as it wriggled and settled itself firmly against his skin, the tendrils now sunk deep into his flesh.

Ulster closed his eyes, a euphoric warmth spreading through his entire body. Another life-force claimed. Another future death countered. He savored the sensation, enjoying the warm tingling feeling that ran the entire length of his body. The tips of his fingers and the edges of his toes thrummed with a delicious pulse. Not only did soul stealing bring wondrous physical pleasure, it also brought a layer of mental security and comfort because he had just given himself another chance at forestalling his final death. You could never have too many chances to avoid that final trip to Hell's Wood.

Tallie watched him quietly, afraid to disturb him. When he opened his eyes again, she pointed to the wooden box. "Can I have one of those?"

Ulster looked at her in a dreamy haze, still enjoying the tingling sensation that permeated his entire body. "You'll have to kill somebody first."

Tallie wasn't fazed. She glanced at the raven-haired whore sleeping on the rug nearby, then looked back to Ulster. "And then you'll give me one?"

Ulster looked at Tallie and grinned. "I'm really starting to like you."

Tallie smiled back. She leaned closer to him and reached for him.

CHAPTER THREE

Junto looked down at the blonde whore's corpse. A ragged wound on her breast marked the spot where the death beetle had fed on her soul.

Junto absently rubbed at the death gem he held in his hand. It was black. Empty of life. Empty of soul. It was attached to a leather cord that he wore around his neck. It was a constant reminder of his failure to save the life-force that had been held within it. A constant reminder of his mission. A constant reminder of his purpose in Moraneesh. Once a life-force was used by a soul stealer, the death gem that had contained the life-force turned black as coal. The life-force, the soul of the unfortunate victim, was gone forever and there was no getting it back.

Death gem. He frowned at the name. It wasn't really a gem. The death gems had earned their death gem name because of their physical resemblance to gemstones; their outer surfaces were hard and shiny, and multi-faceted like gems. But they were anything but precious jewels.

Junto turned the depleted death gem over, staring at the curled up tendrils of the creature. The five tendril-legs on this death beetle were shriveled to the width of sewing thread, nearly non-existent. He knew the tendrils were used to latch on to human skin, to burrow into human flesh. They had a dual purpose. They were used both to feed on a soul by draining its life-force out of a body before its soul had a chance to escape, and then to feed that stolen life-force back into a human body when its host needed an influx of life-force to preserve its own life.

He did not know where the creatures had come from or how they had come into their world, but there was no denying the fact that they existed. They were creatures with an unholy power now harnessed by the soul stealers. They fed on souls. They fed on death. And there was no denying the fact that he and Sekanna and Irchly and the others in their group would have to fight their insidious use to the end of their days. He had no idea how many more death beetles existed in the world, and he had no illusions that they could rid the world of them forever. He didn't know if the death beetles extended beyond the coasts of Moraneesh and had infested other countries on the distant shores of the Panalaga Ocean or on the far side of the Torian Sea, but he couldn't concern himself with their reach right now; they had enough to do in their own home country. All they could do was keep fighting against them, keep fighting those who chose to use their ugly power for their own vile purposes.

Junto glanced over at Irchly who was leaning down over the other body in the room. Irchly was about a foot shorter than Junto, standing five and a half feet tall. He was wiry, muscular but slender.

His right bicep was slightly larger than his left because he preferred to draw his heavy bow with his right hand and that preference caused a slight imbalance in his muscle growth. He seemed to have a perpetual layer of stubble darkening his slender face, and Junto was pretty certain that was as long as Irchly's facial hair was ever going to grow.

"She's dead," Irchly said. "They DG'd her, too."

Junto frowned. Both whores had been death gemmed. Ulster was really getting out of control. It was rare for a soul stealer to death gem two victims at the same time.

Irchly continued to stare down at the raven-haired dead woman at his feet. Junto could see the pain on his face. Irchly never took a death well, but this one seemed to be troubling him much more than usual. "What is it?" Junto asked.

"I..." Irchly started to speak, but then stopped.

Junto rose up and moved over to him. He stared down at the naked woman, at the ugly red gash in her stomach, at her pale, pasty skin. And then he understood the reason for Irchly's discomfort. He felt the same pain spearing through him. They knew her. They knew this dead woman. They knew this woman who just had her soul stolen. Her name was Oriala.

She was Sekanna's sister.

"You'd better tell Sekanna to come in here," Junto said.

Irchly pursed his lips and nodded a sad nod.

17

Sekanna slammed the mug down on the table. "I should have dragged her ass out of that fucking camp!"

Junto stayed silent. Irchly just stared into his mug. They were in Grimroy's Ale and Cheese Shop, sitting in one of the back booths. The tavern was bustling with activity, patrons demanding more ale, serving wenches and serving swains skillfully moving amongst the throng delivering drink and food expertly balanced on serving trays.

Sekanna stared at the two men sitting across from her. "Say something! Yell at me! Blame me! It's all my fault Oriala is dead! My fault!"

It was her fault. They all knew it. Junto didn't even know her sister had been in the whore camp. If he had known, he would have dragged her out of there himself. But Sekanna had never told them. "You should have told me," Junto finally said.

"Yeah, I should have," Sekanna said. She took a drink. "Oriala didn't want me to. She begged me not to tell you. And the fool that I am, I listened to her. She said she liked the coin. She said the men were mostly nice to her and she could easily manipulate them with a smile and a moan, get them to stay a little longer and give her more coin. She made more coin in a month in the camp than she made in a year on the farm." Sekanna stared at her mug. "Little good all that coin does her now." She took another angry drink, quickly tipping the mug up to her lips.

"We need to find Ulster," Junto said. "We need to free Oriala before it's too late."

Sekanna frowned. "You think I don't know that?" The question was laced with bitterness and self-loathing. "I'll kill him if I see him."

"And be tied to his soul for all eternity because you were the one who took his life?" Junto shook his head. "You don't want that Sekanna. Despite what you feel right now, you do not want that."

Sekanna said nothing. She fumed silently for a moment. "No one even knows if that's true," she finally said. "Maybe when you kill someone, they are just gone. Maybe you are not tied to their soul for all eternity. Maybe that just isn't true."

Junto stared hard at her. "Is that a chance you want to take? We're talking all of eternity here. Not a week. Not a month. Not years. All eternity."

"I get what eternity means," Sekanna said.

"Then you should get how foolish you're talking," Junto said. "You would want to attach your soul to a man you hate? You would risk that? He would be with you forever in the Everlasting."

"Yeah? Well, then maybe I could torture him for what he did forever." Sekanna's expression was grim, her words laced with a bitter edge.

Irchly looked up from his mug and frowned at her. "You're really going to get yourself into trouble one day, Sekanna." He absently picked up a toothpick from one of the small cheese cubes that half-filled a plate before them, weighed it in his hand for a brief moment, and then flung it with uncanny accuracy and amazing velocity at a passing patron, sinking the toothpick into the side of the man's mug, right between two of the man's fingers; the man didn't even notice.

"You think?" Sekanna raised her mug and downed the remaining liquid in one gulp.

Junto lifted up the rolled parchment that contained Ulster's portrait sketch. "We need to ask around the camp. I'm sure someone else took notice of him. Maybe they'll know where he's headed or at least in what direction he went."

"Yeah, I seen him," Volina said. Volina was a woman far past her prime. She may have been pretty to look at once, but she was no longer close to being a vision of beauty. Her skin was as wrinkled as a plum left out for too long and her flesh had a fading yellow sheen to it, a sure sign of either a beginning khack leaf addiction or a recently ended one. Her hair was more white than black and it was clearly thinning at the top.

"Here?" Junto asked her. They had made several inquiries around the whore camp and the answers to those inquiries had led them to Volina's quarters. It was a cramped little tent with one small table, a few chairs, and a very old bed frame and mattress in the corner. A few small candles lit the area in a feeble glow.

Sekanna sat next to Junto. Irchly stood near the tent flap, practicing his quick draw of one of the throwing daggers he kept tucked in his belt, adroitly sliding the weapon from its place and mimicking a throwing motion, then sliding the dagger back into place at his waist.

"You saw him here in the camp?" Junto asked.

Volina nodded. "He went off with Tallie. She had one of them death gem things right smack in the middle of her forehead. Looked damned ugly if you ask me."

Junto frowned. It appeared this whore name Tallie had joined forces with Ulster. Now they needed to find both of them. They didn't know which one was holding on to Oriala's life-force. "Where did they go?"

Volina frowned at him. "I look like a tracker to you? I ain't got one fuck of an idea where that bitch went." The whore raised her mug. "Here's hoping she has to travel all five rings of Hell's Wood before she finds eternal peace."

Sekanna frowned at the whore. "What did she do to you?"

"She stole some of my regulars." Volina huffed in indignation. "I was doing fine 'til she got here."

Sekanna looked at Volina's bloated face, her fat forearms. "Maybe you lost some of your regulars because you're—"

Junto grabbed Sekanna's arm, stopping her mid-sentence. He gave her a slight shake of his head. Sekanna was about to say something more, but then closed her mouth. Junto pulled his hand away from her arm. He turned back to the whore. "It's very important that we find her and the man she was with."

"Ain't important to me," Volina said and raised her shoulders with an exaggerated shrug.

Sekanna scowled and curled her fingers around her sword handle. She opened her mouth, but another sharp glance from Junto kept her quiet. She slowly loosened her grip on her sword.

Junto reached into the coin pouch at his waist and pulled out some coins. He laid them down on the scarred wooden table.

Volina glanced down at the glistening coins as they twinkled at her in the candlelight. It was enough for a week's worth of food. Or at the very least a few days of khack leaf. "Getting more important the longer I sit here." Then she shrugged. "But still ain't that important." She took a longer, slower sip from her mug. "Important," she mused. "Import ant," she said, breaking up the word into two. "Import ant. Kind of like bringing in some ants, right? All them little bits of knowledge I got is like little ants churning around in my head and you want to bring them out of my head and into your head. You want to import my ants, get it?" She smiled and seemed very pleased with herself.

"Is this where philosophers end up?" Sekanna asked. "That's kind of what I figured would happen in the end when their words start making no sense." She stared hard at the whore. "Ain't got much else use for them."

Volina looked at Sekanna, then looked to Junto. "Ain't you giving her any? I think you need to feed her some of your meat stick a little more often. She is scrunched up tight."

Sekanna fumed, but said nothing.

Irchly grinned from his position near the tent flap, but made damn sure Sekanna didn't see him doing it. He continued practicing with his daggers.

Junto laid a few more coins on the table. "Now how about those ants? You feel them crawling around in your brain looking for the exit?"

Volina looked down at the growing array of coins set before her on the table. She reached out and slowly pulled them closer to her. "Sure." She played with the coins, stacking them up atop each other, creating a tiny tower of gold.

"Does she live around here? The woman who was with Ulster."

The whore nodded her head. "Sure. Tallie has a room in the Tower."

Junto nodded. "Which room?"

"The purple room on the second floor."

Junto was well acquainted with the Tower. He had visited it numerous times in his younger days. The Tower was one of the structures near the whore camp that drew a lot of visitors from all across Moraneesh. It was a ten story structure, with each floor holding four rooms. Each room was either decorated in one color scheme, or followed a certain theme. There was a red room, a blue room, a yellow room, and on and on. Other rooms were themed to match some outdoor environment or to match an occupation. There was a wooded room filled with fake trees. There was a blacksmith room made to look like a blacksmith shop. There was a kitchen room, complete with various cooking utensils that most likely ended up in unsuspecting orifices. And dozens more themed rooms. The themed rooms made it easy for a patron to remember which room they enjoyed most after a memorable session, and request the same room upon a return visit. Each whore was often attached to a room in the Tower for months, or years, or sometimes even permanently if enough patrons kept requesting her, or him. Once attached to their respective rooms, the whores plied their trades within them.

Junto remembered Layna from the orange room. He wondered if she was still there, but then quickly pushed that memory back down. No time to dredge up the past right now. "What was Tallie doing out of the Tower?"

Volina shrugged. "Some of us girls like to make extra money on the side. No need for the Tower to take a piece of every coin we earn, right?"

Junto said nothing to that. The whore camp was usually where the Tower workers ended up after their services were no longer requested, or if they were simply past their prime earning age and had to make room for the next generation of workers, or if they pissed off the Tower's owners enough and got themselves expelled from the Tower. As far as he knew, Volina's presence in the whore camp could have been a result of all three. "You know where she's from? This Tallie?"

Volina smiled. "We all come from the womb of the Tower, don't you know that? It gives birth to us so we can give pleasure to all who visit."

Junto ignored her glib remark. "What about him? You ever seen the man before?"

She shook her head. "No, I would have remembered him."

"Why?"

"Big man. Lots of death gems all over his body." She nodded to herself. "I would have remembered seeing him before."

"Did he have any other markings on him

besides the death gems?" Junto asked.

Volina frowned. "Markings?"

Junto nodded. "Yes, like scars or pictures painted on his skin."

Volina was quiet for a moment. "Not that I can recall. Don't think that would matter none anyway. Not with all them death gems all over him."

Junto remained silent for a moment. Just how many death gems did Ulster now possess on his body? The more he heard about him, the greater his unease grew. "Did you hear them talk? Maybe they might have said something about where they were going."

Volina shook her head. "I just seen 'em. I didn't hear 'em talking."

Junto nodded. He set another coin on top of her pile of coins. "You ready to tell us what she looks like now?"

"Sure."

Sekanna rolled out a blank parchment on the table and poised her hand above it. She clutched a long, thin piece of charcoal in her slender fingers.

The whore looked at Sekanna in surprise. "She a drawer?"

"Yes, she can draw," Junto said.

"I want one of me, too," Volina said.

Sekanna gritted her teeth. Junto reached out and gently set his hand on Sekanna's arm as he looked at Volina. "Okay. Tell us what she looks like first."

She cocked her head askew at Junto. "You think I'm stupid? You draw me first, then I tell you."

Junto could see Sekanna's free hand curl into a fist. "Okay," he said.

Volina smiled.

Sekanna just stared at her.

"You gonna start?" the whore asked.

"You need to sit still. Can you do that?"

Volina set her mug down. "Sure, I can do that." She sat still, slightly raising her head, facing Sekanna. "How's that?"

"Now you need to keep your mouth shut."

"Sure, I can do that."

"Apparently not," Sekanna muttered. She looked at the woman, then started to sketch her face on the parchment. After a few moments, she was finished. She held up the parchment so the whore could see it. "How's that? I think it captures you perfectly."

The portrait was a gross caricature of the woman. Her eyes were underscored with thick black lines. Her chubby cheeks were distorted into humongous blobs. Her nose was flat and wide. Her thin lips stretched from one side of the sketched face to the other. Her chin was pointy and sharp.

Volina glowered at Sekanna. "You fucking cunt!"

Sekanna feigned a serious frown. She glanced at the parchment, then back to the woman. "What? You don't think it looks like you?"

Junto grabbed Sekanna's arm and pulled her away from the table. Sekanna dropped the parchment sketch on the table and glowered at Volina. "Here, you can have it. You earned it."

The tall square-shaped structure of the Tower loomed in the near distance, reaching up ten stories. Its walls were made of smooth bricks the color of ivory. Very narrow window slits were visible on each floor starting at the second floor; the bottom level of the structure was all just smooth brick but for the massive black metal door that marked the Tower's entrance.

"Was that really necessary?" Junto asked Sekanna as they moved towards the Tower.

Irchly walked a few paces behind them, his bow slung over his shoulder, his quiver filled with arrows.

Sekanna waved her slender pale fingers. "Please. She was just a babbling idiot. Talking about ants in her brain. She wasn't going to tell us anything useful."

Junto said nothing.

"You really would have trusted what she would have told us?" Sekanna asked. "There's no way that sketch would have been accurate. You gave her way too much coin for what little we got out of it."

Junto remained silent.

"Look, she said this Tallie worked the purple room. That's enough to go on," Sekanna said. "If she's really working the purple room, it won't be hard to find her. She's either got purple tattoos, purple hair, or even purple skin cream on. Maybe a purple dress."

Suddenly a young boy raced up to them, panting and out of breath. "Irch, I've been looking everywhere for you. You need to come home. Malladrin is asking for you. He's—" The boy stopped talking and sucked in a few more quick breaths. "He's almost gone."

Irchly looked over to Junto, distress clearly showing on his features.

"It's okay, Irchly," Junto said. "Go and see your grandfather. We got this."

"But what if you run into Ulster?" Irchly asked.

"He's probably long gone by now," Junto said. "He just death gemmed two people. I doubt he's going to stick around."

Irchly hesitated.

"Fuck, Irchly. What the Hell's Wood are you waiting for? Go see your fucking grandfather," Sekanna said.

"You want us to come with you?" Junto asked.

Irchly shook his head. "No, that's okay." Irchly turned to leave, but Junto grabbed his arm and leaned in close. "Tell him I said goodbye and good travels," Junto said softly, his words sincere and heartfelt.

Irchly squeezed Junto's hand and nodded.

Junto and Sekanna watched Irchly move off with the boy for a brief moment. Had Junto known what the future held for Irchly he would have gone with him, but he didn't, so he and Sekanna resumed walking towards the Tower.

They reached the Tower moments later and stood outside its entrance. Junto again thought of Layna. He tilted his head up, moving his gaze up the stone wall of the Tower. There was no way he could not think of her.

Sekanna glanced back at him as he hesitated at the entrance. "You okay?"

Junto looked down away from the Tower wall and met her gaze. "Yes."

They moved inside.

CHAPTER FOUR

The twins greeted Junto and Sekanna as they entered the Tower. The first sight of the twins was always shocking to those who had never seen them before. They were joined at the hip, their bodies fused together as one; one head was a man, the other was a woman. Their names were Esmera and Aremso. Esmera was the woman. The twins were about five feet tall, slight and thin in their upper bodies, both with dark black hair; Esmera had slightly more of a tan than Aremso because she preferred the warmth of the sun while he preferred to stay in the coolness of the shade. She inhaled on a hand-rolled cigarette and Aremso exhaled a cloud of smoke. Junto had never found out what other body parts they shared, nor did he want to.

"Would you like a couples room?" Esmera asked.

Junto shook his head. "We would like to visit the purple room."

Aremso shook his head. "It is occupied right now."

"It's occupied?" Sekanna asked. She looked at Junto with growing tension in her face. She fingered the sword handle of the blade that was strapped to her waist.

Aremso nodded. "Yes." He looked at Junto. "Perhaps you would like to visit the orange room again."

Junto froze, just for a brief moment. He mentally pushed himself to regain control, but he still found himself unable to move or respond for just a quick second.

Sekanna swiveled her head towards him. She cocked a platinum eyebrow. "Again?"

"Youthful indiscretion," Junto said, finally regaining his senses.

"Really?" Sekanna clearly believed none of that.

"I think we need to be more worried about who's in the purple room right now, don't you?" Junto said.

"No weapons," Aremso said, pointing to where Sekanna was touching her sword. Esmera puffed on the cigarette and Aremso blew out the smoke while he finished his sentence. "All weapons must be left here before you can proceed."

"What business do you have with Purple?" Esmera asked. "If you have violent intent, you must leave now."

"We have reason to believe she knows who killed a friend of ours," Junto said.

"She was my sister," Sekanna quickly added. "She knows who killed my sister and stole her life-force."

"This is terrible news." Esmera puffed. Aremso exhaled.

"Was there a man with her? A soul stealer? A man with many death gems on his face?" Junto asked.

"Yes."

"They are here now?"

Esmera puffed. Aremso exhaled. "Yes," Esmera said. "I have already told you that."

Junto exchanged glances with Sekanna. He could see the determination filling her face. The silvery white color of her hair brightened, a sure sign her emotional heat was rising up inside her. He kept trying to train her to keep her emotional level even and flat, but she simply could not do it. Her temper was too strong for her to hold back. The brightening of her hair was slight, unrecognizable if you did not know her well, but Junto knew her well and he could easily see the slight shimmer in her platinum hair. It made her more beautiful, throwing a soft illumination onto her cheekbones, but it also made her more dangerous to be around. Far more dangerous.

To Junto's surprise, the man-head of the co-joined twins recognized the change in Sekanna. Aremso raised his hand and pointed at Sekanna. "No, no," he cautioned, a very clear and obvious nervousness rising in his voice. "She cannot be here in that state. There will be no unwanted violence in the Tower."

Sekanna gritted her teeth as she looked at him. "Believe me, this violence is wanted." She firmly gripped the handle of her sword, but kept the blade encased within its scabbard.

"You must wait for them to leave the Tower. Then you may do with them what you will," Aremso said.

Sekanna turned to Junto. "We cannot let them leave."

Junto said nothing to that. He turned to look at the twins. "Are there other exits out of here? Other ways to get out of the Tower?"

"Only if you want to leap off the battlements at the top," Esmera said.

Junto thought of the window slits hewn into the stone walls of the tower. None of them were wide enough for a human to fit through. They were barely wide enough to let a bird in. Archers could fire through them to defend the Tower if it ever was attacked, but not even a child could wiggle their way out of those long thin holes.

"Junto, we must find them now," Sekanna said.

Junto saw Esmera motion with her eyes to a brunette woman dressed in a plain white smock who was standing in a doorway nearby. The woman nodded and headed for the stairs. "Where is she going?" Junto asked, his tone stern and demanding.

Esmera puffed, long and deep. Aremso coughed, spurting out a thick cloud of smoke.

Sekanna burst forward, racing after the brunette woman, hitting the spiraling stone stairwell at a full sprint, charging up the stone steps after her.

"Stop! Stop!" Both the twin heads shouted the word simultaneously.

"You're trying to warn them, aren't you?" Junto tightened his jaw. "Curse you for a two-headed fool!"

"Purple is one of ours. You are not one of ours." Esmera puffed. Aremso exhaled a cloud of smoke directly into Junto's face.

Junto brushed past them and raced for the stairwell.

The two Tower guards who patrolled the second floor lay battered on the ground; one man was already unconscious by the time Junto reached them. The other man clutched at his bleeding shoulder as he propped himself up against the hallway wall. Junto checked the unconscious man and was relieved not to find any deathly wound on his body. He only had a massive welt on his forehead; Sekanna must have given him a solid strike with the weighted handle of her blade. Junto mentally cursed Sekanna. He knew she was just defending herself, but she was getting awfully close to crossing the line into killing. And once that line was crossed, there was no going back. Not ever. He had tried to convince her to give up her sword and choose a less lethal weapon, but that argument had gone nowhere; she was never going to give up her blade.

Junto glanced up, looking down the corridor. Several whores and patrons were milling about the long hallway, muttering and murmuring amongst themselves about the commotion. One whore was dressed in a vibrant red dress, a red rose tucked into her hair; her patron stood nearby, peering out from the red room. A male whore was dressed as a blacksmith, clutching what looked like a metal penis in his hand. Junto rose up from the guards and drew his battering stick from his belt. His battering stick was a smooth piece of wood about three inches in diameter and about three feet long. He raced for the upwards-curving stairwell at the far end of the hallway, brushing past the whores and their patrons who quickly moved out of his way as he neared.

Junto could hear voices, metal hitting metal emanating down from the third floor as he neared the stairwell. He heard a thick dull thud and then another Tower guard came tumbling down the stairs, his body rolling head over heels again and again as he thumped down the stone stairs. He reached the bottom of the stairs and lay unmoving. A surge of panic threatened to overwhelm Junto, but he quickly calmed when he saw the man's chest still rising and falling. They were in the thick of it now. Junto gripped his battering stick tightly as he stepped over the man's body. He continued on, moving quickly up the spiraling stairs.

Junto moved onto the third floor and froze.

Layna stood in the hallway. She recognized him immediately and stared at him with her beautiful wide green eyes. Her fiery orange-red hair cascaded halfway down her back. She clutched a flimsy piece of orange fabric in front of her naked body.

Junto hesitated. He slowed his pace as he neared Layna, lowering his battering stick to his side.

"Junto," she whispered as he drew near. "What

are you doing here?"

He found no words coming to his lips for a moment. He just stared at her, lost in the beauty of her face, lost in the sweet remembrance of her mouth on his.

"Junto?" she said again, her voice still soft.

"Layna," he finally managed to say. "Are you all right?" He wasn't sure why, but he felt compelled to ask her.

She nodded. She looked down at the club-like weapon he held at his side, then back up to his face. "What's going on?"

"We're hunting a soul stealer."

Layna's big eyes got bigger. "Here? In the Tower?"

Junto nodded.

Layna clutched the fabric tighter against her body. Her long, slender bare legs were very visible, the fabric barely covering her chest and midsection.

Junto glanced behind her, taking in the orange room for just a moment, seeing the orange sheets on the bed, the bowl of oranges on a nearby table. He quickly turned his attention back to Layna. "Where is your patron?" he asked.

"I don't have one right now."

A chilling cry filled the hallway.

Junto whipped his head towards the sound. It was coming from the fourth floor. He turned sharply back to Layna. "Get back in your room and stay there." He raced towards the sound, raising his battering stick.

"Junto!" he heard Layna shout after him, but he did not turn back to look at her.

The cry had come from Sekanna. She sat with her back against the stone wall of the hallway, her hand clutching at her side. Blood seeped through her fingers. Her sword lay on the ground nearby, its blade streaked with blood.

Ulster the soul stealer stood over Sekanna, grinning with his victory, his sword also streaked with blood. He looked up at Junto's entrance into the hallway.

Junto stared with a quick flash of fear at the big man. Death gems covered his sword arm. Only a few of the gems on his arm were dead and black. The rest were alive with trapped souls. The man had at least a dozen life-forces ensnared within those death gems that were still alive and vibrant with shimmering color. The best he could do was hope to wound the man and flee, but he knew that was not possible. He would not leave Sekanna. He grimaced and gritted his teeth. He knew he was about to die right along with her.

Then Junto noticed another body lying in the hallway. He was certain this was Tallie, the whore who worked the purple room; the purple negligee she was wearing and the purple hair that framed her face made that pretty obvious. She was dead, her throat slit. But then he saw Tallie did indeed have one death gem embedded in the middle of her forehead, just as Volina had told them, and realized she wasn't truly dead. He saw the death gem on her forehead pulsing, spreading life back into the woman's body. The ugly gash in her neck slowly healed, the flesh reforming. He knew a slight scar would remain, but that's all that would be left of the death strike. The death gem embedded in her forehead slowly began to lose its color, turning a deep and dark black as its stored life-force drained out of the creature and moved into the whore to give her another chance at living.

Had Sekanna cut her throat? That would have been foolish and just plain stupid. Her sister's life-force could have been contained inside that death gem. If that had been Oriala's, then her sister's soul was now lost forever, devoured by the whore's need for new life.

The soul stealer Ulster stared hard at Junto. "You're in the wrong place at the wrong time."

Junto said nothing. He gripped his battering stick tightly.

Ulster pointed his blade at Junto. Blood dripped down from the tip of the sword to hit the elaborate carpet runner that lined the middle of the stone hallway floor. "Stabber is going to taste your blood next."

Sekanna choked up a mouthful of crimson liquid. She reached feebly for her fallen sword, but it was too far away for her to grab it and she was too weak to move from her propped up position against the hallway wall.

Junto cursed himself. He was too late. If he hadn't been a damn fool distracted by Layna he would've reached Sekanna earlier. He might have gotten there in time to save her. He gripped his battering stick tightly, his choice of weapon suddenly feeling very inadequate and foolish. The only way to stop Ulster was to completely sever his head from his body, then smash his skull to a pulp so his head could not be reattached. He had once seen a soul stealer's decapitated head returned to its body and this had allowed the soul stealer to live again as the head reattached itself to the body. He knew that a severely crushed skull and splattered brains would put a soul stealer down forever. He knew of no other way to stop them permanently, besides burning them to ash and scattering their ashes to the wind. Even badly charred soul stealers could heal themselves if they had enough death gems on their bodies. But that ultimate act of complete destruction, the murdering of Ulster, would also permanently bind Ulster's soul to his for all eternity. That was a prospect he did not relish and would do anything to avoid.

Ulster took a step towards him.

Sekanna gasped and wheezed.

Ulster glanced at her. "Hold on," he said to Sekanna. "Don't die yet." He reached into a pouch at his waist and pulled something out. He held up a dormant death beetle in his hand, displaying it towards Junto. "See this, little man. This is for your friend. I'm going to fuck her and eat her soul at the same time. Then when she's dead I'm going to spill my seed into her corpse." He grinned an ugly grin. The tendrils beneath the death beetle came to life and started wriggling excitedly.

Junto felt rage threatening to overwhelm him.

"And then I am going to do the same to you," Ulster told him.

Junto heard a noise behind him, then felt a rush of wind brush past his ear. Suddenly, there was an arrow jutting out of Ulster's chest. Then another. Then a third. The force of the arrow strikes staggered Ulster back several steps.

Junto whipped his head around to see Layna standing at the end of the hallway, her bow in hand. He knew every one of the whores was trained with a bow to defend the Tower from their rooms in case the Tower was ever attacked; he had even watched Layna practice a few times, but he had never seen a whore actually use one in a fight. Her accuracy was excellent. Two arrows struck Ulster solidly in his chest and one hit him in the stomach.

Ulster dropped to his knees, then collapsed sideways with a garbled gurgle coming from his lips. His eyes were still wide with surprise when his life left him.

Layna hurried to Junto's side. "Come on, he'll be back soon enough."

One of the death gems embedded in Ulster's flesh was already starting to glow, feeding a life-force back into him.

"No, I can't leave Sekanna," Junto said.

"She's gone," Layna said.

Junto looked at his friend. Her eyes were closed, her body motionless. "No," he whispered. "Sekanna, no." He moved quickly over to her.

Just then, Tallie sputtered and started to sit up. Junto looked at the purple-haired whore. He suspected it was the first time she had returned to life and Junto knew she would be disoriented for a few more minutes before she could comprehend what had happened to her. He had seen it happen many times before and it was always the same. The newly resurrected person couldn't comprehend what was going on around them for at least a few minutes.

He looked over at Ulster's fallen body. Two of the arrows had already been pushed out of his flesh by the life-force being fed in from a death gem, and the third arrow was already on its way to being dislodged from Ulster's stomach. They didn't have much time. He didn't have time to hack Ulster's head off his body, not that he would even do that anyway. He scowled. He knew he needed to stop the monster, but he had to get Sekanna away from him. There was still a chance Ulster could steal her life-force before it left her body forever. "I have to get her away from here," he said to Layna.

"Bring her to my room," Layna said, keeping her voice low. She put another arrow into Ulster, sinking it into his stomach near the arrow that was nearly pushed out. "That'll keep him busy."

"No more arrows," Junto said to Layna. He raised his hand and put it on her bow, pulling the weapon down. "Every death gem on his body that goes black is a soul we can't save anymore."

Layna frowned at him, clearly not understanding what he was telling her. But she lowered her bow further anyway.

A cold resolve came over Junto. This was his chance to capture Ulster. It might be his only chance. He couldn't avoid his responsibility. "I need to stop him first," Junto said. He reached into a pouch at his waist and drew out a glass vial filled with a creamy white liquid, its top sealed tightly with a cork. He was determined to put an end to Ulster's reign of terror forever. The vial held enough blackout juice to knock five men unconscious.

Sekanna sputtered, spitting blood onto Junto. Startled, he lost his grip on the vial and the glass shattered on the stone hallway floor, its contents spilling across the runner. Junto glanced with shocked eyes at Sekanna. She was still alive!

"You have to get her out of here," Layna said. "Come on. We need to stop her bleeding. Hurry!"

Junto stared at Ulster, at the glowing death gem on his body, then glanced at the spilled contents on the floor. No matter now. He had to see to Sekanna first above all. He reached for Sekanna and lifted her up, cradling her in his arms. She moaned and winced, spitting up more blood into his face. He ignored the blood dripping down his cheeks and over his lips and chin. He turned to follow Layna, moving quickly back down the stairwell.

CHAPTER FIVE

"Is she going to live?"

Layna gave a soft shake of her head. "I don't know. Those cuts were pretty deep." She rose up away from Sekanna who lay on her bed, her eyes closed, her body still. She adjusted the blanket, pulling it up around the wounded woman to keep her warm. "But at least the bleeding has stopped and the cuts are sealed. She might make it. She seems pretty strong."

Junto nodded. "She is strong." He looked down at Sekanna's sweating face. He wiped a cloth tenderly across her wet brow. "She is very strong."

"Is she your lover?" Layna asked.

"No. Just my friend." Just my dearest friend in all of Calkut, he thought.

"Come," Layna said. "Leave her be."

Junto obeyed her wishes, following her over to a small table, sitting in a plush chair positioned near it. A small fire burned in a fireplace nearby, giving the room an orange-red glow. The glowing light cast from the flames made Layna's hair appear as if she was wearing a headdress of flames. She took a seat near him. She was dressed in the same flimsy orange piece of cloth that she had clutched in front of herself when he had seen her in the hallway. Her full breasts, her dark nipples, and her orange-dyed pubic hair were very visible beneath the thin fabric. He supposed one could call it a dress, but it was not something most women would wear out in public.

"You are certain Ulster is gone?" Junto asked.

Layna shrugged. "I think so. I heard two of the girls say they saw them leave the Tower."

They both sat quietly for a moment.

"I have no idea how to get you out of the Tower safely," she said. "The Enforcers will probably be here soon. The twins don't like any kind of violence, at least unpaid for violence, happening in the Tower, so I'm certain they sent for the law. And others saw us. They will be quiet for a time, but eventually someone will say something. They always do."

Junto nodded.

Layna stared at him. "What exactly are you doing here, Junto?"

"My job."

"Your job? And what exactly is your *job*?"

"I hunt soul stealers." He looked up at her. "You know that."

"And who exactly is paying you to do this *job*?" Layna asked.

"No one."

"Then I wouldn't call it a job, would I? A job is something you get paid for." Layna rested her hands on the arms of the chair as she looked intently at Junto. "What you are doing, is an obsession."

Junto shrugged. "Call it what you will. It's something I need to do. No one else seems to give a damn."

"So why are you giving a damn?" She looked at him. "You can't stop them all."

He frowned. "So that means I shouldn't try? I should just give up and stop?"

She looked away.

"I should let the soul stealers keep on doing what they do? I should let them keep an innocent's soul trapped in a death gem?" Junto's frown deepened. "I should let them use someone else's life-force so they can keep on living? Would you want that to happen to your soul?"

"No," she said softly.

"I wouldn't either." He looked at her. "Isn't that reason enough for me to keep fighting?"

"Don't fight for me," she said. "You don't need to fight for me."

"That's what Sekanna's sister said." He looked at her. "And you know where she is now? Most likely devoured by that whore Tallie. You saw that death gem on Tallie's forehead? That probably held Oriala's life-force. She told Sekanna she could fend for herself."

Layna remained quiet. "So you are going to save the entire world?"

"If I have to."

"Seems like a lonely battle."

He shook his head. "I have friends on my side. There are others who believe as I do."

Layna looked at Sekanna lying on the bed. "Like her."

Junto nodded. "Yes, like her."

"She maimed three Tower guards." She looked

away from Sekanna, bringing her gaze back to Junto. "They were my friends. Rinalto's wife just had a baby, too. His first. A son. She broke his arm and shattered his knee."

Junto looked away from Layna to glance at Sekanna. "She..." His voice trailed off for a moment. "She doesn't always think rationally. She was just defending herself."

"She maimed them all the same."

"I..." Again, he had no words. "Yes. Yes, she did." He lowered his head.

"Who should I hire to stop her?" Layna asked.

Junto lifted his gaze to her and frowned.

"You fight to stop the soul stealers. Who fights to stop you?"

"No one needs to fight against us."

Layna frowned. "Really? That is what I tell Rinalto's wife? That is what I tell Rinalto's son when he grows up and asks me why his father limps all the time? I should tell him to let his father's attacker go free without any punishment?"

Junto said nothing for a moment. "He will heal," he finally said.

"How many innocent men have you killed in your pursuit of soul stealers?"

Junto answered without hesitation. "None," he said. "I have killed no one. I don't even kill soul stealers. We imprison them. We don't kill them." He looked at her. "I don't want a soul stealer connected to me for all eternity."

"You are a believer in the Everlasting?"

"Yes."

She pursed her lips, studying him for a

moment. "As am I."

The followers of the Everlasting had a very strong belief in the life-force. Life and death were intertwined and inseparable. If a life-force was willfully taken by another life-force through an act of willful murder, then that life-force of the victim was forever attached to the murderer. It was not fair that a victim should suffer such a fate for all eternity, but Junto didn't make the rules. Life was sacred and needed to be protected at all costs. The discovery of the death gems perverted the power of the life-force, turning it into something it was never meant to be.

Junto had no desire to allow his soul to be eternally attached to psychopathic killers and monstrous murderers. He did not know what the great afterlife would bring, but he did not want it to be filled with the ugly souls he hunted in this life. Even if his belief in the Everlasting was wrong, it was a chance he wasn't willing to take. Not at the expense of his eternal soul. That was why they did not kill the soul stealers. That was why they captured them and imprisoned them instead of taking their lives.

Sekanna moaned, but moved only slightly; her eyes remained closed.

"She should not be moved for at least a few days," Layna said. "Those cuts need to heal."

Junto nodded. "Can you hide us for a few days?"

Layna was quiet for a moment. "Probably not. I am sorry, but someone will talk before that. I know the Tower. There are no secrets in the Tower." She was quiet for a moment, then looked towards the bathroom as an idea came to her. "You could probably escape through the chute. You'll land in a pool of piss and shit, but you'll be able to get out."

Junto shook his head. "I can't leave her."

"It will be easier for me to hide one person than to hide two."

Junto was quiet.

Layna looked at him. "You don't trust me, do you?"

Junto looked over at her. She was achingly beautiful. The firelight caressed her face in a golden glow, making her skin shine with a smooth sheen. "I—" He paused. "I don't really know you."

"I just put four arrows into a soul stealer for you. What else would you like to know?"

Junto's expression remained serious. "I know. And I thank you for that. Truly, I do." He looked over at Sekanna. "I just cannot leave her. It's not you. I wouldn't leave her with anybody. I've already let her down enough. She nearly died because of me."

"Because I distracted you," Layna said.

Junto said nothing.

A knock sounded at the door.

Junto looked with alarm at Layna.

She shrugged. "I knew someone would talk. That was quicker than expected, though."

Junto glanced around the room, searching. "Is there somewhere to hide?

"We can't move her."

"Can't you... cover her or something? Pretend she's a patron?"

The knock sounded again. "Orange?" a voice called from the other side of the heavy wooden door.

"Give me a moment," Layna called out. "I am entertaining."

There was silence from the other side of the door. "Entertaining who? You have no one scheduled until tomorrow night."

Junto finally recognized the voice on the other side of the door. It was Esmera.

Layna motioned for Junto to move towards a wardrobe closet, ushering him inside to hide behind the numerous orange-colored and orange-tinted costumes hanging within. She pushed him deep into a back corner. The darkness of the unlit corner of the closet hid him thoroughly.

Layna moved to Sekanna and pulled a cover completely over her body, covering her from any casual inspection. Then she moved to the door and opened it slightly to peer at her visitors.

Esmera and Aremso stood there, flanked by three other Tower guards she knew. "Where are they?" Esmera asked.

"They ran," Layna said. "I told them to run."

"You told them to run? Why?"

"It was Junto." That's all Layna said.

Aremso frowned. "I warned you not to have feelings for your patrons. It makes you do stupid things. Very stupid things. You fuck them and forget them. That is the first cardinal rule."

"I know, Aremso. I am trying to forget him."

From his hidden position in the wardrobe closet, Junto could hear them speaking. He squinted his eyes curiously as he listened to Layna speak of him.

"Who is with you?" Esmera demanded, peering over Layna's shoulder into her room. "Is that someone in your bed."

Layna stepped out of the room, moving into the hallway. She pulled the door behind her, leaving only a crack of it open. "It's Rorek," she said, lowering her voice to just above a whisper. "You know how he doesn't like attention."

"He didn't pay," Esmera said.

"I know. But don't worry, I'll collect and give you the coin. He always pays, you know that."

"I don't like this, Orange," Esmera said. "You helped those two escape and now you are entertaining patrons in secret. You are giving me a headache every time I see you now."

Aremso held his hand over his forehead. "And me."

"I will make him pay double," Layna said. "Rorek should pay extra for wanting to stay so secret."

Esmera smiled. "Suddenly, my headache is receding. Yes, double. That is only fair. We can accommodate his wishes, but wishes aren't free. Not in the Tower."

Aremso laughed.

"What about the other two who were causing all the disturbances?" Layna asked. "The soul stealer and Purple. Are they still here?"

Esmera shook her head. "No, they are gone. He wanted your head, but we made them leave."

"We fear Purple is no longer in our employ,"

Aremso said. "We will need to find someone else to play the purple room."

A faint moaning sound slipped through the crack in the door.

"I had better get back," Layna said.

"It sounds like a woman's voice," Aremso said.

Layna leaned closer to the twins. "I dressed him like a princess," she said in a conspiratorial whisper and smiled. "He really likes to play the part." Layna turned to go back into the room, but Esmera's cautioning voice made her pause.

"You best be careful," Esmera said. "That soul stealer had the look of death in his eyes when he spoke of you. He is not going to let this go, Orange. You had better be on guard when you leave the Tower. He could be waiting for you out there right now."

CHAPTER SIX

Ulster looked at Tallie with a scowl as she lay sleeping on a bed nearby. They were staying at an inn on the outskirts of Calkut. The room was small, with only one bed and a small table where an oil lamp burned, but it was sufficient for now; they weren't going to stay here long. The death gem on her forehead was a dull black now. The life-force was gone, absorbed by the purple-haired woman. It was her first re-birth, so he knew she would be disoriented by the experience for a while. She would be asking him a million questions that he would have no tolerance for.

He looked at the pale hint of a scar on her neck where the silver-haired bitch's sword had cut her and he felt his anger rise. He would exact vengeance on those who attempted to destroy what was his. Tallie was his now and he would do what it took to protect her and avenge any wrong perpetrated upon her. Those who had wounded her would pay.

He absently rubbed at the healed wounds in his chest and belly. And the orange-haired whore who shot the arrows into him would pay dearly. He glanced at a blackened gem on his arm; it had been a glimmering yellow only hours ago, but now was a dull black because he had drained the life-force from it in his healing and re-birth. He would make her suffer a great suffering before he stole her life-force. It would be a suffering such as the world had never seen before.

And then a thought struck him. A thought so brilliant that it made him as giddy as a school boy getting a secret look at his teacher's tits. He would plant death gems all over her body so that he could torture her to death over and over and over and over again. He would slash her throat, let her heal and re-birth, then cut her open like a ripe melon, then let her heal and re-birth, then gouge her eyes out.

He smiled and felt his excitement growing in his mind and in his loins.

He looked at Tallie again. She needed some more gems. One was never enough, especially since she had already used up its stored life-force.

His smile grew. There was a lot of killing to be done.

He removed his breeches and climbed into bed with Tallie. There was no need for further foreplay.

CHAPTER SEVEN

"Help me move the bed," Layna said. She grabbed at one of the bedposts and started to slowly tug at it.

Junto glanced at Sekanna, who was lying on the bed, her eyes closed, her chest rising and falling slightly. "Sekanna's still asleep."

"I know, that's why we need to move the bed, and not her. She needs to rest and not move so her wounds can finish healing."

"Why do we need to move the bed?" Junto asked.

"Because I have a patron coming in."

Junto froze. "You have a patron coming in?"

"Yes." She looked at him. "I still work here," she said. She cocked her head at him. "Don't you have a job? A place you need to be?"

"You know what my job is."

"Where do you get your coin?"

He hesitated. "I get by."

"You get by. That's not an answer." She tugged at the bedpost again, shifting the bed slightly, but then paused to look at him. "You steal it, don't you? You take it from the soul stealers you capture."

"Seems appropriate, doesn't it?" He pulled on a

different bedpost, slowly moving the bed.

"Ha. Mister high and mighty stealing like a common thief. So the high ground only applies to everyone else, not to you."

"I make no claim to walking on this so-called higher ground of yours. I do what needs to be done so I can keep doing what needs to be done."

"That was a mouthful."

They continued to ease the bed into the back alcove, moving it out of the main room. To say the apartment was full of orange would be an understatement. The table was hewn from orange wood, the chairs as well. Several lush paintings of the Torian Sea adorned the walls, one of a sunrise, the other of a sunset, both paintings splashed with the vibrant orange color of their respective dawn and dusk skies.

"Where are you going to... entertain your patron?"

She waved her hand. "He just likes to bend me over things anyway. He probably won't even notice the bed is moved. We hardly ever use it."

"He likes to bend you over things?"

"Yes. He only takes me from behind."

Junto stopped moving the bed and looked at Layna. "Doesn't he like to look at you?"

She shrugged. "I guess not."

"Damn fool doesn't know what he's missing," Junto muttered.

Layna squinted at him. "What?"

"Hmm? Oh, nothing." Junto returned his attention to the bedpost.

They finished moving the bed into the alcove.

Once the orange curtain that separated the alcove from the main room was pulled closed, the bed would be completely hidden from view.

Layna adjusted the blanket covering Sekanna, pulling it up higher over her chest. Then she stepped out of the alcove and moved over to a desk. "Here, help me move this a little. Put it near where the bed was. He probably won't notice, but I don't want to be blatantly obvious about the big empty space."

Junto helped her ease the desk over towards the space the bed had occupied. She pointed to a nearby statue. "Let's move that, too."

They both reached down to take an end of the statue and their faces drew very close to each other, their lips nearly touching. They both froze for a moment, neither one speaking, neither one moving. Junto inhaled the sweet heady scent of her and he felt his desire for this exquisite woman rising up. Her lips were so close to his, so achingly wonderfully close.

"Are you going to help me lift this?" she asked.

For a moment, he didn't answer. And then he moved, helping her lift the heavy statue. They set it down where the foot of the bed used to be.

"When is this patron going to arrive?" Junto asked.

Layna moved over to a nearby wall and slid a panel aside, revealing a calendar that was hidden behind the panel. The eight months of the year were neatly arranged in two rows of four. Each day within each month was marked by a thin peg, forty for each day within their respective months. There were several colored circular rings marking various dates, the rings inserted over various pegs throughout the months, each colored circular ring designating an upcoming patron visit. She took a white ring, the only white ring used on the calendar because it denoted the current date, and moved it over one peg to the right, inserting the white ring on top of one of the colored rings. "Some time today."

She glanced over to a small shadow clock illuminated by the sunlight streaming in through the narrow window slit nearby; the position of the shadow it cast indicated what time of the day it was. "Soon."

"Where am I supposed to hide?"

Layna looked around the room. "I suppose back in the wardrobe closet again. I have to change first."

He followed her over to the wardrobe and watched her finger through various outfits before settling on one. It was a long, flowing, light orange dress, more of a peach color, made of a sheer material that left little to the imagination. There were dark designs woven into the material to cover her breasts and the mound of her womanhood, but everywhere else the fabric was nearly transparent.

She started to remove her clothes, sliding the strap off her left shoulder, exposing her breast to him. He immediately spun around, looking away from her. "What are you doing?" he sputtered.

"I can't change my clothes unless I take off what I'm wearing first."

"Of course," he said. He heard more ruffling of fabric, then nothing.

"I thought you liked to look at me," she said.

"I do," he said.

More silence.

"Isn't your patron going to be here soon?" he asked.

"Yes."

More silence.

"Are you still standing there naked?" he asked, not daring to turn around and look.

"Yes."

He felt her move closer, could feel the presence of her body right behind him. "You're right behind me, aren't you?"

"Yes," she whispered.

He could smell the sweet scent of her filling his head. Blood raced down to his loins, roaring into him, thickening him. He couldn't take it any longer. He had to see her. He had to taste her mouth again. He had to touch her flesh again. He had to—

"Will someone bring me a fucking cup of water!"

The sound of Sekanna's angry voice both excited him and deflated him all at the same time. She was going to be okay! He just knew it from the demanding tone in her voice. He turned to Layna to see her standing before him, a hint of disappointment in her features. She was stunningly beautiful and still stark naked. "I—" he started to say, but then could think of no more words.

Layna pointed to an ornate silver pitcher with a pumpkin orange handle and some silver goblets rimmed with a similar pumpkin orange coloring on a nearby table. "You'd better do as she asks."

Junto nodded. He quickly moved to the table

and poured some water into a goblet. He moved quickly to the alcove area, sloshing some water over his hand in his haste. He entered the alcove area to see Sekanna sitting up against the headboard. She rubbed at her temples, wincing.

"Junto," she said as she saw him come into view. "Are we still in the Tower? What happened?"

"I hate to say it, but Ulster kicked your ass." He handed her the goblet and she took an eager drink, obviously relishing the liquid, ignoring the dribbling stream that ran down her lips. "How are you feeling?" he asked.

She lowered the goblet and wiped the back of her hand across her mouth. "Thirsty." She took another drink.

"Take it slow. You have some sword wounds in your side that are healing."

"Yeah, I can feel them." She took another drink.

"Easy," Junto said.

She handed the goblet back to him. "Did you get him?"

Junto shook his head.

"You saved me instead." She stated it and did not ask it. "You fucking idiot."

Junto smiled at her. He reached over to her and brushed a lock of her platinum hair away from her face.

"So where is he?"

"Gone."

"And Tallie?"

"Probably gone, too."

Sekanna frowned. "And now she's probably

absorbed my sister's soul."

Junto lowered his head. "I am sorry about that." He wanted to chastise Sekanna for being so impulsive, for just charging into the fray, but he didn't feel like now was the time. She would suffer enough on her own without his help. The death gem on Tallie's forehead had most likely contained her sister's life-force. If they had captured Tallie without killing her, they could have attempted the removal of the death gem. The extraction process was the only method they knew of that could free a trapped soul, and they were improving their extraction techniques every time they performed one, so they might have had a chance to save Oriala. But now it was too late. Tallie had probably already absorbed her sister's life-force, using her sister's energy to heal her wounds and to live again. Her sister's soul was gone forever. It was an ugly brutal truth. It only made him want to find every soul stealer in the world and imprison them forever. No one should go through this agony. And now Sekanna would have to live with it forever.

"Why did you kill her?" Junto asked. The question came out reluctantly; it was a question he didn't want to confront Sekanna with but he had to know the answer.

Sekanna shook her head. "I didn't mean to. I was swinging at that Ulster fucker and he blocked my blade. It deflected off his sword and sliced right through that dumb whore's throat." Sekanna fought back tears, angrily wiping at the moistening corners of her eyes. "Oriala, I'm sorry," she managed in a choking whisper. "I'm so fucking sorry..."

Layna appeared. "You have to be quiet now," she said in a low voice. "He's here. He just knocked at the door."

Sekanna looked at Layna and frowned. She turned to Junto, still wiping angrily at the tears that threatened to stain her cheeks. "What the Hell's Wood is going on, Junto?"

"Layna saved both our lives. Now she's hiding us."

"Please, just be quiet," Layna said. She pulled the curtain shut that enclosed the alcove, sealing them within, and then disappeared back into the main room.

"Junto—" Sekanna started, but Junto hushed her with a finger to his lips.

Junto listened to the rapturous moans and the heavy grunts coming from the main room.

"Are they doing what I think they are doing?" Sekanna asked in a whisper.

Junto motioned for her to be quiet. The panting and ecstatic groaning continued.

"Aren't you going to take a look?" Sekanna whispered.

Junto glowered at her.

Sekanna wasn't fazed by his irritated look. "I think I'm getting aroused," she muttered.

The sounds of sex continued. They went on for what seemed liked hours.

Layna moved into the alcove, pulling the orange curtain open.

"All finished?" Junto asked.

Layna nodded.

For a moment, Junto thought he saw a flush of embarrassment on Layna's cheeks, but he couldn't be sure.

"Quite a boisterous fellow," Sekanna said.

Layna said nothing to that. "How are you feeling?"

"Better," Sekanna said. "My side hurts like hell, but I'm still breathing." She looked at Layna. "I hear I have you to thank for that."

Layna looked at Junto, then back to her. "You have both of us to thank."

Sekanna looked at Junto. "Him, I already owe." She looked back to Layna, "You, now that's a new one on me. You're on the list now."

"The list?" Layna asked.

"It's her way of saying thanks," Junto said.

Layna looked puzzled.

"She owes you a favor. She'll do whatever you ask," Junto said. "You are on the list."

Layna nodded.

Sekanna nodded. "Yeah, thanks."

Layna smiled softly.

Sekanna turned to Junto. "So can we get out of here now? I think we've disrupted this lady's life for long enough now."

"You feeling up to it?" Junto asked. "You think you can walk?"

Layna stepped forward, shaking her head. "No. You need to give that wound another day or two. You move too much and you'll rip it right open."

"We've already troubled you enough," Sekanna said.

Junto nodded. "I'll make her go slow," he said.

Sekanna looked at Layna. "Do you have any clothes I can wear? Something without blood all over them? Mine are starting to stink." She glanced at the sheer dress Layna wore. "Something a bit more — demure."

"Now you are modest all of a sudden?" Junto asked.

"Staring at the tunnel of light gives a woman perspective," Sekanna said.

Junto looked at her for a moment. "You saw the tunnel?"

Sekanna looked at him.

"You were that close?"

She didn't answer.

"Sekanna, you were that close?" Junto asked again.

"Yes." She paused. "I almost went into it." She looked up at him. "But I heard you. I heard you calling me back."

He reached over and hugged her. "I'm glad you didn't go in. It's not time for you yet. I need you." He pulled back and stroked her platinum hair. He looked over to Layna. "Do you have some clothes Sekanna can use? I'll pay you for them."

Layna hesitated.

"Layna?"

"Yes, yes, of course. You don't have to pay me.

I have plenty of extras." She motioned towards the other room, motioning for Junto to follow her.

Junto looked back at Sekanna before exiting the alcove. "Don't worry, I'll pick out something demure for you." He grinned.

Sekanna groaned.

Junto followed Layna over to the wardrobe closet and she began fingering through all the dresses and ensembles contained within the large closet. She suddenly stopped and whirled to face Junto. "You can't leave," she said, blurting it out.

"She'll be all right. I'll watch over her and make sure she takes it easy."

Layna shook her head. "I'm not worried about her. She's a strong woman."

Junto looked curiously at her. "What? What is it, Layna?"

She hesitated. "I'm scared."

"You're scared? Scared of what?"

"That soul stealer. He looked right at me. He knows my face now." She hesitated. "He wants my soul. I saw it. I saw it in his eyes." Tears started to pool in the corners of her eyes. "I don't want him to steal my soul."

"Hey, hey," Junto said, trying to soothe her. "It's okay." He reached out and put a comforting hand on her shoulder. Her skin was warm under his touch, and smooth, so smooth.

Layna shook her head. "No, it's not okay. I've been trying to pretend I'm not scared, but I can't do it anymore." She looked at Junto with desperation clearly etched into her face. "Please don't leave me." She grabbed at his arm. "I'm scared. I know he's going to come for me."

Junto understood her fear. It was the greatest fear a person could ever know. The fear that their soul would be destroyed. The fear that their life-force would be extinguished forever. Most people didn't give it much thought during their lives, but when you saw a soul stealer up close, when you confronted the actual threat of someone capable of stealing and destroying your soul, it was a very sobering experience. He remembered the first time he had learned of the soul stealers. There were nights he still woke up in a cold sweat, consumed by his own nightmares.

Tears streamed down Layna's face and Junto felt his heart break. He pulled her close and hugged her tightly against him. Don't be scared, he wanted to say. It will be okay, he wanted to say. But he didn't say any of those things. He knew she should be scared. He was scared for her. He was scared for Sekanna. He was scared for himself. The soul stealer knew all of their faces. He most likely wanted to see them all dead. He most likely wanted to steal all of their souls right about now for what they had done to him. He pulled back from the embrace, keeping a hold on her shoulders. "I won't stop hunting him down. I promise you that. You asked me why I am doing what I'm doing. This is why. I don't want anyone to feel as scared as you do. Ever. Someone has to stop them. Someone has to stop all of them."

Layna wiped a tear away from her cheek, nodding softly.

"He'll be after all of us now. You, me,

Sekanna. I'm sure he wants all of us."

"And now Purple is with him."

Junto nodded. "Yes, now Tallie is with him. That makes both of them even more dangerous."

"How do you stop them? And him. How do you stop him? He had a dozen death gems on his body that I could see."

"We can cut off his head and smash his skull. That's one way." He glanced towards the direction of the alcove, but he couldn't see Sekanna from this vantage point. "That's the way Sekanna would prefer we do it."

"I like that way," Layna said.

Junto looked back to her. Her grim expression didn't change. "Or we take him alive and put him through the extraction."

Layna frowned.

"We extract the death gems from his body. One at a time."

"Why? Just kill him and be done with it."

Junto shook his head. "If we do, then all the souls trapped in the death gems are tied to him forever. They go into the afterlife with him, attached to him for all eternity. I wouldn't wish that on anyone, would you? Would you want your soul attached forever to the person who took your life? I sure wouldn't."

Layna was quiet for a moment. "So what happens with this — extraction?"

"We remove one death gem at a time."

"How?"

"There is a way. It's very time-consuming but we're starting to be successful with it."

She waited for him to continue.

"The soul is trapped in the death gem, so when we remove the death gem from the soul stealer, the soul comes with it."

"Then what do you do with it?"

"We release it."

"Release it?"

Junto nodded. "We release it."

"And then the soul goes free?"

Junto nodded.

"So there is still a chance for the Everlasting even after a soul stealer steals your soul?"

"Yes."

Layna wiped away another tear from her cheek. "And those black death gems? I saw he had some on his arm. What are those?"

Junto shook his head. "That means the souls they contained are gone. They are gone forever."

"Forever?"

Junto nodded. "Forever. They are gone forever. The soul stealer absorbs their life-force to keep himself alive. They can never be saved. They just — they're just gone…"

Layna was quiet. He could see some of the unsettling fear returning to her eyes.

"That's why we can't just kill a soul stealer who has living death gems on his body. Then they'll just absorb someone's soul and extinguish their life-force forever."

Layna was quiet for a moment. Then a full blown panic filled her features. "But I — I killed him. I shot him full of arrows. Does that mean — does that mean I helped destroy someone's soul forever?"

"You were saving us. You had to, Layna. You had to do it."

"I destroyed someone's soul..."

"No, you didn't. *He* did it." Junto gritted his teeth. "That fucking soul stealer is the only one responsible for that, Layna. Not you. Not me. Them. Only them. That is why I have to stop them."

Layna was quiet. Junto frowned. She was too quiet. "What are you thinking, Layna."

"I'm thinking how much I hate you right now."

Junto was taken aback. He took a few steps away from her. "I didn't mean for this to happen. I didn't mean to involve you."

She looked up at him with red-streaked eyes. "And I'm hating myself even more."

He just looked at her.

"Hating myself for living in the Tower. Hating myself for entertaining patrons with my sweet little pussy. Hating myself for pleasuring others for money. Hating myself for hiding in ignorance while you are out fighting to save people's souls." She scoffed. "How pathetic is that? I'm worried about what dress to wear before I take it up the ass and you are out there fighting to save people's eternal fucking souls."

Junto had no words for that. "I'm sorry for involving you," he said again.

"What? I'm not. You finally opened my eyes." She stared at all the clothes in her wardrobe for a long moment. "I can't do this anymore. How am I supposed to keep on doing this? I can't."

Junto just listened.

Layna started yanking dresses off their hooks and dumping them onto the floor. She grew more agitated as she continued to dump the clothing onto the floor. She grabbed at one thin dress and savagely tore at the fabric, destroying the garment with angry rips. She grabbed another dress but the fabric was too thick to rip; she kept trying, straining to tear it. Finally, she gave up and tossed it to the ground, stomping angrily on it.

Junto just watched.

"What the hell is going on over there?" Sekanna shouted. She could hear ripping and stomping and cursing and crying coming from the main room. Then there was a long period of silence.

After a moment, Junto stepped into the alcove, carrying a black tunic and some leggings. Layna trailed behind him.

"What the hell were you two doing over there? Entertaining yourselves while I'm wallowing in pain over here?"

"Layna's coming with us," Junto said.

Sekanna put her finger in her ear, pretending to clean it out. "What?"

"Layna is coming with us."

Sekanna looked at Layna, then back to Junto. "Why?"

"She's joining us."

"She's joining us." Sekanna looked at Junto. "The Tower trollop is joining us to fight soul stealers?" She looked at Layna. "Sorry, that just came out wrong."

Layna said nothing.

"She can't stay here anymore," Junto said.

Sekanna nodded. "Okay, I get that. But joining us? That's a whole different story."

"Where else is she supposed to go?"

Sekanna shrugged. "I don't know. We can take her to the Temple on Galapos. Or to the Druindi on Valakan. She would be safe there."

Junto looked at Layna. "Those are good ideas. You would be safe on Valakan. The Druindi are very protective of their islands."

Layna looked hard at Sekanna. "You owe me, right?" Layna didn't expect an answer and Sekanna did not give her one. "Then I want you to accept me as part of your group. Then we call it even."

Sekanna opened her mouth, then closed it. She looked over to Junto. "She's a crafty one, isn't she?"

"I am finding that out," he said.

Sekanna looked at Layna. "Well, Junto said you are good with a bow."

"Better than you, I'm sure," Layna said to her.

"No need to get nasty," Sekanna said, then let the corner of her mouth quirk up into a slight smile.

The three of them were silent for a moment.

"So now what?" Sekanna asked.

"Now we set a trap for Ulster and take him down," Junto said.

"You picked this one out on purpose, didn't

you?" Sekanna adjusted the very tight fitting tunic by cupping her breasts and shifting them around. The tight black tunic pushed her breasts up and out, giving her very ample cleavage.

Junto looked at her cleavage.

"Umm, eyes up," Sekanna said.

Junto just smiled. "It's tight to help keep your wounds secure."

"Sure it is," Sekanna said.

"You look hot," Layna said.

Sekanna glanced at her. "Don't get any ideas," she said. "I don't play with girls."

Layna gave her a slight shrug. "Not yet."

Junto looked at Layna, then at Sekanna, then back to Layna. She gave him the same slight shrug.

"Oh, boy," Sekanna said. "We've got some interesting times ahead, don't we?"

"What the hell just happened here?" Junto asked.

Sekanna patted him on the shoulder. "Never mind. We've got other things to worry about."

Layna was dressed in a vibrant orange dress, her hair done up in an elegant style. She looked stunning. There was no way to miss her. And that was the plan. Junto felt uncomfortable using her as bait for Ulster, but they all agreed it was the best way to flush him out.

They just didn't expect the soul stealer to show up so quickly, nor did they expect to pay such a high price when they encountered him.

CHAPTER EIGHT

Ulster dressed himself in a cloak that covered his death gems, and a cowl that covered his head and kept his face hidden in shadow. Tallie wore a silken bandanna across her forehead to cover the blackened death gem embedded in her flesh. She had two more death gems on her right shoulder now, but they were hidden beneath her tunic shirt. She also wore a dark brown cloak, but the cowl was pushed back, leaving her face exposed. Her hair was dyed black now, but there were still some purple streaks visible because Tallie had done it herself in a rush.

They had returned to the Tower to look for the woman who had put three arrows into Ulster, but Orange was not there. He was convinced the double-head who managed the Tower was telling him the truth, especially after he told them their life-force was twice as strong and they would make an excellent addition to his collection of death gems if he ever found out they were not telling him the truth.

The man-head started blabbering like he was drunk on brale. He told him that Orange had just vanished. One of her patrons had come calling, but she was not in her room. They searched high and low for her in the Tower, but she was not there.

Ulster asked him about the other two, the man and the silver-haired woman. Double-head said they had seen the man before, that he was once a patron of Orange but that he had not visited her in quite some time. They did not know who the other woman was.

But then they had told him something that disturbed him. They told him the man and the woman were specifically looking for him. And then double-head told Ulster something else. They told him they thought the man was hunting him. The woman-head specifically had emphasized the word hunting. Was that man one of the extractors? Was he the man he had heard rumors about? Was he the man who ran the torture chamber? Was that man the extractor Torek had spoken of? Was he the one who had extracted all of Torek's death gems before Torek had escaped from his prison?

Ulster had a hint of an unsettling feeling churn his stomach, but he quickly squelched that sensation. He wasn't going to fear this man. He was going to become the hunter, not the hunted. He was going to take this extractor's life-force and put it in a death gem smack in the middle of his forehead for all to see. He would wear his soul proudly. And then once he took his, he would go after the rest of his so called team of extractors. None of them would survive.

"There she is," Tallie said.

Ulster looked over to Tallie. She pointed into the crowded market, towards the line in front of a baker's shop. The delightful aroma of freshly baked bread wafted to his nose. His stomach growled. After he took care of these pesky extractors, he would treat himself to an entire loaf. Maybe even two. Tallie was right. Orange was there, dressed in a bright orange blouse and white leggings. Brown boots adorned with orange fringes covered half her legs, running up to just below her knees. She was making no effort to hide herself and Ulster immediately wondered why. Unlike Tallie who had her contract terminated (by mutual agreement between Ulster's threatening glare and double-head's desire to avoid being a victim of Ulster's violence), Orange was still under contract with the Tower. She knew they would be out looking for her. Why be so blatant? Why make your presence so obvious that you could instantly be picked out even in a thick crowd of people? Ulster frowned. Why indeed?

Ulster paused, scanning the surrounding area, studying the faces of the people in the throngs of customers bustling through the market. He looked at the candle maker dipping a wick into a vat of wax, then at the bowl maker spinning his pottery wheel, then at the meat strip seller hanging freshly salted slices of meat up to dry. He could spot nothing out of the ordinary.

He handed a small curved dagger to Tallie. It had a viciously serrated edge to its blade. "Here," he said. "Get in line behind her and shove this into her side. Give it a good twist and rip her open. She'll bleed to death very quickly."

Tallie looked down at the dagger, then looked

up at him, a nervousness evident in her features. "What are you going to do?"

"After you cry out for help, I'm going to run over to you and help the poor woman who just collapsed right in front of you." He held up a dormant death beetle. "But unfortunately she's just not going to make it."

Tallie hesitated.

"Her friend cut your throat. You do remember that, right?" Ulster asked. "Her friend cut your throat and she just left you there to die. I'm the one who gave you a second chance at life and she put three arrows into me. You can do me this little favor, can't you?"

Tallie took the offered dagger.

"Just hold her up for a minute, let her bleed out some, then put the creature on her. Then let her fall and give it your best scream. Once the commotion starts, just back away. You can disappear back into the crowd."

"Just like that, huh?"

Ulster nodded. "Just like that." He held out the dormant death beetle towards her.

"Maybe we should wait until there isn't such a crowd," Tallie said. "We can follow her and do it when she's alone." She licked her lips. "I'm really thirsty. We should get something to eat."

Ulster shook his head. "No, we see her now, we do it now." His tone was insistent, with zero chance of him changing his mind.

Tallie looked at the death beetle for a moment, then took it from Ulster, handling it gently by grabbing the edges of its shell, clearly fearful that it might come alive at any moment and bite her.

"Put the death beetle on the back of her neck so I'll know where to find it quickly, but slide it down a bit under her clothes," Ulster told her.

Tallie nodded, but didn't move.

Ulster leaned in to her and it was apparent that Tallie thought he was going to give her a good luck kiss, but he just grabbed the edges of her cowl and pulled it up to shield her face. "Go," Ulster said, biting back a growing annoyance at her timidity.

She looked away from him towards Orange, then headed in her direction.

Ulster watched Tallie move off into the crowd.

Junto stood in the shadows near a stall where a man and his wife were selling newly woven tunics. They had taken the chance and exited the Tower early in the morning. Just about every occupant of the Tower slept late into the day, as their nights were full of activity, so the mornings were usually very calm and very quiet with very few whores or patrons moving about so early in the day. The twins were not on duty, either, so that had made it much easier to leave the Tower without the unwanted distraction of dealing with Aremso and Esmera.

His gaze roamed through the crowd, coming back to rest on Layna. She was like a beacon, her orange tunic clearly visible even amongst the wild variety of clothing being worn by other shoppers. This was the only marketplace within Calkut. The next nearest market was in Berjon, a full day's walk from Calkut going west. So either Ulster and Tallie were long gone by now, or they would eventually come here to the Calkut market to replenish their supplies. They all agreed to give it a week. If they saw no sign of Ulster or Tallie, they would move on. He wasn't sure where they would go, but he suspected they would head towards Berjon. It was the next closest town. Maybe someone had seen them there. Of course, they could head in the opposite direction and move east towards Greywood, but that was a two day walk at a brisk pace and they'd have to pass through that quarter mile stretch of the Horgan Fields where the khack growers grew their khack. There was very little traffic lately between Calkut and Greywood because of that; no one enjoyed the hassle of dealing with paranoid khack growers.

He found Sekanna on the other side of the market. She was casually inspecting some apples, turning one over in her hand before putting it back in one of the baskets that lined a rack of shelves in front of her. She glanced up to look around the marketplace, then moved to the next basket of apples, reaching in to inspect another one. Junto saw her squeeze her legs together and do her little sideways squirm. He smiled. He knew she had to urinate; that was her little 'I gotta pee' dance.

Junto moved his gaze back to Layna. The line in front of the baker slowly shuffled forward. The baker and his daughter were moving as quickly as they could, selling loaf after loaf to the eager customers waiting for the fresh bread, but there were so many waiting that the line just crawled slowly forward.

Some grey clouds in the distance threatened some rain, but he didn't think that would happen for at least a few hours, and the storm might miss them altogether.

He glanced back towards Sekanna, but she was no longer near the apple vendor's stall. He looked in the nearby vicinity of the vendor, but he didn't see her. She was probably just using one of the bathroom facilities nearby.

A shrill scream caused him to whip his head back in the direction of Layna. A feeling of dread lurched into his chest. She was gone.

CHAPTER NINE

Tallie twisted the blade just like Ulster had told her to. Orange screamed a piercing scream. The loudness of Orange's cry startled Tallie. She withdrew the blade and quickly hid it back on her body. The orange-haired woman collapsed back against her and Tallie held her up for a moment. She held Orange up against her body, feeling her blood seeping through her own clothes, then lowered her to the ground. "Help! Tallie cried out. "She's been stabbed." She pointed in a random direction towards a throng of people. "There!" she yelled. "That man did it. He's trying to get away. He just stabbed my friend!"

A commotion arose, people talking, pointing, gathering.

Tallie quickly took out the death beetle and bent down over Orange's body, doing her best to shield what she was doing from anyone's view. The creature sensed the presence of a life-force so its tendrils descended down from its body and started wriggling wildly, clearly anticipating what was to come. She stuck the creature down Orange's back, making sure it was below the neckline of her blouse and out of plain sight. She felt the creature take hold of the woman's flesh and she released her grip on the death beetle.

A man dressed in a loose-fitting yellow tunic and brown breeches standing nearby frowned deeply. "You did it," he said.

Tallie turned towards him.

"You did it," the man in the yellow tunic said. "I saw you do it." He faced the gathering crowd. "She did it." He pointed at Tallie. "I saw you stab her."

Tallie looked at the gathering crowd, the darkening faces. She could hear the anger rising in their voices even without being able to hear distinct words amidst the growing noise. The crowd closed in. Come on, Ulster, she thought. Where are you?

Junto pushed his way savagely through the crowd, shoving people aside left and right, the sound of Layna's scream still ringing in his ears. A huge man was in his way and he tried to shove him aside by nudging him in his ribs with his elbow. The huge man turned to look at Junto with a scowl. "Move asi—" Junto started to demand but the huge man's fist connecting with his face shoved his word right back into his mouth before it could come out. Junto staggered backward, feeling a warm rush of blood immediately filling his mouth. His vision blurred for a moment and he staggered, dropping to one knee.

The huge man stepped towards him and Junto threw up a hand, motioning for him to stop. "No," he muttered. "That's my friend," he said, pointing a shaking hand in Layna's direction. He spit out some blood. "Please, I have to help her."

The huge man reached down and gently lifted him back up to his feet. "My apologies, my dear fellow. Your sudden thrust at my ribs startled me into immediate action. I was of the notion you were attacking me." The huge man was nearly seven feet tall, if not taller. His black hair was short, his head large, his neck thick, his body swarthy under his loose-fitting tunic. His eyes were a deep brown, almost black, his nose wide and flat.

Junto pointed towards Layna. "Please."

The huge man nodded and led Junto to Layna, a path clearing before the huge man without him having to say a word or make any gestures. They reached Layna quickly. She lay on the ground, unmoving. Her eyes were open and staring at nothing. Sekanna was already there, kneeling next to Layna, just staring down at her. She looked over to Junto and slowly shook her head.

Rage twisted Junto's face. He looked over to see a crowd gathered around Tallie. Two men gripped her, refusing to lessen their tight holds on her arms no matter how hard she struggled. Her cowl was down now, her face exposed.

"She killed her," the man in the yellow tunic said. "I saw her stab her."

Tallie glared at Junto. She made no effort to deny it.

"I saw it, too." A woman in a plain green smock came forward. "I saw her stab her. She just stuck her knife into her and twisted it. I saw her do it."

Junto tightened his fingers into a balled fist.

"Hang her!" someone shouted.

"Hang her!" another voice cried out.

Within moments, the gathered crowd was shouting as one, demanding immediate justice. The two men holding Tallie started to move, clearly meaning to drag her over to the scaffold erected on the edge of the market. It was the public punishment area, with a scaffold, a stocks, and several other means of public humiliation to teach criminals a lesson or dole out punishment depending on the severity of the crime. There were still many who didn't believe in the Everlasting, many who cried out for death without truly understanding the eternal consequences of their actions. Junto was against public execution because he feared even those who willfully watched such an event would still have the criminal's soul forever linked to theirs for all time. It wasn't worth the risk to anyone's eternal soul. Let the guilty suffer for the rest of their lives imprisoned in a cell, stewing in their own self-inflicted misery; that was the justice they deserved.

"Hang her," Sekanna said, her words calm and quiet but dripping with venom.

Junto looked at Sekanna with a stern face. "No," he said, his jaw tight, his mouth set in a grim line. Sekanna knew better.

No one listened to him. The two men shook Tallie roughly and started to drag her towards the scaffold.

"No!" Junto said, louder.

The two men stopped and turned to him.

"She's a soul stealer," Junto said.

This quieted the crowd.

Junto walked over to Tallie, still staggering a bit as he moved. His head was still a bit groggy from the mighty blow he took from the huge man, and his nostrils still felt wet with blood. He reached up and yanked the bandanna away from Tallie's forehead, revealing the blackened death gem that once contained a soul, a soul Junto feared had been the soul of Sekanna's sister. "She's already stolen one life."

The crowd stopped making any noise at all. The two men gripping Tallie released their hold on her and stepped back. Tallie remained standing defiantly where she was.

"She probably has more death gems on her," Junto said.

The huge man grabbed hold of Tallie's dress beneath her cloak and ripped off her top with one sharp yank, exposing her upper body and her breasts. A death gem glittered on Tallie's upper body, positioned above her right breast near her shoulder.

The crowd remained quiet, but there was a palpable outrage starting to form in their silence.

Junto saw the second death gem near Tallie's left breast, positioned across from the one on her right side. He scowled. She and Ulster had been busy. She might even have more death gems beyond these two hidden somewhere on her body. "I will take her."

The huge man just looked at him.

"I need to extract those souls." He stared hard

at Tallie.

The huge man looked at Junto with keen interest. "You are an extractor?"

Junto looked at him. "Yes."

The huge man bowed his head humbly, then looked back to Junto. "You had better take her before any Enforcers get here." He moved behind Tallie and gripped her, holding her shoulders firmly in his hands, pulling her tight against him.

Junto nodded. He quickly scanned the area but saw no sign of the white tell-tale uniforms worn by the Enforces. The Enforcers were the guardians of the public peace, but Calkut only employed a few of this newly created group so the odds of one showing up so quickly, unless they were already present in the marketplace, were very low.

The huge man followed Junto's gaze, also scanning the area for any sign of an Enforcer.

Tallie tried to take advantage of this momentary distraction by stomping on the huge man's foot, but he simply tightened his grip on her shoulders and ignored her stomping attempt altogether.

Ulster scowled. Things were not going as he had hoped. He stood in the crowd nearby, his face masked in the shadow of his raised cowl. The gathered crowd was far too thick, and far too much attention was being paid to Tallie for him to step forward. She had been sloppy in her strike, her movements much too blatant, almost vulgarly obvious. He knew that was his fault. She wasn't trained in the art of subtle killing, in silent assassination. And her pointing blindly into the crowd and shouting at an imaginary killer was just foolish; it had only served to draw more attention to herself. He had asked too much of her. And now the crowd was on to her.

He also realized his earlier plan of torturing the orange-haired whore again and again and keeping her alive with death gems was not going to happen; it would have been too much of a hassle to make that happen anyway. Seeing her murdered right before his eyes was not as satisfying as that would have been, but at least it was something.

But there was a glimmer of hope that had come out of this.

He now had eyes on one of the extractors. They may have used Orange as bait, but he now realized Tallie was serving just as useful of a purpose for him. Maybe that was my plan after all, he thought. He knew sometimes his mind formulated plans that appeared to be one thing on the surface, but upon execution they turned into something else entirely. He knew his subconscious thoughts were often far smarter, far more devious than his conscious thoughts. He didn't question how it worked anymore; that's just how his mind functioned. It had only taken a few hours of being alone with Tallie before he started to find her tiresome. Maybe this was his sub-mind's way of ridding himself of her annoying presence. Maybe he had really meant to sacrifice her all along. Maybe. But he still enjoyed fucking her. He mentally shook his head. No, he wasn't quite ready to give her up completely yet.

He would follow them and rescue Tallie. He could still take the death gem from the orange-haired whore's corpse; he was well aware that the life-force would remain viable within the death beetle for weeks, as the creature could continue to get sustenance from the body of a dead host for quite a while as long as it remained attached to the corpse. He would find out where the extractors took any captured soul stealers to extract the death beetles, find out where they were holding their prisoners, and then he would also release all his incarcerated soul stealer brothers and sisters.

And then he would kill all the extractors he could find. He frowned, realizing he wasn't quite ready for that part of his plan yet. He would need more death beetles. There were a lot of souls he was going to harvest.

His stomach rumbled. He was hungry enough to eat three loaves now.

CHAPTER TEN

"I'm sorry, Junto," Sekanna said. "I know you really liked her."

Junto said nothing. He stared down at Layna, his face filled with sadness. She truly was a beautiful woman. Her eyes were closed now, her face peaceful. She was lying on a bed, her head resting on a feather-filled pillow. Her hands were folded across her chest. A wool blanket was pulled up to her chest, the blanket covering the bloodied portion of her blouse. They were in one of the guest rooms on the upper floor in their manor home. The room was modestly furnished with two twin beds, a small desk between them. A dresser rested against a far wall, an unlit candle resting atop it. Cloth curtains, embroidered with the patterns of flowers, hung over the single window that looked out over the Masupi River beyond; the curtains were closed, muting the afternoon sunlight.

He cursed himself. What a stupid plan. He should never have used Layna as bait. The plan had not even come close to being successful. It was a complete and utter failure. And now Layna was dead because of him. Entirely because of him. It was a guilt he knew he would never forget for the rest of his life. "I don't even know if she has a family," he said softly. "I don't even know if we should send a messenger to someone." His words came out funny because his swollen lip made it painful to talk. A bit of blood was still smeared on his chin.

"We can ask that double-head from the Tower," Sekanna said.

Junto nodded sadly. They were probably the only ones who might know, but even they might not know anything more about Layna; he knew many of the women who worked the Tower had dark pasts they preferred to keep to themselves.

"We need to take her to the pyre," Sekanna said.

Junto nodded. "Let's take care of business first," he said. He fingered the small blade he used in the extraction process and slid it behind his belt.

The huge man was still present in the holding area when they returned to the room. The holding area was a large room on the first floor in the rear of the manor home filled with four iron-bar cages positioned along two of the walls, two cages per wall. Each cage was built in isolation, a good twenty feet from each other, so they shared no common bars. A wooden table with numerous chairs was positioned near the two walls that contained no cages, the chairs positioned to face the cages. The huge man sat in a chair on the side of the table near the cage where Tallie was being held captive.

Tallie was bound to a pole within the cage, her hands and feet tied tightly. They knew from experience they had to keep their soul stealer prisoners heavily bound so they didn't try to kill themselves and destroy the souls stored in their death gems just for spite. And after Torek's escape, they knew they had to be more careful in how they handled their prisoners.

"Thank you for helping us," Junto said.

The huge man nodded a slight nod. "Thank you for the food." Four empty bowls rested on the table near the man.

Junto motioned towards the doorway that led out of the holding area, indicating the way out to the huge man.

The huge man looked at him with his dark eyes. "My preference would be to stay."

Junto looked at him curiously, then finally asked, "Why?"

"I am of a curious nature. I have not been in the presence of an extractor prior to my crossing paths with you. I would be keen on watching you perform this — extraction."

Junto stared at him. "Who are you?"

"I am Elcor. Elcor Boriondi. I am from Velandia. Traveling here looking for spices to bring back to my homeland."

"You're a spice merchant?" Sekanna asked.

"I am."

"You don't look like a spice merchant," she said.

"And you don't look like a saver of souls."

Sekanna frowned a playful frown. "What? The hair? You don't like the hair, do you?"

Elcor turned his gaze fully on Sekanna, looking earnestly at her. "On the contrary. I find your silver locks most appealing."

Sekanna said nothing. She held Elcor's stare for a moment, then looked away.

"I'm afraid this is something we must keep secret," Junto said.

Elcor swiveled his gaze to Junto. "Why?"

"It's…" Junto paused.

"It's not pretty," Sekanna said, finishing for Junto.

"Not pretty?" Elcor questioned.

"It's brutal and ugly and messy," Sekanna added.

"I am quite familiar with all three of those."

Sekanna looked at Elcor. "Yeah, I believe you are."

Junto frowned at Sekanna. She frowned back at him, then looked to Elcor with a flustered face. "I didn't mean to say you were ugly. I just meant that—"

Elcor held up his hand. "No need. I knew what you meant."

They were all quiet for a moment. Junto motioned towards the doorway with his head. "Thanks again."

Elcor remained seated. "I still prefer to stay," he said.

Junto shook his head. "I'm sorry, I must insist."

Elcor rose up from the chair, but he made no move to actually leave the room. He began pulling up his sleeve. "No. *I* must insist." He continued to pull up his sleeve, revealing a row of death gems embedded into his flesh, half a dozen in all, all of them still vibrant with color, all of them still containing a trapped life-force within.

"Get me out of here!" Tallie shouted at Elcor.

Junto acted quickly. He took advantage of the few seconds that Elcor was distracted by Tallie's cry. He drew his extraction blade and swept it low, cutting across Elcor's calf muscle, severing tendons. He reversed the direction of his blade and swept it upwards, cutting across one of his meaty thighs.

Elcor howled in pain and rage and clutched at Junto's throat. Junto avoided his groping fingers and slashed again, slicing the blade across one of the huge man's groping arms.

"Kill them!" Tallie screeched from her prison cage. The bindings held her tight, but her body still shook with rage as she yelled.

And then Sekanna was there, cutting and slashing and stabbing, driving her blade deep into Elcor's gut. Blood sprayed out, splashing over her hands, making ruby pools on the stone floor. He howled mightily and reached for her. She couldn't avoid his grabbing hand and his fingers encircled her throat, squeezing tight.

Junto brought his blade down on the back of Elcor's wrist, cutting deep. He swung again, cutting deeper.

Sekanna jerked away from Elcor's weakening grip and spun away from him. She quickly spun back, stabbing and slicing at him, thrusting her blade into his gut again.

The huge man finally collapsed to the floor. Dead. At least for the moment.

"Hurry," Junto said. "Get him into a cage."

They both struggled with Elcor's body, dragging his bulky weight into a nearby empty cage. They bound him as best they could, tying his hands and feet tight with ropes, immobilizing his soon-not-to-be-a-corpse-body as best they could. One of the death gems on his arm started to glow and Junto scowled. Elcor was absorbing one of the souls into his body, devouring the life-force to refuel his own. There was nothing he could do about it. That soul would be lost forever, utterly destroyed as Elcor absorbed it into his being. It wouldn't be attached to him or Sekanna, or to anyone else ever again; the absorbed soul and its life-force would simply cease to exist. Junto wondered who it was. And then he forced himself to stop wondering. It would do them no good to be distracted.

They finished binding Elcor and then moved out of the cage, locking the heavy metal door behind them as they exited. They both panted, stopping to catch their breaths. Blood splatters and smeared crimson pools covered the floor; dark red patches stained their clothes, their flesh.

Elcor was going to be a dangerous soul stealer to keep around. A very dangerous one. He wondered how many death gems Elcor had on his body. It would take weeks just to extract the souls from the gems on his arm, let alone what other gems he might have on his body. Wushwan wasn't going to like this one, Junto thought.

He cursed himself a fool. That was twice in a matter of hours that he had made terrible mistakes. He had blindly trusted this big man simply because he had offered to help. He knew he had to stop thinking of others as if they all would act and think as he did. He hated to admit it, but he had to stop trusting people. The only people he could trust was Sekanna and Wushwan and Irchly and—

Irchly. Junto frowned. What had happened to Irchly? He had gone to check on his dying grandfather but then had never returned. Irchly was known to disappear for days, so that part wasn't surprising, but he usually stuck around when he knew they were close to finding a soul stealer. He was probably still dealing with his ill grandfather. Perhaps the old man had passed. Irchly would want to give him a proper send off into the Everlasting.

He thought of Layna. She had trusted him and now she was dead. I should trust no one and no one should trust me, he thought bitterly. Who am I to lead them against the soul stealers? I should just go back to being alone, go back to tracking them down myself. But he knew that wasn't possible. They needed to keep the extraction room operational. It was the only way to save souls. He couldn't run it by himself. He couldn't hunt down soul stealers and extract souls by himself. It just wasn't possible.

There were too many soul stealers.

"Are you okay?"

Junto looked up to see Sekanna watching him. He nodded.

She reached over to him and wiped away moisture from his cheek. It wasn't blood he saw on her fingers. It was his tears.

CHAPTER ELEVEN

The pyre room was a small room, isolated in the far corner of the manor home, accessible only through a long bare hallway made of sturdy stone. They made sure to keep any flammable materials away from the pyre room, so the hallway was left purposely bare of any decorations or ornamentation. The ceiling in the pyre room was high, reaching up over thirty feet, with a small opening to let out the smoke. Junto stared down at Layna as her body rested atop the wood platform that was set up beneath the stacked cords of wood. He was again struck by her beauty, deeply saddened that her faith in him had been terribly misguided.

Almost no one buried bodies anymore for fear of soul stealers. It gave the bereaved a feeling of comfort to watch a dead love one burn on the pyre. Once the flesh was burned away the loved one's life-force was gone and they were safe from the thieving clutches of soul stealers.

Layna looked so beautiful. They dressed her in a bright orange dress. Sekanna had done up her fiery red hair in an elegant style that framed her face. Junto reached down and moved a lock of hair away from Layna's cheek. He put his fingers on her face and lightly caressed her cold skin.

They had found the death gem on the back of Layna's neck after they had brought her back to the manor home. The gem was still alive with color, Layna's life-force still contained within it. Ulster and Tallie had clearly planned to harvest her life-force for their own vile purposes. Then a discussion arose as to what they should do with it. Did they need to extract it even though it was still attached to Layna's body? It was her life-force after all, so it had not been separated from her body. After much discussion, it was agreed that they could safely leave the death gem attached to her body and perform the pyre ritual as normal. Her soul would be freed with the burning of her flesh and rise up into the Everlasting.

Sekanna stood slightly behind Junto, holding a small burning torch in her hand. The fire gently crackled and popped.

Wushwan, Nadrini, and Velit stood slightly behind Sekanna. They hadn't known Layna, but were there to give their silent respect to the dead.

Wushwan was a dark-skinned man, slender of build, his body firm with muscle. He had been vital in the creation of the extraction process, his knowledge of biology and herbs and the function of the human body integral to its current success. He was dressed in his usual attire of well-worn leather breeches and a wool tunic.

Nadrini and Velit were Wushwan's slaves from before he started extracting souls. They were both pale-skinned women, with small delicate noses and softly rounded chins. Nadrini was slightly taller, with a little more meat on her bones than Velit. They were mostly hairless, the flesh on their arms and legs smooth and sleek, but each of the women still had a thin tuft of blonde hair coating their scalps. They were no longer slaves as Wushwan had granted them their freedom before he began his work with Junto. They had volunteered to stay with Wushwan and help in their fight. Wushwan had treated them well with great respect, even when they were his slaves, and they loved Wushwan fiercely. Junto sometimes wondered if their love for Wushwan was because of some master-slave affliction, because of some weird emotional control Wushwan had over them, but he tried not to dwell on it. The two pale women didn't speak often so Junto did not know much about them personally; Wushwan needed them and Junto was glad they were there for him. They still dressed in plain yellow smocks, seeming to prefer their old slave garb to any newer, more elaborative dress. Junto glanced down at their feet and was not surprised to see their feet were bare; at no time did he ever recall seeing them wear any shoes or boots, let alone a simple pair of slippers.

"Are you ready?" Wushwan asked of Junto.

Junto nodded and took a step back away from the pyre. Wushwan stepped forward and raised his arms to the level of his chest, his palms up. "May the fires consume your flesh and free your soul. May your soul roam the eternal heavens and find comfort with those who have gone before you. Keep watch over us and guide us, for one day we will also join you."

Junto took the torch from Sekanna and touched the flame to the cords of wood stacked beneath the platform upon which Layna rested. "I hope you find peace in the Everlasting."

They watched her begin to burn together. Wushwan, Nadrini, and Velit exited the room after a few moments. Sekanna stayed a little longer, but then she too left the room, leaving Junto alone with Layna.

The smell of charred flesh mingled with the smell of the burning wood. Junto watched quietly as the flames ate away at Layna's flesh. Then, a chilling sound came from the funeral pyre, a bone-chilling sound that penetrated into the very core of his being. His entire body tensed. Was that a wailing cry? He moved closer, feeling the heat waves from the crackling flames buffeting his face. No, Layna's mouth was still closed, the fire starting to eat away at her face now. The sound seemed to be coming from somewhere near her head, but it was definitely not coming from her mouth. It seemed to be coming from behind her. And then he thought of the death gem on the back of her neck. The death beetle. It was a living creature after all and it was still attached to her, still feeding on her. Perhaps they should have extracted it first, but that point was moot now, the opportunity long passed.

Junto leaned in closer, listening, feeling the hot waves of the fire pushing at his face, but the wailing sound was gone. All he could hear now was the crackling of burning wood and the singeing of flesh. He moved back away from the pyre and continued to watch Layna burn.

After a while, Layna's flesh had burned away, leaving darkened piles of ash. Junto produced a small metal vial from his pouch and gently put some of the ashes into the vial, sealing the vial firmly with a cork stopper. He returned the sealed vial to his pouch. It joined two other sealed vials already stored within his pouch. Layna was gone, but he would always keep a part of her with him, both to remember her and to remind himself of the fatal mistakes he had made that caused her death. That was now three deaths he was responsible for. Soon, he knew his pouch would be filled with vials. He was no leader. He scoffed at himself. The other two vials in his pouch didn't make him smarter, didn't make him more careful, even though they should have. The guilt of their deaths did nothing to sharpen his judgment, did nothing to elevate his caution. He just kept on making rash decisions and foolish plans.

He watched the dark smoke rise up to the ceiling as the final remaining pieces of the wood continued to burn, eying swirling grey strips of haze as they escaped through the narrow hole in the high ceiling above, the twirling tendrils of smoke reminding him of a death beetle's tendril-like legs. He wondered what part of the smoke had contained Layna's soul. He thought of the ceremonial words Wushwan had spoken. Could she really still see us? Could she watch over us? Would she even *want* to watch over them? They had caused her death, after all. Why would she want to watch over someone who caused her demise? He wasn't sure if he would if someone had done something like that to him. Would he really watch over someone who caused his death? He had no answer for any of those questions. He was just glad that no soul stealer had devoured Layna's soul before they released her. There was small comfort in that, but he would take that comfort. It did count for something.

He turned away from the pyre.

There was a lot of work to be done.

"Ulster forced me to do it. You have to believe me."

Junto stared down at Tallie. They had taken her from the cage and chained her down to the extraction table in the extraction room. She was naked, spread-eagled, her arms and legs securely bound with thick manacles and thick chains. While the hair on her head had only a few visible strands of pastel purple left within her thick black mane, her pubic hair was still a bright violet color. A metal clamp secured her neck to the metal table she lay upon. Another large metal brace secured her chest just below her bare breasts, and another metal brace was clamped down over her thighs. The blackened death gem in the middle of her forehead looked like some monstrous third eye.

"I liked Orange. I didn't want to kill her. Ulster made me do it. He said he'd kill me if I didn't do what he said." Tears streamed down Tallie's face. "I was scared of him. You saw what kind of monster he is. You know what he can do."

"Her name was Layna," Junto said.

Tallie said nothing, her face wracked with torment and fear.

Junto stared at the two death gems in Tallie's shoulder area, looking first at the gem near her right shoulder, then shifting his gaze to look at the one near her left shoulder. Both gems shimmered softly with pale color, the one on her right shoulder a topaz color, the left one more of an aqua blue.

Tallie followed his gaze with her eyes towards her left shoulder. She couldn't move her head because of the tight clamp over her neck. "I didn't kill them. Ulster did."

"You could have refused the death gems," Junto said.

"No. No, I couldn't! Ulster made me take them!"

Junto had enough of her pathetic pleading. He shoved a gag in her mouth and pushed it in tightly, muffling her voice. She made noises from behind the gag, but her words were unintelligible.

Wushwan, Nadrini, and Velit were near the metal table, busy preparing the creams and implements that were necessary for the extraction.

Nadrini had three bowls of ingredients before her, ready to mix them upon Wushwan's command. Once the ingredients were mixed, their potency only lasted a few minutes. They needed to smear the compound thoroughly over the death beetle and the surrounding area of skin where the creature had embedded itself into its host. The ingredients were very hard to come by, a mixture of rare herbs and animal secretions, so they treated them with precious care. They could not afford to waste a drop.

Junto checked all the bindings. "She is secure," he said.

Wushwan nodded. He looked to Nadrini and gave her a nod. Nadrini mixed the ingredients, quickly stirring them together, creating a white paste-like substance. She handed the bowl to Wushwan and he dipped his long fingers into the container, scooping out some of the paste. He quickly smeared the white mixture onto the death gem on Tallie's right shoulder, wiping it across the facets that gave the death beetle's shell its gem-like appearance, expertly covering the entire surface of the creature with practiced motions. He had done this many times before and was quite adept at the task. He finished covering the death gem, completely encasing it with the paste, then dipped his fingers back into the bowl, gathering up more paste. He wiped the white mixture around the area of flesh in Tallie's right shoulder where the death beetle had embedded its tendrils.

Behind the gag in her mouth, Tallie screamed. Her entire body went rigid, the clamps holding her in place as her body shook with wild spasms.

Wushwan, Nadrini, and Velit remained calm amidst Tallie's buckling and wild gyrations. They knew the clamps and manacles and chains would keep Tallie secure. Wushwan held his white-streaked fingers up to Velit and she wiped away the residue on a cloth. It was a weirdly intimate gesture, the way in which Velit caressed Wushwan's fingers, but Junto didn't let his thoughts take it any further. He had no idea what the three of them did behind closed doors and he had no desire to find out.

The writhing and trembling went on for a few minutes. Tallie kept screaming behind her gag.

They could only extract one gem at a time. The pain of two simultaneous extractions would kill the host. They knew this from direct experience. Junto and Wushwan had those two souls on their conscious. Their attempt to speed up the process resulted in two souls being destroyed forever. They never talked about it, but Junto knew they both thought of it often. It had been his own idea and Junto knew that Wushwan still blamed him for it. Once again, it had been a bad decision that he had made.

Finally, Tallie's body went limp. Her fingers and toes uncurled. He could see the tension just fall off her body. That signaled the second phase of the extraction. The creature was weakened, its hold tenuous on its host, the components in the mixture Wushwan had concocted doing its part, acting like a toxin to the death beetle.

Wushwan moved back up to Tallie and held out his hand, palm up. Velit put an implement into his hand, a long, pointed blade. Nadrini grabbed at an edge of the death gem and very gently eased it up, revealing one of the tendrils that grew out from its body and had pierced Tallie's flesh. The white-paste mixture also served to loosen the death beetle's grip, allowing them to get the separation they needed between the death beetle's body and its host so they could get at the tendrils. Wushwan put the blade to the nearest exposed tendril and slowly began to cut, sawing at the tendril.

Tallie went rigid again, another muffled scream filling her mouth.

Wushwan continued to cut. Nadrini continued to hold up the death gem. Velit waited close nearby, her fingers poised. As Wushwan reached the halfway point cutting through the width of the tendril, he paused so that Velit could reach in and grabbed the portion of the tendril that was between his blade and Tallie's shoulder. Once Velit had a secure grip on the tendril, Wushwan finished the cut, severing the tendril. Wushwan backed away slightly, giving Velit room to get closer. Velit slowly pulled on the exposed portion of the tendril, gripping it tightly in her fingers, easing its length out of Tallie's body one slow inch at a time.

Junto never ceased to be amazed at how long the tendrils were. They were usually three to four feet long, but he had seen some as long as seven feet. Once the death beetle latched on to a new host, the tendrils extended into the host's body, weaving themselves deep into the host's body, growing alongside veins and arteries, sometimes reaching into the heart, or the lungs, or sometimes even the brain.

Tallie screamed the entire time that Velit was pulling out the tendril.

Velit finished withdrawing the tendril and moved over to the fire burning in the hearth nearby. She tossed the limp, four-feet-long bit of tendril into the flames and watched it burn.

Nadrini released her hold on the death gem, letting it rest flush against Tallie's body again. Wushwan set the blade down on the instrument table nearby. One tendril down, four to go.

Now they had to wait a few hours for Tallie's body to react to the loss of the tendril. This was something they had learned during their first extraction. They had lost that soul by trying to extract all of the tendrils at once. Neither he nor Wushwan blamed themselves for that soul. There was no way they could have known. Still, it was their fault.

He thought of all the death gems adorning Elcor's huge body. Who knew how many the huge man had all over him. It could take them days, if not weeks, to extract them all. That was something he was not looking forward to at all. The man was incredibly dangerous.

CHAPTER TWELVE

"What do you intend to do with me, little man?" Elcor asked. He was sitting in the cage they had put him in after they had *killed* him, his back to the wall, bound hand and foot, thick manacles securing his wrists and ankles, these manacles attached to thick chains that were embedded in the rear stone wall of the cage. A toilet and a small water basin were positioned near him. A mattress and blanket were positioned in a far corner of the cage. There was just enough give in the chains for him to reach the toilet and water, as well as lie down on the mattress if he so chose.

Junto looked at the huge man through the iron bars of the cage. "I think you already know what we intend to do with you."

"You think you are going to extract every one of them from me?"

"Yes."

Elcor laughed. "Do you know how many I have?"

Junto studied his exposed arm, seeing the five visible remaining shining death gems embedded there; the sixth death gem was now a dull black, the life-force it had contained now gone forever, absorbed by Elcor. "At least five."

"Try again," Elcor said. "I have twenty seven, little man. Three of them are blacks." He paused, correcting himself. "Now four."

The number hit Junto like a hammer blow to the head. Twenty seven. The number went through his head over and over and over. Twenty seven. He had a hard time processing the amount of death gems Elcor had on his body. How many could a body hold? Twenty seven. He had never seen, nor even heard of, anyone with more than ten. Torek had three when they performed his extractions, and that had been one of the most difficult extractions of all. Twenty seven. Taking away the four blackened death gems, that left twenty three souls to extract, but he still couldn't get the number twenty seven to stop ringing about inside his mind. Twenty seven. "You stole twenty seven souls?"

"Five of them were given to me."

Given. Junto froze.

Elcor narrowed his eyes. "Ahh, that changes things, doesn't it?"

Junto said nothing. He had no idea if the huge man was telling him the truth or not.

"They all came to me together. They even had their own death beetles. Each one offered themselves to me. And you know what? I took them. They were determined to give themselves to someone, so why not me? Someone else would have taken them anyway." Elcor smiled. "You should have seen it, little man. It was glorious. They all patiently awaited their turn, watching the one before him die in my hands. Then, they just stepped up to me and gave themselves to me. One after the other. Men and women."

Sacrificials. Junto had heard of such people, but he had never encountered them. People so worn down by their own lives that they were willing to give their life-force to someone else. They didn't want their souls to continue on into the Everlasting. They wanted to be extinguished forever. It was a mindset he hoped he would never understand.

Elcor looked at Junto with his dark eyes. "And even a child. She was the best of all. So much life in her." Elcor closed his eyes and tilted his head back, as if bathing in the remembrance of the event. "So much life." He lowered his head back down and raised his hand to touch a spot on his tunic near the middle of his chest. "I keep her close to my heart." He smiled grimly at Junto. "They don't want to be saved, little man," Elcor said.

"They were not in their right minds," Junto countered.

"And who are you to decide that? Who are you to decide what someone wants to do with their eternal soul? They gave themselves to me willingly, knowing full well the consequences of their actions. And now you want to save them? You want to save those who begged *not* to be saved?" Elcor paused. "I ask you again. Who are you to make such decisions for them? Who are you to deny them their true wishes?"

"They were not in their right minds when they gave themselves to you," Junto said.

Elcor shook his head, his chains rattling slightly with his movement. "You are wrong. They were. They were of the clearest minds I have ever encountered. They knew exactly what they wanted. And I gave it to them."

"They will be extracted." Junto's voice was firm.

Elcor set his jaw. "So your way is the only way? You are the one who decides the final fate of others?"

"I will extract every soul I can. Including the souls of sacrificials."

Elcor's jaw tightened even further and his eyes narrowed. "I hope they hound you in the Everlasting for all eternity."

Junto shrugged. "They may be the only company I'll have."

Elcor scowled, tugging at his chains. "They gave themselves to me!"

"And I will be taking them away." Junto turned and walked towards the door of the room.

"You'll pay for this, little man!" Elcor shouted after him, the veins in his forehead bulging with his rage. "I promise you that. If not in this life, then in the next!"

Junto hesitated at the doorway, then continued out of the room.

The extraction of Tallie's death gem continued. Each tendril removal brought about the same reaction from the woman. Muffled screams, tremendous trembling, then she fainted from the pain.

It was late into the night before they reached the final tendril. Velit had the box ready to put the creature in. Nadrini held on to the creature's shell with both hands, gripping the death beetle firmly. They wanted no surprises. There were no windows in the extraction room so they didn't need to fear the creature escaping that way. They shut the door and placed a strip of metal just under the bottom of the door, blocking the tiny gap between the door and the floor, leaving absolutely no way for the creature to get out of the room if it did somehow manage to escape from Nadrini's grasp. It had happened before, but with each extraction performed, they learned more and more and tightened up the procedure to eliminate as many potential mistakes as possible. The only way out was up the fireplace flue, but the death beetles had a fear of fire so they never even attempted to go that way the few times one of them had gotten free. The fire blazed high and hot in the fireplace right now, awaiting the final tendril.

Sekanna watched the proceedings from a corner in the room, keeping silent, just observing, staying out of the way.

Junto stood near the extraction table, watching Wushwan slice at the final tendril. Junto gripped the sliver of the tendril that was visible beneath the blade as Wushwan cut. It was his job with this final tendril to remove it from the host. Wushwan made the final cut and Junto pulled, sliding the tendril up and up and up and out of the host. He used both hands, pulling the thick slimy cord hand over hand, slowly but efficiently extracting the tendril from

Tallie. Thankfully for them, the purple-haired whore had already passed out from the pain, so she was mercifully quiet. He moved quickly over to the fire and tossed the gooey tendril into the flames. It popped and crackled and immediately shriveled into black ash. He moved back to the table.

Nadrini held the death beetle in her hands, cupping it between them. A soft, pulsing light emanated from the creature. Junto wondered who it was inside the creature. Whose soul was it? Was it a man, a woman? A child? Was it Oriala's? Was it Sekanna's sister? There was no way of knowing just by looking at it.

Junto looked closer at the creature. They were an endless source of fascination. Where had the death beetles come from? How had the soul stealers discovered their power? Who was the first soul stealer? Was that person still alive somewhere? He could be, he realized. He could be hundreds of years old, maybe even older, with scores of death gems all over his body. He felt in his heart that the first soul stealer had been a man, not a woman. He wasn't sure why, but that's what he felt. There was something so ugly about the process of stealing a soul that he felt only a man would be the first to consider actually doing it. He might be wrong, but that's what he felt about the first soul stealer.

He had no idea how long the soul stealers had been working their ugly game. He just knew they had been around since before he had been borne and before his father had been borne. And they were growing in numbers, not dwindling. It was a battle he feared would never end. But he also knew it was a battle he could never stop fighting. He owed that to his mother and father and his sister.

Nadrini set the creature down on the elegantly designed padded pillow that lined the ornate box. The box was shaped like a coffin, its design taken from ages past when people buried their dead instead of cremating them on a funeral pyre. This step wasn't absolutely necessary, but all of them felt it was the right way to do it. They surrounded the dying creature in beauty and softness, hoping that the soul within would sense the peace and serenity around them and their departure from this world would be a calm and peaceful one. Nadrini held onto the creature for a few moments longer, making certain the death beetle was lying inert and unmoving before letting go of her grip on it.

Sekanna moved closer to Velit, staring down into the coffin-like tiny box, staring at the lightly glowing death beetle. She said nothing, keeping her expression even, almost coldly unemotional.

Nadrini took the box from Velit and they all moved out of the room, following Nadrini as she carried the box to the Everlasting room. She climbed the few steps that led up to the lavishly decorated pedestal that rested at the far end of the small room. Velit lit the candles that were situated on the wall near the pedestal as Nadrini set the box down on top of the pedestal. She bowed to the box, then stepped back down the steps.

There was no brilliant flash of light, no blinding glare, nothing to signify the release of the soul. The soft pulsing light emanating from within the creature just slowed and dimmed, and then eventually just stopped altogether. That was it. It was very anti-climactic the first time someone witnessed it, but that was simply what happened.

Sekanna stood slightly away from the others, just watching.

Some could argue that the soul wasn't even released. Some could argue that the soul just died within the creature and vanished forever. Some could argue the death beetle's demise also brought about the trapped soul's death. Junto had listened to those arguments, and then had very simply chosen not to believe them. They would never have proof one way or the other. No one could prove the soul escaped into the Everlasting, nor could anyone prove the soul was destroyed forever.

He chose life. He chose to have faith in the path they had chosen. And he would never falter from that belief. He knew Wushwan, Nadrini, and Velit felt the same as he. They would never falter. He sometimes wondered about Sekanna. He sometimes sensed a doubt in her, but she had never expressed it openly to him.

He looked back to the pedestal, to the box, to the death beetle. The light dimmed and then faded out completely. The creature's shell was now a solid thick black. There was no life left in it at all. Not the life of the creature, nor any trapped soul. It was empty. It was now just a hard black gem. After their first extraction they weren't sure what would happen to the death beetle, whether it would keep on living after the extraction, but they quickly came to discover that once the light faded the death beetle was dead. Its shell hardened as it died, forming an outer surface that was difficult to crush let alone chip or even scratch. It truly did look like a black jewel upon its death.

He had heard of collectors who valued the black gems, but he had never actually seen one being used for barter. The thought sickened him that anyone would put a monetary value on some creature that once housed a human soul, but nothing surprised him anymore. Some people paid exorbitant sums for illicit plants, some for exotic animals, some for the carvings of the Riashini tribes, some for the fabric woven by the Seamers. Obsessive collectors would always be around somewhere. There were also rumors of a group that hunted soul stealers for the blackened death gems, murdering the soul stealers and just chopping the death gems out of their flesh, but he had only heard that story once and had never seen any evidence of such a group.

"It is done," Wushwan said.

Sekanna immediately turned away and walked out of the room.

Nadrini gathered up the box and closed the lid. She would take it to join the others in the Room of the Freed Souls, a small room in the front area of the manor house near the study that they had dedicated for that purpose.

Junto sighed. They would have to repeat this process one more time with Tallie, and then two dozen times with that brute Elcor. He was not looking forward to that, but he knew it had to be done. There was no rushing it; there was no quicker way to save them. Every one of those poor souls the huge man had stolen deserved their own chance at reaching the Everlasting. Every single one.

"I just think we are wasting an opportunity," Sekanna said.

Junto rolled his mug absently between his hands.

Sekanna and Junto were seated in the small dining area just outside the kitchen. Velit was busy preparing a meal in the cooking area behind them, dressed in her yellow smock, her feet bare. The dining area, the kitchen, and a small study nearby, were rooms located near the entrance to the manor home, away from the areas deeper in the home that were involved in the captivity of soul stealers and the extraction process.

The Room of the Freed Souls was located just beyond the small study, a thick curtain marking its entrance. They tried to soundproof the walls as best they could up in this area of the manor home by building an extra layer of bricks over a layer of thick clay, but occasionally the angry screams of a prisoner would still reach their ears.

But now there was quiet throughout the manor home, even in the back areas; the only prisoners they held at the manor currently were Tallie and Ulster, and both were either resting or stewing in silence, or eating a meal. Soul stealers with active death gems embedded in their bodies had appetites above all others, as if the death beetles themselves kept demanding sustenance. Junto thought of the four empty bowls he had seen in front of Elcor just before the huge man had revealed the death gems on his arm. He shook his head, disgusted at himself; another obvious clue that he had missed seeing.

"Are you listening to me?" Sekanna asked, leaning towards Junto.

Junto stopped rolling the mug and looked over at Sekanna who sat opposite him across the small table. "I can't even believe you are suggesting such a thing."

"Are you telling me the thought has never crossed your mind."

He looked directly at Sekanna. "Yes. That is what I'm telling you."

Sekanna looked at him for a moment. "Then I'm glad I just planted the seed in your head." She leaned back in her chair.

Junto frowned. "Why would I ever want to do such a thing? That is the exact thing we are fighting to stop."

"There is a difference."

Junto shook his head slightly. "I don't see it."

"We are fighting the good fight. They are not," Sekanna said. "You don't think that's a difference? That's a big fucking difference, Junto."

Junto was silent. He glanced up and looked out the window, absently staring at the thick growth of trees that flanked the side of the manor home. The rising sun was still mostly hidden behind the trees. The manor home was located on the outskirts of Calkut, far enough away from any other homes that no one would just accidentally stumble upon it (or hear the screams of their *guests*), but close enough that they could get into town to restock supplies relatively quickly if necessary. There was no road leading up to the house, just narrow dirt paths they had beaten down and trod upon over the years.

"You really need to think this through," Sekanna said. "If you die, this all ends."

Junto shook his head. "Wushwan will continue."

"Sure, here, in this place," Sekanna glanced about the room, then looked back to Junto. "But who's going to bring him the souls to save? Who's going to hunt soul stealers out in the big ugly world? You know it ain't gonna be me. I'm not the leader type."

Junto was sad to hear those words coming from her, but he knew she spoke the truth. She would not pick up the mantle and carry on the fight by herself. He knew she wouldn't.

"Use the power of the death beetles for good," Sekanna said.

"What could possibly be good about stealing someone's soul?" Junto asked.

"What could possibly be good about you dying and giving the soul stealers free reign to act as they please?"

"I don't plan on dying any time soon."

Sekanna laughed a choked off laugh. "Shit, I don't plan on it, either. But I know that day is coming. Probably sooner rather than later. Our list of enemies is getting long. Probably enough to fill one parchment and part of a second." She paused and took a drink. "You think my sister had that on her list of planned activities for the day?" Sekanna paused again for just a brief moment, then looked at him. "You think Layna planned on dying?"

His hands tightened around his mug and the muscles in his jaw clenched.

"You're pissed at me. I can see that," Sekanna said. "You know what? That's okay. Because you need to listen. You need to plan for the inevitable, Junto. You need to think long and hard on this. You need to keep fighting this fight. We both do, but you do more than me. What the fuck is going to happen if you die? You have to think about that. Right now. You have to think and think and fucking think until your brain's about to explode. There is no other choice. It may take you a while to come to that conclusion, but you will."

Velit moved out of the kitchen, carrying two bowls of steaming food that was a mixture of eggs, chicken, and spices that seemed to change every time she served this particular meal.

Junto raised his mug and slammed it down on the table, sloshing some of the ale over the rim of the cup. "I am not stealing someone else's soul so I can keep on living!"

Sekanna said nothing. They sat in silence for a long moment. "You could use a sacrificial," she finally said.

Velit reached the table and set a steaming bowl down in front of Sekanna. Velit appeared calm and even, as if oblivious of the emotional outbursts taking place around her.

"No! Absolutely not." He shook his head firmly.

"Why not?" Sekanna asked, her tone sincere.

"They would give it to you willingly."

He looked hard at Sekanna. "No, Sekanna. I will never take the soul of a sacrificial. They are lost and troubled and need help. They don't need more encouragement to give up their soul. You can wipe that thought right out of your head right now. I mean it."

Sekanna looked away from his intense stare.

"That will never happen," Junto said.

They sat in silence while Velit set the steaming bowl of food down before Junto. She reached over to Junto and smiled at him, gently caressing his cheek. Junto looked up at her curiously.

"Thank you, Velit," Sekanna said.

Velit gave her a slight frown and a bit of a glare, then gave her a resounding slap across the side of her face. She returned to the kitchen, silently padding across the floor in her bare feet.

Junto looked after Velit, squinting curiously at her. He looked at Sekanna.

"One of their friends was a sacrificial," Sekanna said as a way of explanation for Velit's behavior. "They... weren't able to save her." She absently rubbed at her cheek. "I guess I deserved that."

Junto look towards the kitchen but Velit was no longer in sight.

Sekanna started eating, enjoying heaping spoonfuls of the aromatic meal. Junto absently picked at some of the morsels of meat in his bowl, eating in silence for a while.

"So what are you going to do with Tallie?" Sekanna asked. "Just keep her as a prisoner? Feed her, clothe her, give her a roof over her head?"

Junto didn't answer. He spooned up a small scoop of eggs and ate them.

"She murdered Layna. And maybe my sister, too."

"I know what she did, Sekanna. You don't need to keep on reminding me." He kept his eyes focused on the food in the bowl before him.

"She doesn't deserve to just sit peacefully in one of our cages."

Junto looked up at her. "You want me to torture her?"

"I want you to use her damn soul. That's what I want you to do. She killed Layna by sticking a knife into her belly. She deserves to have her life-force forfeited. She had two more death gems on her. And that third one in her forehead was already black. She already took a soul. Most likely my sister's soul!"

There was a hope that they had just released Oriala's soul in the extraction, or they would soon in the next extraction, but they did not speak of it because they knew they could never be sure whose soul was contained in each of the death gems on Tallie's body. And they had no desire to ask Tallie if she knew because they knew full well that her answer could never be trusted.

"She wiped out a soul forever, Junto," Sekanna said. "Forever."

"I am not going to become what I am fighting to stop," Junto said firmly.

Sekanna was unfazed by the strong declaration in his words. "I think you are just afraid to think this all the way through to its logical conclusion."

He looked at her with a disappointed sadness in his eyes. "I can't believe you are even asking me to consider such a thing."

Sekanna kept her resolve. "Whether you like it or not, it's the only thing that makes sense in this war we are fighting."

CHAPTER THIRTEEN

Ulster scowled at the death gem dealer. "I need half a dozen more."

The dealer was a tall thin man with a pointy goatee. He had a hooked nose and thin lips. He wore a thin robe, tied loosely around his waist with a red sash. His eyes were deep set, a deep brown that was nearly black. The dealer shook his head. "Oh, no. That is too many. The most I can sell you is three. I have other customers who need them."

The dealer's shop, if one could call it a shop, was located in the barn situated near the man's farmhouse. The interior of the barn was murky, a lone torch burning in a sconce on a nearby wall barely throwing off enough light to even reach the dealer's face as the man stood near a row of stalls with low walls. Each stall was about five feet wide and twenty feet deep, the walls of the stalls about three feet high. The place always smelled repulsively of wet animal fur to Ulster, but it was the nearest place he knew of to buy additional death beetles so he had no choice but to tolerate the stench and get his business done as quickly as possible.

"I need six," Ulster said.

"I will sell you three."

Several dozen small animals skittered about within the stalls, snorting and sniffing at the dirt floors of the stalls, screeching and squealing with their annoying screechy squealing voices. Ulster didn't even know what the real name of their breed was; he just knew everybody called them sniffers. They had six legs on their long and slender pink bodies. They had a very fine layer of what could be hair on their bodies, but Ulster had no desire to touch one to be certain one way or the other. They looked hairless to him. They reached anywhere from two feet long to four feet in length on some of the bigger sniffers. They had a flat snout that they pressed firmly against the ground to sniff out what may lay underneath. They also had a sharply tipped tongue they used to spear into the ground, using it as some sort of probe. To Ulster, they looked like a nightmare version of a pig crossed with a caterpillar because of the segmented portions of their body that separated each pair of their legs.

The dealer tossed a spoonful of some form of food into one of the stalls, scooping the food out of the bucket he was holding. The sniffers in the stall squealed with delight and scurried over to the food, noisily devouring it.

The death gem dealers used the sniffers to track and hunt down death beetle nests, or so Ulster had heard the stories say. He didn't know if those stories were true or not, but the death beetles did have to come from somewhere, so someone had to be hunting them down. That explanation was as good as any other.

One of the sniffers lifted its head, staring at

Ulster with its wide eyes. It had a look on its face that made Ulster feel uncomfortable as he stared at it. Sniffers always looked like they were on the verge of hysterics, with their amber eyes wide and intense on their round, heavily wrinkled faces. He couldn't look at it for more than a few seconds without wanting to cringe. He looked away from the sniffer, looking back over to the dealer. "I already have plans for three and I like to keep extras with me," Ulster said. "Just in case a situation presents itself."

The dealer nodded. "It's good to be prepared." He tossed another spoonful of food into another stall. The sniffers reacted with the same delight to the food, snorting and snuffing and attacking the food with great relish.

"So you'll give me six?" Ulster asked.

The dealer shook his head. "I will sell you three."

"How about I buy three and then just take three," Ulster said, not being subtle with the obvious threat.

The dealer looked down at the bucket he held in his hand. He slowly, deliberately, set the bucket down on the ground near the stalls. He raised himself back up, making a soft whistling sound as he moved.

Every single one of the two dozen sniffers stopped screeching and squealing and stopped moving. Every single sniffer swiveled its head towards Ulster, rising up to stand on its two hind legs. Every single sniffer glared at him with a wide-eyed, intense stare that was far more ominous and menacing than hysterical. Every single sniffer extended claws out a few inches from its front paws. Every single sniffer showed Ulster razor sharp teeth behind a snarling grimace.

The death gem dealer looked at Ulster. "I will sell you three."

Ulster said nothing.

"I will see your coins, please," the dealer said. He held out his hand, palm up.

Ulster unhooked a coin pouch from his belt and dropped it into the dealer's waiting hand. The heavy pouch jangled with the sound of many coins grinding against each other as it plopped down into the dealer's palm. The dealer held the pouch still for a moment, staring at the small leathery bag, then he looked up at Ulster. "You are one short."

Ulster frowned, but produced a loose coin from his pocket and flipped it towards the dealer. The dealer snatched the coin out of the air and added it to the pouch.

Behind him, the sniffers returned to feeding on their meals, snorting and grunting and squealing in the dirt.

The dealer raised his hand into the air, extending his index finger. As if appearing out of nowhere, a young boy stepped out from the shadows and approached the dealer. He was about twelve years old with long blond hair, dressed in a plain tunic and brown breeches. The dealer bent down to the boy and whispered in his ear. He handed the boy the coin pouch and the boy raced out of the barn.

Ulster studied the dealer for a moment as he

waited for his order of death gems to be delivered. The tall man had no visible death gems on him. "You do not partake of the death gems?" he asked the dealer.

The dealer shook his head. "One life in this miserable place is enough for me."

"If you're tired of it, you can give it to me."

The dealer looked at him. "Do I look like a sacrificial to you?"

Ulster smiled. "Only when the torchlight catches you just right."

The dealer stared at him for a moment with a distasteful twist to his lips. "I find you very unpleasant," the dealer told him.

Ulster shrugged. "But you'll still take my coin."

"Of course."

Moments later, the boy reappeared, carrying a leather pouch. The boy handed the pouch to the dealer. "May I go to the Races now?" the boy asked. "The Reds have a great team this year!" The boy was genuinely excited, his tanned face beaming.

"There are Races?" Ulster asked. "Here?"

The boy nodded his head enthusiastically. "Oh, yes."

Ulster felt a tingling rush of excitement. He loved the Races. He hadn't seen one in years, let alone participate in one as he had done so many years ago. The Races! He had to go.

"What did I tell you about talking to the customers," the dealer said, chiding the boy. "We will speak of this later."

The boy lowered his head and shuffled away, going back to his hidden spot somewhere in the shadows.

The dealer reached into the leather pouch the boy had brought him and pulled out a death beetle. Ulster felt a nervous thrill just at the sight of the creature. Its tendril-legs were barely visible, curled up tight beneath its hard outer shell. It was in its dormant stage and would remain so until he placed it on a dying body. This one had a greenish color to it, almost an emerald quality to its shell.

The dealer set the death beetle down on a nearby stool, then pulled out the second death beetle and set it down next to the first. This one also had a greenish color to it, but it had more of a jade quality to its shell. The third death beetle had a deep red color to it, a ruby-like sheen to its shell. The colors seemed to make no difference in how the creatures worked. One worked just as well as the other no matter what color the shell was. He wondered if there was a difference that he wasn't aware of. Ulster thought of asking the dealer, but he had a great dislike for the man and he had no desire to engage him in any further conversation. He just wanted his death gems, and then he would depart.

The dealer gestured towards the three death beetles on the stool and Ulster quickly scooped them up, dumping them into another leather pouch which he then promptly tied very securely to his belt so that it was positioned snugly at his waist, near his right upper thigh. He hated touching the things; he had a superstitious fear that a death beetle would unfold its tendrils and stick them into his flesh if he held on to one of them too long. He handled them as little as possible. The next time he would even look at them would be when he was ready to use one of them.

He turned and exited the death gem dealer's shop.

He couldn't get the thought of the Races out of his head. The thunderous sound of the horses' hooves pounding in the dirt. The cracks of the whips as the Drivers urged their teams to go ever faster and faster. The raucous cheering of the crowd. All of the women shouting lustily for their team, then letting their lusts get the better of them in the dark corridors of the stadium. It had been far too long since he had attended one.

He thought of the orange-haired whore and his plan of revenge. He chastised himself for losing track of the extractor and his minions. The damned smell of the bakery had been just too strong for him to resist. He had been so damned hungry he couldn't take it anymore. And that bread had been so very tasty. He was confident he would come across the extractor again anyway, especially if he stayed near Calkut. The extractor seemed to have a base of operations somewhere close to the town. And now that he had more death beetles on hand, he was much more prepared to take advantage of his true plans — to destroy anyone and everyone who threatened his way of life and feast on their souls.

But the Races. Oh, the Races...

He would just go take a quick peek at them to satisfy his curiosity.

CHAPTER FOURTEEN

"Just kill me," Tallie pleaded as she writhed on the mattress. "I can't take the pain." She was still naked, bound tightly to the bed with ropes around her wrists and ankles to prevent herself from doing any harm to herself, each wrist and ankle bound to a separate bedpost. A metal collar was attached around her neck, but there was no chain attached to the collar at the moment. There was a bright red welt on her right shoulder where the death beetle had been embedded in her flesh. Within the welt, five dark holes were visible, marking the areas where the tendrils had burrowed into her skin. The darkly red patch of skin was starting to show the beginnings of a permanent scar already starting to form, a scar that would be a permanent record of her crime for all to see.

They had moved Tallie into a small bedroom next to the extraction chamber. It was a sparsely furnished room where they held the extractee while they were in the middle of the extraction process, containing only a bed, a small side table and two chairs. A toilet was positioned in the far corner, a tiny basin next to it.

Sekanna looked at the red welt on Tallie's right

shoulder. She was the only one in the room with her, sitting in a chair near the side of the bed. There was an herb Sekanna knew of that she could give to Tallie to help alleviate the lingering pain of the prior extraction, but she chose not to give it to her. She fingered the length of chain in her hand as she stared at Tallie. "You should have thought of that before you stole someone's soul." Sekanna pointed to the remaining death gem on Tallie's left shoulder; the gem glimmered very faintly with an aqua blue glow. "Who was it? Whose soul did you take?"

Tallie didn't answer.

"You think you feel pain now?" Sekanna asked. "That's nothing compared to what you are going to feel next if you don't answer me."

Tallie remained silent.

"We can extract one tendril every two days and make this last." She looked hard at Tallie. "I think I might even enjoy that."

A flash of fear crossed Tallie's eyes.

Sekanna saw the distress in Tallie's face. "That puckered up your little purple-haired pussy, now didn't it?"

Tallie remained silent.

Sekanna felt the disgust and hate for this woman churning up inside her. She clenched her jaw tight, gripping the cold metal chain in her fingers tightly. Her platinum hair shimmered. "Tell me," Sekanna said.

"It was just some old man," Tallie said, looking away.

"What was his name?"

Tallie frowned. "How should I know? It was just some old man we grabbed off the street."

"Wrong place at the wrong time, huh?"

"Yeah."

Sekanna patted Tallie's bare leg, the force of her pat getting harder and harder each time she touched her leg. "Well, lucky for you it's the right place and the right time." Sekanna attached the chain she held in her hand to the metal collar around Tallie's neck, then attached the other end to a hook on the wall, keeping the woman rigidly bound while she untied one of Tallie's hands, freeing it from the bedpost. "Time for your final extraction." She finished removing the remaining bindings, freeing Tallie's other arm and her legs. She unhooked the chain from the wall and tugged on Tallie, jerking her head forward a bit roughly. "I will drag you if I have to," Sekanna said.

Tallie resisted, but another sharp tug on her neck chain forced her to her feet. She stood shakily on her feet near the side of the bed. "What are you going to do with me after the — extraction?"

"We haven't decided yet. I told Junto he should use your soul." Sekanna made the statement casually, then started to head out of the room, clutching the chain as she moved. The chain grew taut and Sekanna turned to see Tallie frozen where she stood. Her face was filled with absolute fear. "Gee, you don't think that's appropriate?" Sekanna asked. "After you stole three souls?"

"No…" Tallie said, the word coming out more as a terrified gasp.

"You don't think we should just wipe you out

of existence forever?"

"No, please don't."

Sekanna looked at her curiously, with no remorse. "But that's what you did to my sister."

"I—" Tallie started, but then had no words.

Sekanna cocked her head towards the woman. "You what?"

Tallie stayed silent.

"You thought maybe no one would stop you?" Sekanna took a threatening step towards her. "You thought maybe no one would ever catch you? You thought maybe no one would care what you did?"

"I — I'm sorry," Tallie said.

"You're just sorry you got caught, you piece of garbage." Sekanna tugged violently on the chain, yanking Tallie down to her knees.

"Sekanna!"

Sekanna looked up to see Junto entering the room. She looked at Tallie, then back to Junto. "She fell."

Junto reached down to Tallie and gripped her under her elbow, helping her back up to her feet.

"Don't steal my soul," she said to Junto, begging for mercy. Tears pooled in the corners of her eyes, threatening to wash away what little remained of her purple eye make-up.

Junto looked at Sekanna. Sekanna raised her eyebrows and gave him a slight shrug. He kept his gaze on Sekanna as he replied to Tallie. "No one is going to be stealing your soul," he said.

Sekanna looked away from his gaze.

"What are you going to do with me?" Tallie asked.

"We are going to extract that soul from you," Junto said, indicating the slightly shimmering death gem on her left shoulder.

"After that. What are you going to do with me after that?" Her voice trembled.

Sekanna didn't hesitate. "I vote to put a death gem on you and extract *your* soul." Sekanna raised her hand that was not holding on to the leash.

"Just let me go," Tallie begged, keeping her gaze on Junto. "I'll leave Calkut. I'll leave Moraneesh. You'll never see me again. I swear it."

"That's never going to happen," Sekanna said.

"I'll tell you where Ulster is," Tallie blurted out. "He's the one you should really be after. He's the one who did all this." She reached for Junto, clutching at his tunic. "I'll tell you where to find him."

Junto looked down at where Tallie was clutching his clothing, at her bare breasts thrusting into his own chest, but he made no move to remove her grip on him. He looked back up at Tallie's begging, pleading face. "Yes you will," Junto said. "Yes, you will."

Tallie talked. Junto and Sekanna sat with her at the table in the dining area just outside the kitchen. They fed her a delicious meal prepared by Velit and listened to her talk and talk and talk. They gave her some sweet wine and she drank the first goblet-full as if she had just walked out of the Arindia Dunes and was dying of thirst. They filled her goblet again and patiently watched her eat. They had even given her a thin blanket to throw about her shoulders to cover her nakedness. The metal collar was still around her neck with the chain attached; Sekanna held the other end of the chain in her hand.

Tallie told them about her childhood, about growing up on the verge of starvation every day, about her brother, how he abused her and raped her. Sekanna listened with an utter lack of sympathy, if not outright contempt, for every word that came out of Tallie's mouth. Junto had a disturbing feeling that Sekanna wouldn't hesitate to slit the whore's throat if he had told her to do so after the final extraction, Tallie's soul attached to her for all eternity be damned.

Tallie was obviously trying to evoke some kind of pity for her plight, but Junto had none for her either, nor did he even pretend to have some. He just listened with a flat expression. Finally, after the story of her third rape, he had enough of her troubled past. He suspected there were far more lies than truth in everything she had told them anyway; he was pretty certain of that. The woman reeked of falsehood. "Where's Ulster?" he asked.

Tallie took a drink of her sweet wine and set the goblet down. "He has a room on Farindall Road. That little inn right near the cobbler's shop."

"Is he there now?" Junto asked.

Tallie shrugged. "I don't know. He was supposed to come and get me out of the crowd after—" Her voice cut off.

"After what?" Junto asked. "Go on, you can finish. After what?"

"You know what," Tallie said. She stared down at the goblet in front of her.

"I would like you to say it," Junto said. "After what?"

"After I stabbed Orange." She raised the goblet and took a deep drink.

Junto fought to keep his expression even. "Her name was Layna." Beautiful Layna. Beautiful, stunning Layna. A flash of anger lit up his thoughts and he ground his teeth together. Why was he trying to be polite to this whore? She had killed Layna. Stuck a knife in her gut and murdered her in cold blood. He felt his fingers curl into hooks and for a brief, flashing moment envisioned them going around Tallie's neck and squeezing tight. He quickly forced that image out of his mind and uncurled his fingers.

Tallie said nothing.

"And then what?" Junto asked. "What was the plan after that?" His voice was tight as he spoke.

Tallie took another drink of her sweet wine. "He was supposed to come find me in all the confusion and pull me out of the crowd. But he didn't."

"And then what?" Junto felt his voice get tighter.

Tallie wiped at her mouth with the back of her hand. "He wanted her life-force. I know that much. He was going to follow whoever took the body and steal her soul. At least that's what he told me. That's why I put the death gem on her."

"How did my sister die?" Sekanna asked. She yanked on the chain, jerking Tallie's head forward.

Junto looked at Sekanna curiously, but said nothing. She had been quiet the entire time before this question. He turned back to Tallie, also wanting to know the answer.

"Did you kill her, too?" Sekanna said.

"Ulster made me do it." Tallie raised the goblet back up towards her mouth, but Sekanna reached across the table and swiped the cup out of her hand before it could reach her lips. The red liquid splashed across Tallie's chest, the table, the floor at her bare feet.

Sekanna stared at the woman with venomous hate. She tugged on the chain, pulling Tallie's face closer to her. The shimmering emanating from Sekanna's platinum hair cast a faint glow on Tallie's terrified face. "Your final extraction is going to be very slow and very painful. And I am going to enjoy every second of it."

The fear on Tallie's face was absolute. It covered her features, moved deep into her eyes. Her lips trembled. Her fingers shook. "No," she whimpered. "No, please. No..."

"Sekanna, that's enough," Junto said. "We don't use the extraction process to torture anyone."

"We should," Sekanna said immediately without any hesitation. She loosened her tugging grip on the chain and Tallie jerked back away from her. She glared hatefully at Tallie. "I'll find a way to make you pay." Sekanna's silvery locks shimmered. Then she jerked sharply on the chain, pulling Tallie's head violently down, sending her face smashing into the plate on the table, the force of the harsh yank cracking the plate as Tallie's face collided with it. Tallie yelped in pain and sputtered as she lifted her head back up. A trickle of blood oozed down out of her nose, and a few bits of food stuck to her cheeks and chin.

"Sekanna!" Junto said, his voice firm.

The dark resolve in Sekanna's face never wavered despite the disapproving look and harsh reprobation from Junto. "I slipped."

Junto glanced up to see Velit standing quietly nearby in the kitchen doorway. "Tell Wushwan and Nadrini to prepare for the final extraction."

Velit gave him a slight bow and hurried away to inform the others.

Tallie wiped at the food on her face, whimpering in pain.

Junto looked disapproving again at Sekanna, but she kept her expression calm.

Had Junto known what Sekanna was really thinking of doing with Tallie, the disturbing feeling he had felt earlier would have amplified itself a hundred-fold.

CHAPTER FIFTEEN

Over the course of the following day, they finished extracting the final death gem from Tallie and then freed the trapped soul, releasing whoever it was who had been trapped within the death beetle that had been embedded on Tallie's left shoulder. They placed the blackened death gem in the Room of the Freed Souls along with the others. Perhaps it was Oriala whom they had freed. Perhaps it was someone else besides Sekanna's sister. They would never know. At least not until they reached the Everlasting themselves and found out who was waiting there for them.

The ugly rage Junto had felt towards the purple-haired whore had not fully subsided. He was seated in an overstuffed chair in the small study that was located in the front area of the manor home. Several tall shelves filled with books lined one wall. Three other chairs, all of them empty, were positioned near the one he was sitting in; he was alone in the room with his thoughts. Several small tables were positioned near the chairs, their wooden surfaces gleaming with a fresh polish that Nadrini or Velit must have just put on them. He still needed to figure out what to do with the woman. Was he really going to be able to keep Tallie in a prison cell for the remainder of her days, feed her, give her shelter, knowing that every time he saw her he would think of Layna? Did Tallie even deserve to live out her days? He wondered if he should just leave her a vial of poison in her cage and let her take her own life? Should he let her starve to death? Would that count as murder? Would that still bind her soul to his? And whose souls would that bind if they just left her to die? His? Sekanna's? Wushwan's? Everyone who was aware of what they were doing? Could a soul be attached to multiple people if they each had an equal hand in that person's death? It was a tricky question that had no definitive answer, and he had no desire to test any of those theories specifically because there was no answer.

Should he wait for Zerin's return and let Zerin behead her and be done with it? Should he let Zerin burn her on the funeral pyre? No, she didn't even deserve that dignity. Junto knew he had to decide soon before pity overtook his anger. And he knew it wasn't fair to ask Zerin to perform an execution, even though Zerin already had a dozen murdered souls connected to him for all eternity. Zerin was sincere in his attempt to atone for his past soul-stealing crimes. He had even gone so far as to take a pilgrimage to Tholg, seeking some kind of enlightenment, or perhaps forgiveness, from the Anchii priests. Regardless, he knew bringing Zerin into the equation was a moot point; the man wasn't even around. He had left for Yoknari weeks ago, and his expected return was a few weeks away, but

Junto knew it may be far longer than that before Zerin returned. If he even returned at all. He wasn't sure what Zerin would do. Ever.

Junto thought of Irchly again and wondered where he was. He felt like he could really use his presence right about now. He was a calming presence that balanced out Sekanna's hot-headed flashes of temper.

And what of Ulster? Sekanna had already finished scouting the inn near the cobbler's on Farindall Road, and had returned to the manor home just after they had finished the releasing of the soul rescued from Tallie's death gem. Junto had told Sekanna they didn't need her for Tallie's final extraction and she hadn't put up a fight. Junto was grateful for Sekanna's concession on that point. He knew she would have enjoyed watching Tallie suffer through her final extraction, which was exactly the reason why he had not wanted her in attendance for the extraction.

Sekanna had willingly stayed away and had gone out to scout the area near Farindall Road to see if she could gather more information on the whereabouts of Ulster - with the strict instructions that she was not to engage him if she found him. If she did find him, she was to immediately return to the manor home and report back to Junto. But she didn't find him, and had already returned home with only hints of his whereabouts. Many people said they had seen Ulster days ago, so Tallie had been telling the truth about him having a room there at least, but no one had seen him lately. The trail was cold for now.

The next place they needed to look for Ulster, or least try to find more clues to his whereabouts, was at the death gem merchants' shops; they needed to question the men and women who sold the death beetles. Junto detested the merchants who peddled the death beetles, and put them on a level just above the soul stealers but not much higher. They were next on his list to wipe out after the soul stealers, but he also knew they were still important to him. They were often the only lead he had.

He had yet to take down a death gem merchant's shop. They were too well protected, too well guarded. And he knew the Enforcers in the towns where the shops were located were very well compensated to keep the merchant shops safe and secure. Any town that allowed a death gem merchant shop to set up was a dirty town. No one could be trusted in a town like that. No one. There was far too much coin involved. And now Calkut was rumored to have its own death merchants, possibly even several. He had heard stories of one merchant setting up shop on a remote farm on the edge of town, and then also another rumor of a merchant setting up shop on the fringes of the marketplace itself. It seemed the merchants were getting more and more brazen, becoming more and more visible, creeping ever closer to the hearts of towns, spreading their vile ways deeper into the population.

His thoughts returned to Tallie. And to Layna. What would Layna want him to do with her killer? How would she want to be avenged? He thought of keeping Tallie alive. Keeping her as a constant reminder of his failure. Every time he saw her it would remind him to be more vigilant, more alert, plan better, plan smarter. Would she serve him better by remaining alive? Or would Tallie's death bring him at least some semblance of satisfaction, give him closure over Layna's death?

He thought of Layna more and more. Of her sweet face. Her soft skin. That fiery orange-red head of hair. And he had cried. He had sat on his bed last night with his head in his hands and just let the hot tears fall through his fingers. And then the tears had made him angry and he thought of running a blade across Tallie's throat and listening to her splutter and choke while she died. Or maybe he would just cut her a little at a time, he had thought, killing her with excruciating slowness. But that only brought more angry tears, anger directed at her for making him think such ugly things. There was no solution that would ever end his misery. There was nothing he could do with her that would ever take away his guilt and his pain.

Keeping Tallie alive would become a tedious chore. They would have to feed her, clean her, guard her. They already had limited resources as it was. They were not prepared to keep adding to their stock of prisoners. Their two current prisoners, Baisk and Liesh, were already a major pain in the ass to take care of. He should just let Zerin whirl through them with his blade and be done with it. Lop off their heads and throw them into the river. The thought sickened him, but he feared they truly needed a cold-blooded killer as part of their group, someone who didn't give a damn about their own eternal soul, someone who could just do the horrific things that needed to be done. He would never be that person. And he certainly didn't want to turn Sekanna into that person. Irchly would never do it, either. Wushwan, Nadrini, and Velit wouldn't even be part of any such discussion, so they were out.

He cursed and clenched his teeth. Keeping Tallie alive just wasn't going to be practical. But then he thought of something else. What if they let her escape? Make her think she did it on her own. Or what if they just let her go? Make her promise never to steal a soul again and then act as if they trusted her word (even when they knew they never really could). Would she lead them to Ulster? Would she even try to find him after he had betrayed her? She might, he knew. She might do it just to spite Ulster. She seemed like that kind of woman. She might just track him down to spit in his face and walk away. She might just lead them right to him.

"Have you lost your mind?" Sekanna asked. "You want to let her go?"

"She might lead us to Ulster," Junto said. "We can have Nadrini and Velit track her while we search for Ulster ourselves. We might be able to find him quicker this way."

They were sitting at the kitchen table, some half-eaten bowls of food resting on the table before them.

"And she damn well might not lead us to

Ulster," Sekanna countered. "Then what?"

"Then we bring her back here and put her in a cell."

"And how long do we give her to find Ulster? A day? A week? Two weeks?"

Junto didn't answer.

"And what if she eludes us? What if Nadrini and Velit lose track of her?"

"They won't."

Sekanna shook her head. "You can't say that, Junto. Shit happens. How would you feel if we lost her and she was out there living her life without paying for what she did? How would that make you feel?"

"Just think about it," Junto said. "Maybe we can make it work."

Sekanna pushed her chair back sharply and rose quickly away from the table. "That woman cannot be set free!" Her face was aflame with a wild fury he rarely saw so brazenly displayed on her features. Her hair shone a bright silver. She stormed out of the room.

Junto should have gone after her. He should have tried to calm Sekanna down, but he had no idea to the extent which the very thought of releasing Tallie had pushed her. Her thoughts had already been going to dangerous places, places on the verge of a precipice from which there would be no returning if she stepped over the ledge. He should have gone after her before her wildly angry thoughts plunged her into the uncharted territory hidden in the dark recesses of her mind. But he didn't.

CHAPTER SIXTEEN

Junto awoke feeling strange, as if he had been in the middle of an unpleasant dream but could remember none of what was happening in the dream, only that it was disturbing and weird. He felt a slight tingling itch on the back of his right shoulder. He usually slept only with a light pair of cloth pants on, so his torso was bare. He reached over his right shoulder with his left hand and touched something hard. It felt smooth, but had several facets to it. His hand froze and then he bolted upright, every muscle in his body tensing, squeezing tight. No, no. It can't be. He leaped out of his bed, his bare feet slapping against the cold wood floor. He tried to look at his shoulder, spinning in a mad circle like a cat chasing its tail, but he couldn't see what he had just touched. He slowed his motion, fighting to catch his breath. He slowly reached up with trembling fingers and touched the object on his right shoulder again. No!

It was a death gem. He had a death gem embedded into his flesh!

Junto stormed through the hallways, his mind awhirl with dizzying thoughts. He had thrown on a shirt to cover the hideous thing attached to his skin. A death gem! He had a death beetle embedded in his flesh! How could that be? When had that happened? During the night? But how? He hadn't felt anything.

He continued to march angrily through the hallways and found Velit near the kitchen. "Where is Sekanna?" he demanded. Velit shook her head and gave him a casual shrug. Junto grabbed her shoulders and roughly shook her. "Where is Sekanna?" He released his grip on Velit when he saw the fear in her eyes. He spun away and moved on, shouting her name over and over. "Sekanna! Sekanna!"

He moved deeper into the manor home, entering the holding area where they kept their most recent prisoners in their cages as they awaited extraction. He immediately saw that Tallie was not in her cage. Had they moved her downstairs to a prison cell after the final extraction? Was she with Baisk and Liesh? No, no one had even consulted with him on which cell to put her in. He glanced over at Elcor's cage, but the huge man was asleep on his cot, snoring loudly.

Junto exited the holding area and saw Wushwan stepping into a nearby hallway. Junto hurried up to the slender dark-skinned man. "Where is Sekanna?"

"She left," Wushwan said.

"She left? Where did she go?"

"To the death merchant's shop," Wushwan

said.

"By herself?" Junto frowned.

Wushwan said nothing.

"Why didn't you stop her?" Junto asked.

Wushwan gave him an incredulous look.

Junto knew no one could stop Sekanna when she had her mind set on something. "Forget it," he said to Wushwan. "Did she say anything else?"

"She said you would be very angry when you woke up."

"Oh, she did, did she? Did she tell you why I would be very angry when I woke up?" He could feel every muscle in his body tensing up again, tightening with a growing fury.

Wushwan did not answer.

Junto grabbed the collar of his own shirt and yanked it down, shifting his right shoulder towards Wushwan to reveal the death gem to him. "That's why. Prepare for extraction."

Wushwan did not move.

"Wushwan, prepare for extraction."

Wushwan did not move.

Junto frowned angrily at him, his eyes narrowing to a glare. "What's wrong with you? I want this off of me. Now!"

Wushwan did not move.

Junto studied him, intently looking at the man he thought was his trusted friend. "You knew about this." But then it became a question because he could not believe it. His shoulders drooped. "You knew about this?"

"It is for the greater good," Wushwan said. There was not even a hint of any doubt, or guilt, in his voice.

"The greater good? The greater fucking good?"

"She took a life. She can now save a life. Your life. It keeps the world in balance." To Wushwan, this was a simple, logical matter and the words came out in a calm, even tone.

Junto threw his hands to his head. "Is everyone crazy around here? I don't want to steal someone's soul! Prepare for extraction. Now!"

Wushwan did not move. "Sekanna needs your help. She needs you to stay alive."

"Sekanna can rot in Hell's Wood!" Junto stormed off. "Sekanna!"

CHAPTER SEVENTEEN

Sekanna moved slowly through the Calkut market, moving towards the western fringe of the marketplace where they had heard rumors of a death gem merchant setting up shop. A slight dollop of rainfall during the night left only a slight glistening vestige of its visit on some rooftops and on the edges of a few merchant wagons. The ground beneath her boots was already back to its normal dry-brown appearance and there was little left of the rain's scent in the air, perhaps a hint of its departing humidity. It was mid-afternoon and the early rush of morning customers had subsided. Only a few handfuls of people wandered about the market, moving lazily in and out merchant stalls; no one seemed to have any real purchase intent and just appeared to be content to browse and make idle talk with the merchants.

She had used her death beetle on Junto. Now he had one. It was done. She had done it. Junto had a death gem embedded in his flesh. There was no taking it back. She absently rubbed the inside of her thigh, running her hand over her inner thigh, fingering the death gem embedded in her leg. Now they both had one. Is that why she had done it to

Junto? So she wouldn't feel so guilty about hers? Did she put the stain on Junto so she wouldn't feel so alone? Did she mark him so her mark wouldn't be so ugly? Or did she do it to save his life, to give him a second chance if the unthinkable happened?

She knew it was some of both.

She knew it wasn't funny, not even in the slightest, but she so wanted to see the reaction on Junto's face when he felt the death gem she had put on him. She was surprised it hadn't woken him up, but she knew he had drunk pretty heavily before he went to bed because of his tormented emotions over what to do with that purple-haired bitch, so he probably didn't even feel the slight pinch as the tendrils went into his flesh. Plus, the crushed blackout root she had waved under his sleeping nose had most assuredly put him into a deeper slumber as well.

She remembered the apprehensive fear she had felt when she had attached hers. She had been ready for some serious pain, but had only felt a very slight tingling when she had put her death beetle against her skin. It had almost been pleasant. It hadn't been the wisest choice to put it on the inside of her thigh, but there was nothing she could do about that now. It had been a crazy, impulsive thing to do it in the first place and that was the spot on her body that seemed the most hidden from any prying eyes, especially since she had no sexual relations with anyone, be it a man or a woman, in quite some time.

She wondered what Junto was feeling right now. He was most likely storming up and down the hallways in their manor home, cursing her name.

She reached what she believed was the death gem merchant's shop and paused. Two big men stood guard outside. She pretended to ignore them and started to walk past them. That didn't work. One of them blocked her path, putting a beefy hand directly on her chest. She slapped his hand away from her breasts.

The man was not fazed. He looked down at her. "State your business." He had a big squarish head with a square haircut to match his square jawline. His skin had a slight olive-drab hue to it and she surmised he was probably from Yoknari as most of the Yoknari had a similar tint to their flesh that had come from generations of exposure to the khack leaf. It seemed to give them an immunity to the addictive effects of the khack leaf, which made them greatly effective as dealers in the powerful herb. Well, she didn't know if their skin color actually gave them any immunity, but the olive-drab color of skin on a person usually did indicate someone who would not succumb to the intoxicating effects of the khack. Khack dealers often worked hand-in-hand with death gem merchants. Both kinds were the bottom dwellers of society as far as Sekanna was concerned.

"I want to speak to the merchant," she said to the Yoknari guard.

"And of what subject do you want to speak?" he asked.

"That is between the merchant and myself."

"No. It is not," the guard said.

"I want to ask him a few questions," Sekanna said.

"What questions do you want to ask him?"

"Questions that are meant for him."

The Yoknari guard's facial expression did not change. "You are now tiresome. Be on your way."

Sekanna stared at him. She reached up and took his hand, putting it against the cloth of her breeches that covered her inner thigh. "Feel that? I need another one."

The Yoknari man pulled his hand immediately away from her when she let go of him. "I don't know what that is."

Sekanna frowned. "It's a death gem. I need another one."

"You say it is a death gem."

"It is."

"So you say." The Yoknari man did not move from her path, continuing to block the entrance to the shop.

"It's a death gem," she repeated.

"I heard you," the guard said.

She stood still for a moment. Then, she loosened the belt around her breeches and pulled the fabric away from her waist. "Feel it," she told him. She motioned down to the opening between the fabric and the smooth skin of her belly. "Feel it. It's a death gem."

"I've already felt it," he said.

"Then let me in to see the merchant," Sekanna said.

"I have not seen it," the guard said.

Sekanna paused, the fabric still in her hand. She released her grip on her clothing. She glanced around the area. The shop was near the end of a narrow strip of road but there were still people milling about, talking, walking past, visiting other shops nearby. She sighed. She pulled her breeches down to reveal the tops of her thighs. She also exposed the curls of her platinum womanly hairs. The man looked at the patch of silvery-haired curls for a moment. Sekanna pointed to the death gem embedded in the inside of her thigh. "Down here, big boy," she said.

The Yoknari guard looked up at her face, then moved his gaze down to the death gem in her thigh. He crouched down to get a closer look, putting his face near her crotch area. Sekanna glanced around to see a couple watching her curiously. She waved to them and smiled. The guard reached towards her thigh and touched the death gem.

"One inch higher and I'll slice off your fingers," she said as he glanced up at her.

He smiled at her, then withdrew his hand. He moved back up to a standing position.

She pulled her breeches back up and tightened her belt. "Now are you going to let me in?"

The man motioned to the other Yoknari guard. The second guard was a big man as well, but not as big as the first guard who had blocked her way. His dark hair was a bit longer and he had a slight growth of beard starting to stubble his chin. He had been standing silently, watching them with bemused eyes. He disappeared inside the building, following the commanding gesture of the first guard's head tilt.

"We will see if the merchant wishes to see you," the first guard said.

She jangled her coin pouch. "I have coin."

The Yoknari man wasn't impressed. "So do I."

Sekanna frowned. "Doesn't he want customers?"

"He does. They need to be the right customers."

"And what kind of customer is that? I thought any customer with coin was the right customer."

The guard made no reply to that.

The second Yoknari guard came back out and shook his head at the first guard.

The first guard looked at her. "Move along."

"You had your face in my crotch and now you are telling me to move along?" Sekanna shook her head. "I don't think so."

The Yoknari man slowly eased his hand down to the handle of his sword. "Move along."

Sekanna remained where she was. "Look, I need to talk to him."

"I need a mansion in the hills of Valeo. Doesn't mean I am going to get one."

The second guard sniggered.

Sekanna reflexively reached for her sword.

The first guard shook his head. "Don't do that."

Sekanna glanced down at her hand, then moved her fingers away from the leather handle of her weapon. "Hell's Wood! I need to talk to him."

Neither Yoknari man moved, nor even pretended to care.

"I'm looking for someone," she finally said. "Maybe you can help me. He's covered with death gems. A big guy. Goes by the name of Ulster. You seen him?"

"I've seen him," the first guard said.

Sekanna's expression brightened. "You've seen Ulster? When? Where is he? Where was he headed?"

The first guard glanced at her coin pouch, then back up to her face.

Sekanna reached into her coin pouch, plucked out a coin, and handed it to him.

He took the coin and put it into his coin pouch. But said nothing more.

"When did you see him?" Sekanna asked.

"I've seen him several times."

Sekanna glowered. "When did you see him last?"

He said nothing.

She gave him another coin. "When did you see him last?"

"A few days ago."

"He was here?"

The Yoknari man did not answer. She handed him another coin.

"Yes," he said.

"Did he say anything?"

The guard did not answer.

She gave him another coin.

"He said several things."

She stared at him. "You are trying to piss me off, aren't you?"

He stared at her, then raised up an open palm. She handed him a coin, slapping it into his open hand.

"Yes," he said.

The second guard chuckled softly, clearly

enjoying his partner's shenanigans.

Sekanna gritted her teeth. "I need to find Ulster. What do I need to do to talk to the merchant?"

The first guard deposited the coin she had just given him into the coin pouch secured to his belt. "The merchant won't tell you. He won't reveal anything about his patrons."

"Oh, he might." She fingered her sword handle. "If the price is right."

"If you threaten violence against the merchant one more time I will kill you where you stand."

She took her hand away from her sword. "I need to find Ulster. He stole something from me that he shouldn't have taken."

"Why didn't you say so? Thieves leave a bad taste in my mouth," the guard said. "He's probably over at Kral's. He likes the food there. If he's not there now, he'll probably show up in a day or two." He handed her back the coins she had given him, digging them out of his pouch and presenting them to her in his open palm.

She looked at him curiously.

"I don't need your coin. The merchant pays us quite well."

Sekanna took back her coins and dropped them into her coin pouch.

The Yoknari man pointed to the inside of her thigh. "Who is it?"

"What?"

"Whose soul?"

"Oh." She looked down at her leg, then back up at him. "Someone who didn't need it anymore."

The man touched his chest, near his heart. "I have my wife's. She gave it to me."

"That was — nice of her." Sekanna had no idea what else to say.

The Yoknari man shook his head. "No. She was very ill, but too afraid of the Everlasting. She begged me to take it. I didn't really want it, but she begged me. I didn't want it."

The second guard reached out and gently put his hand on the first man's shoulder. The first guard put his hand over the second guard's hand and squeezed it. The second guard withdrew his hand.

"Why was she afraid of the Everlasting?" Sekanna asked after a moment. She knew it might not be an appropriate question of a stranger, but her curiosity got the best of her.

The first guard hesitated, but then decided to answer. "She killed a woman. It was many years ago, before she met me, but she was afraid to go into the Everlasting. Afraid she was there waiting for her."

Sekanna was quiet. "So you took her soul?"

"She begged me. I could not say no to her." The first guard paused. "We had a good life together. That's what she wanted."

Sekanna was again quiet. "But you'll never see her again. Not even in the Everlasting."

The first guard touched the area near his heart, obviously feeling the death gem embedded in his flesh beneath his tunic. "She's always with me now."

"But..." Sekanna closed her mouth. She did not want to get into a deep discussion with the man. She was quiet again, not trying to move forward, but also not turning around to leave.

The Yoknari guard looked at her. "What did Ulster take from you?"

"My sister."

CHAPTER EIGHTEEN

Junto was sloppy drunk. He couldn't reach the death gem embedded in the back of his right shoulder. He tried to rub it against a post, struggling to dislodge it, but the death gem was too embedded in his flesh to move. He took a dagger and stabbed at the flesh around it, trying to dig it out, but the angle was too awkward and he couldn't get the leverage he needed. Plus the pain was excruciating. He couldn't keep it up for more than a few seconds before feeling like he was going to black out.

He had wandered the streets aimlessly, looking for Sekanna, wanting to strangle the life out of her but knowing that he couldn't. Maddening frustration threatened to consume him. He found himself in front of Croate's Inn, a small inn located near the whore Towers, went inside and started drinking.

He sat huddled in a far booth, hidden in the murky shadows of the inn. His back itched and ached where he had poked and prodded at the death gem.

The fireplace was on the other side of the large main room. Tables filled the middle of the room, with booths lining both walls. The kitchen area was up and off to his right. The inn was about half full, patrons drinking and smoking and chewing khack leaf. Some of the Tower girls were working the room. He thought of Layna and cried over his drink.

He felt very alone. He felt betrayed. He thought of telling someone to just slash the death gem right out of his flesh, but he knew that would kill him and he would just absorb Tallie's soul and take her life energy. He was certain the tendrils were already spread deep and wide inside his body, so just cutting the death gem out of his shoulder would serve no purpose other than causing debilitating pain and extinguishing Tallie's soul. That would defeat the entire purpose of his mission. He was here to save souls, not use them. He slammed his mug down on the table, cursing Sekanna, cursing Wushwan, cursing the world.

"Having a bad day?"

Junto looked up to see a Tower girl smiling down at him. Layna. He blinked twice, three times, trying to clear the vision he was seeing in his drunken haze. No, it wasn't Layna. It was the woman chosen to be the new Orange in the Tower. Not Layna.

She was dressed in a vibrant orange dress, her slender fingers dressed in white half-gloves that were fringed with orange fabric. Her fiery orange-red hair framed her beautiful face, making her radiant with the sexy glow of a sunrise. The double heads hadn't wasted any time in filling Layna's room with a new girl. Junto just stared at her. Sorrow and anger and self-pity and lust all swirled around in his fogged brain. He staggered to his feet, staring at her. And then he grabbed her and kissed her. He didn't care, nothing mattered. He felt himself growing hard and he deepened his kiss, thrusting his tongue into her mouth.

She pushed back against his chest, but he held her tight, keeping his lips clamped down over hers. She finally broke away from the kiss, laughing at his drunken advance. "Okay, save your energy for the Tower." She grabbed his hand and started to lead him away from the table. He pulled her back and kissed her some more. She broke away, laughing. "You're very eager, aren't you?"

He fumbled into his coin pouch and splashed coins across the table. Her eyes lit up at the sight of the glittering gold pieces as they spun on the scarred wooden table top . She reached down for a coin and he continued to push her down to the table with one hand on the back of her neck. With the other hand, he started hiking up the orange fabric of her dress. She continued to pick up the coins. "It's all yours, honey," she said, squirming her now bare buttocks in his direction. "Take as much as you'd like."

He took a huge drink of ale, spilling it down over his lips. Some of it splashed across her bare buttocks, dripping down between her butt cheeks. She hissed a giggling hiss as the cold liquid hit her naked flesh. He fumbled at his pants awkwardly with one hand, trying to tug them down but his belt kept them up.

Another Tower girl came over to the table, a look of concern on her face. She was dressed in a deep green dress, her hair adorned with fresh green leaves. A bright green eyeliner decorated her eyes.

"Are you okay?" she asked Orange.

Orange nodded. "Help him out, will you?"

The other Tower girl, known as Green, nodded. She brushed Junto's fumbling hand away from his breeches and worked at his belt, undoing it. She tugged his breeches down, freeing his manhood. Junto pulled the second Tower girl closer and kissed Green hard on the mouth. Nothing mattered. Nothing mattered at all.

Green laughed and pushed him away.

"Is he ready?" Orange asked.

"Oh, he's ready," Green said, glancing down at Junto's stiffness. She looked over to Orange. "You ready?"

"Yes." Orange lowered her voice. "Is everybody watching?"

The second Tower girl leaned down closer. "Yes."

"Oh my Gods, I'm so ready," Orange said.

"You're going to be a very popular Tower girl after this," Green said.

"Don't I know it," Orange said. "Put him in."

"Junto!"

The room became very quiet. Every patron in the inn stopped what they were doing, the sound of the commanding voice giving them no choice but to pause their activities.

"Junto!"

Junto turned a wobbling head towards the sound of the voice. Through the smoky haze filling the room he saw Sekanna marching towards him.

"Pull your fucking pants up," she said, her tone commanding and firm. She ripped the mug out of his hand and set it down on the table.

Junto pushed at her. "Get the fuck away from me," he said, his words slurred.

Orange stood up, and for a moment Sekanna froze at the sight of her. She did have a close resemblance to Layna, especially because she was dressed up in the vibrant orange attire she had been known for.

"What are you doing?" the new Orange asked. "He paid. Leave him alone."

Sekanna took a very threatening step towards her, her jaw set tight, her eyes thinned to narrow slits. Her platinum hair shimmered. "Get out of here."

Orange did not move. Green moved away, quickly finding other patrons to mingle with; she wanted no part of this fight. Drunk men were one thing, and usually easy to deal with. Angry women were another matter entirely.

"You had better listen to me." Sekanna tightened her jaw. "Get out of here now."

"He paid," Orange said.

"Keep the fucking coins. Get out of here."

Orange hesitated, then reached down and grabbed a few more loose coins from the table and glared at Sekanna. "For my troubles," she said with a snarl.

"Yeah," Sekanna said back. She fumbled with Junto's pants, tugging them back up around his waist.

"No, stay," Junto said, pointing to Orange. "Don't leave, Layna. Stay with me."

Orange hesitated, looking at Junto, then

glancing at Sekanna. "What did he just call me?" Orange asked.

Sekanna looked at the woman with the fiery hair, trying to keep herself calm. It wasn't her fault that Junto was acting like an animal. "Look, he's not in his right mind. Please, you need to leave."

"He wants me to stay," Orange said.

"He thinks you're someone else, okay? You need to leave."

"For that much coin, I'll be whoever he wants me to be." Orange reached out and caressed Junto's face. "Isn't that right, honey? You can call me whatever you want."

Sekanna scowled. The Tower whore wasn't getting it and she was quickly becoming aggravated again. Sekanna slapped Orange's hand away from Junto. "I will fucking kill you and steal your fucking soul," she whispered to Orange. She hated herself for uttering those words, but she had to get this woman away from Junto at any cost.

This brought a flash of fear to Orange's face. She turned and moved quickly away, heading out of the inn. She paused in the doorway and looked at Junto. "You come and see me in the Tower any time you want," she said, then gave Sekanna a spiteful stare. "But leave her at home." The woman exited the inn.

Sekanna turned away from Orange to see Junto staring at her with the most miserably sorrowful eyes she had ever seen. Tears streamed down his face. "You betrayed me," he said. "You betrayed me, Sekanna." More tears fell. "Now I have no one."

The energy seemed to suddenly drain out of him and he collapsed in her arms. She nearly stumbled, but held him up, keeping him upright. She clutched at him tightly, feeling his chest heaving against hers.

CHAPTER NINETEEN

Junto opened his eyes to see Sekanna sleeping in a chair next to his bed. He was back in his room, lying on his bed. His head ached painfully and the bright light streaming in from the window near his bed made him squint.

Wushwan suddenly appeared, holding a steaming cup of something. "Here, drink this. It will clear your head."

Junto did not take the cup. "I don't want anything from you, Wushwan. I don't trust you anymore. I don't trust any of you."

Wushwan held the cup out for a moment longer, then withdrew the offer. He set the cup down on the table near the bed. He lowered his head and turned away, moving out of the room.

Junto looked over to see Sekanna staring at him.

"Feeling better?" she asked him.

"No," he said. "Please leave." He sat up in the bed, groaning softly as he moved, leaning his back against the headboard. The death gem embedded in his shoulder made a slight scratching sound as it rubbed against the wooden headboard and Junto shifted his position slightly. He tightened his jaw.

Sekanna looked at the steaming mug on the table near the bed. "You should drink that. You'll feel better."

Junto ignored her suggestion.

"Do you remember what you once told me?" Sekanna finally asked after a long moment of uncomfortable silence between them.

He didn't answer.

"You told me to never waver in your beliefs no matter what. Even if no one else believes in what you believe in. If your heart of hearts told you to believe in something, then you should keep believing it. No matter what."

He kept silent.

"Keeping you alive is what I believe in. No matter what." Sekanna leaned forward in the chair. "If you die, then all of this has been for nothing. There is no one else who will fight this fight like you will. No one. If that means you have to use the life-force energy of soul stealers then so be it. Who better? Why does that whore's soul deserve to go peacefully into the Everlasting after what she did? Anyone who steals a soul should forfeit theirs. To us."

Junto looked her square in the eyes. "You stole Tallie's soul."

She shook her head. "No, that's where you are dead wrong. She forfeited her right to it." She leaned back into the chair. "The way I see it, she won't be attached to me in the Everlasting either, because her life-force is in the death gem now. And if you…" her voice trailed off, but she felt compelled to finish her thought aloud. "If you use…

it… then she's… gone. Just gone. And that will be that for that stupid bitch. I feel zero guilt for that, not after what she did."

Junto was quiet for a long moment. "Sekanna, I feel like you poisoned me in my sleep."

"I am sorry about that. But you would never have done it willingly. You are too proud and too stubborn."

"I can never trust you again," he said.

"You are wrong. You can trust me more than anyone else in the world."

"No, I can't."

Sekanna rose up out of the chair, moved to the door and closed it. She returned to the side of the bed and pulled her breeches down, revealing the silvery-tipped platinum hairs of her female mound.

"Sekanna, no. What are you doing?" Junto raised his hands in front of his eyes and turned his head to look away from her.

"Shut up. I'm not doing *that*." She pointed to the inside of her thigh. "Look."

He looked. And he froze for a long moment, just staring at the death gem on the inside of her thigh; the gem shimmered faintly, ever so faintly, with a soft yellow glow. He shifted his bewildered gaze up to her face. "When—"

"I've had it since before we met. I took it from the soul stealer who killed my friend. Vanya was the only friend I had in the whole world." She looked earnestly at Junto. "Before you."

"You've had that the whole time?"

"Yes."

Junto frowned. "So you keep secrets from me

and you betray my very beliefs. Tell me again why I'm supposed to trust you."

"Because I would do anything to keep you alive, to keep you fighting the good fight," Sekanna said.

"Is that what you are doing? Fighting the good fight?"

"Yes. We can't fight if we are dead."

"You really don't see how wrong all of this is?" He stared at her. "This is what we are fighting against, Sekanna!"

"What happens to all those souls when you die?"

Junto said nothing for a moment. He put his hand to his head, wincing at the pain pounding at the inside of his skull. "You can pull your pants up now."

Sekanna gave an exasperated grunt and tugged her pants back up. "You still need to answer that question, Junto. What happens to them? What happens to those hundreds of trapped souls that you know are out there? What happens to all those souls being held hostage by soul stealers when you die?"

"Someone else will free them."

Sekanna scoffed. "Who? Who, Junto? Who the fuck is going to free them? Who is lining up to take our jobs?"

"Someone will."

"Who? Name them!"

Junto said nothing. Then he said, "Irchly."

"Irchly?" Sekanna was blatantly flabbergasted by his remark. "Irchly? We don't even know where he is. As far as we know, he's already decided to quit helping us." She returned to the chair and plopped herself heavily back into it.

Junto was pensive for a moment. "Someone should check up on him. Maybe he's still with his grandfather."

"You know who needs to check up on him?" Sekanna asked. "Us, Junto. *We* need to check up on him. No one else is going to."

Junto said nothing. He put his hand to his head, wincing at the lingering effects of his overzealous bout of drinking from the night before.

Sekanna thrust a finger at him. "Stop lying to yourself! There is no one else but us!"

"We can't steal souls, Sekanna!" Junto shouted back at her, lowering his hand away from his head but still wincing with pain. "That makes us just like them! That makes us just like what we are trying to stop! Why can't you see that?"

"You just want this to be easy, don't you? You just want to fight until you die. Then you'll be free. You don't really care about all those souls. You're just buying time until you die."

"I care. You know I care. It's why I am doing this."

Sekanna waved her hand dismissively. "Ha. Just talk now." She leaned back into the chair.

"We can't save souls and steal them at the same time," Junto said. "We just can't."

She threw up her arms, exasperated. "We are not stealing souls. They have forfeited them to us."

"That's just the way you rationalize it to yourself."

"That's just looking at it truthfully." She stood

up and paced the room, whirling about abruptly after a few strides. "Look at Elcor! He's got a over a dozen death gems on him. Two dozen. You want to extract them and then just let him live out his life here in a prison cell until he dies of old age? Let him go freely into the Everlasting?" She shook her head. "No, he doesn't deserve it. He made his choice and he needs to suffer the consequences."

"No one needs to suffer."

"He does! He took over twenty souls. Three of them have gone black! That's three souls he extinguished forever! You don't think we should use his life-force for our cause? You don't think we should use his evil and turn it into something good?"

Junto was silent for a long moment. "What you did to me was wrong, Sekanna. Tallie doesn't deserve that. Ulster, maybe. Tallie, no."

Sekanna was quiet for a moment, then looked hard at him. "Junto, she had three death gems on her. One of them was black. She could have resisted Ulster if she had really wanted to. You don't have three death gems on you without being a very willing participant."

"One of them was black because of us," Junto said.

"She murdered Layna! And most likely destroyed my sister's soul. I don't think I've even comprehended the magnitude of that. My mind won't let me. She might have destroyed my sister's soul, Junto! What possible forgiveness does she deserve?"

Junto was quiet for a moment. "I feel — tainted

with her — on me."

"It's not her. It's her life-force."

"It's her," Junto said. "It's her soul. And it's inside me, waiting for me to use it. Waiting for me to completely wipe out her very existence for all eternity." He looked at Sekanna. "Would you want Elcor — on you? In you? Doesn't that feel — wrong to you?"

"I don't look at it that way. It's just energy to me now. A second chance for when I really screw up. Because I *will* really screw up one day." She looked at him. "And so will you. We deserve a second chance." Her voice grew more determined. "And a third and a fourth."

"Doesn't everyone deserve a second chance, Sekanna?" His voice was soft, his words low.

"Does Tallie really deserve a second chance? Does Elcor deserve a second chance? And what about Liesh and Baisk? Do they deserve second chances? Baisk murdered two babies, Junto! Two infants because he thought their life-force would be at full charge since they had just been born."

Junto thought of Liesh and Baisk. They were still alive, prisoners deep underground beneath the manor home, locked tight in their cells. They still hadn't decided what to do with those two soul stealers, either. "Zerin deserved a second chance," Junto said.

Sekanna shook her head. "Only to you. Not to me." She resumed her pacing. "I think you're only keeping Liesh alive so you can keep the memory of Jamilla alive in your heart. She's the only thing left that connects you to your grandmother. When she's gone, your connection to her will be gone."

"Is that why you think I am keeping Liesh alive? So I can keep thinking about Jamilla?"

"Why else would you let that vile piece of garbage keep taking a breath?"

Junto waved his hand dismissively. "Okay, this isn't about them. This is about me. About us. About what you did to me. About what you forced on me without my consent."

"I didn't rape you, Junto."

"Didn't you? It sure feels like you did. It feels like you raped my fucking soul while I was asleep."

Sekanna was quiet. "Is that how you really feel?"

Junto looked at her with an earnest expression. "Yes. Yes, Sekanna. That is how I really feel. I feel like you violated my body and my trust." His expression darkened and saddened at the same time. "I will never trust you again."

"Isn't that a little extreme?"

"What you did went beyond extreme. I'm still having a hard time comprehending how you could have done this to me. I really am." He looked at her with widening eyes, his head cocking to the side, the anger growing in his voice. "You put a fucking death gem on me, Sekanna!"

"To save you, not to hurt you!"

"I don't need to be saved!"

"You do! You just won't accept it, but you do!"

"So you decide what's best for me, is that it? Is that how this works?"

"Yes!" She calmed herself. "In this instance, yes. Because you refuse to see the logic in it. You refuse to see the real necessity of it."

"I don't refuse to see it. There is a ring of truth in what you say. But I still reject it. I choose not to go down that path, Sekanna. I chose *not* to."

Sekanna was quiet.

Junto was quiet for a long moment. "How did you do it?" he asked. "How did you put it on me without me knowing?"

Sekanna didn't answer right away.

"How Sekanna? You need to tell me."

"I put some crushed blackout root under your nose when you were sleeping. A few whiffs of that, and you were out."

"You knocked me out with blackout root to put a death gem on me?"

Sekanna said nothing. She looked away from him.

"And you don't think you violated me in any way?"

Sekanna said nothing, still keeping her gaze averted.

"I want it extracted." His tone was calm, matter-of-fact, as if his mind had already been made up and there was no possibility of convincing him otherwise.

Sekanna looked up at him with a growing alarm in her face. "Tallie does not deserve to be released into the Everlasting, Junto. She doesn't deserve it! We have to draw a line somewhere. Not everyone deserves a second chance. They just don't!"

"I don't want a death gem on me!" Junto shouted.

"I don't want her following me in the Everlasting!" Sekanna shouted back. "You want her to be attached to me for all eternity?" Her voice rose even higher. "Don't do that to me, Junto! Don't you dare free her fucking soul!"

A hesitating doubt crept into Junto's face as he stared at Sekanna.

A knock came at the door, then Nadrini's voice followed without waiting for their response to the knock. "We found Ulster," she said loudly from behind the door.

Junto and Sekanna froze for a moment. They both looked to the door, then glanced at each other, then looked back to the door. Sekanna moved to the door and opened it to give Nadrini entrance. Nadrini padded into the room in her bare feet, dressed in her yellow smock.

"We found Ulster," Nadrini said again.

Sekanna and Junto just stared at Nadrini for a moment.

"Where?" Junto finally asked.

"He's at the Oval."

Sekanna looked curiously at Nadrini. "Watching the Races?"

Nadrini shook her head. "No, he's *in* the Races."

Junto just stared at Nadrini, as if not believing what she had just said. "In?"

Nadrini nodded. "And he's already won two of them." Nadrini paused. "The crowds love him."

"He's on a team?" Sekanna asked.

Nadrini nodded again. "The Reds."

"When the hell did this happen?" Junto asked.

Nadrini shrugged her dainty shoulders. "Over the last few days."

"And he's already a favorite?" Sekanna asked.

Nadrini shrugged yet again. "You know the crowd. Their favors blow in the breeze and change direction as easily as a leaf in a windstorm."

"Thank you, Nadrini." Sekanna said.

Nadrini bowed and departed.

Sekanna looked at Junto. "We should've known this was going to get worse. It always does."

Junto shook his head sadly. "Doesn't anyone care that he's a soul stealer?"

"We do."

Junto was quiet for a moment. He slowly looked up at Sekanna. "Why? Why do we even care?"

Sekanna reached out and touched his shoulder. "Because we do, Junto. Because we do."

He said nothing. He put his hand on hers, then gently lifted her hand and shifted it off of his shoulder.

"I think others care, too," Sekanna said, withdrawing her hand back to let it fall to her side. "I just think they don't know what to do about it. Or they're too afraid to do anything about it. It's much easier just to look the other way."

"Maybe we should just look the other way, too" Junto said, hanging his head.

Sekanna laughed a tiny laugh. "You couldn't do that if you tried. You'd grow eyes in the back of your head just so you could keep looking." She paused for a moment. "That's why I'm with you, Junto. That's why I'll always be with you."

Junto looked up and Sekanna felt her heart seize in her chest. A lone tear rolled down his cheek. "You poisoned me, Sekanna. Why did you do that to me?"

"Damn it, Junto. I didn't poison you. I'm trying to keep you alive!" She looked at him, her face animated with a mixture of anguish and guilt. "I did it for me, okay? I did it for me. I don't want you to die. I would be lost without you. I need you not to die. Do you understand that? Damn it, Junto. I need you to stay alive. For me! I did it for me, damn you. I did it for me!"

"That was very selfish of you."

Sekanna laughed, wiping away a tear of her own. "Of course it was. Why would I act any different than I always have?"

"And Wushwan?"

"Wushwan loves you like a brother. And like a father, even. You have given him a purpose, Junto. You have given us all a purpose. Without that, we'd have meaningless lives."

"You can't always depend on me, Sekanna," Junto said. "Someday, I will be gone and you'll have to live your own life."

"I am living my own life now. I just want you to be part of it. And I want to stay a part of yours."

Junto was quiet.

"You know, there is a very simple solution to all of this," Sekanna said.

Junto looked up at her.

"Just don't die. Then you'll never have to make use of the gem." She smiled a half-hearted smile. "Now what are we going to do about Ulster?"

CHAPTER TWENTY

Ulster raised his hand and smiled at the crowd as he took his victory lap. He maneuvered his chariot around the corpses that littered the racing arena, gripping the reins in one hand as he waved at the roaring crowd with the other. The Oval was packed thick with crowds today, with barely an empty seat visible.

He noticed one of the fallen drivers was still alive, feebly crawling toward the safety of a carved slot in the stone wall that lined the inside of the track. There were slots etched into the stone every dozen feet or so, about the width of a man, carved both into the inner and outer stone walls of the track to provide a means for track workers to be safely out of the way during a race, or to provide a safe haven for a fallen driver to flee to if he was knocked out of his chariot during a race. Ulster steered his horses towards the crawling man.

Ulster had died during the race, but he didn't think anyone even noticed. One of the other drivers had managed to slash his throat when their two chariots had been racing neck and neck, the other driver getting in a lucky slash with the blade that was strapped to his left index finger when Ulster tried to lean hard on his chariot and drive him into the outer stone wall of the racetrack. One of the gems on his forehead had gone black as he absorbed the life-force into him. He couldn't see the gem but he knew it had gone black. He could feel the life-force seeping out of it and refueling his own. He knew he had blacked out during his death, but it had only been for a very brief moment. His team of horses had kept on racing on their own since all four of them knew the layout of the figure-eight track, having traversed the track thousands of times in practice and hundreds of times in actual races. He had come back to life just as they had neared the crossing. Another chariot was approaching the crossing from a different direction and they had nearly collided, but the other driver had slowed to allow him to pass through the dangerous intersection first.

He was getting very good at countering death with the death gems. It was as if his body now understood exactly what to do immediately when he *died*. Instead of taking minutes to be re-born, it now only took a few dozen seconds, as if the more deaths he experienced, the quicker his body knew how to absorb a life-force from a death gem and return him to life.

They really should be called life stones, he thought. Death gems really did not do them justice. To him, they were life. He had nine remaining now, but he knew he was going to keep adding more. He even dreamed of seeing his entire body covered in life stones. They would be like a shell, like a coat of armor protecting him. Yes, that was a most pleasant dream. He thought of putting one on his cock, but he still hadn't gotten up the nerve to do it yet. He didn't know how well that would go over with the ladies. It would probably hurt like hell and rip up their insides. Maybe he could put one on his ball sac. Or two. They might even offer him some good protection down there. That could work.

He approached the fallen crawling driver and felt a slight jarring bump as he drove right over his back. He heard several cracking noises and a meaty crunch and wondered if that was the man's ribs being crushed beneath the weight of his chariot. It probably was.

The raucous roar of the crowd grew even louder as he continued his victory lap.

He didn't realize how much of a thrill racing would be. He had entered the tournament on a whim, buying out the position of another driver and his chariot with a ridiculous sum of coin. The man hadn't even hesitated. He took the coin, gave Ulster a few tips about how to handle each horse on his team, and handed him the reins to his chariot. The guy never even looked back as he walked away. Ulster wondered if he had made a bad decision if the man was so eager to give up his chariot, but that feeling quickly faded the moment he stepped onto the chariot. It felt good. It felt right. It felt like he belonged on it.

He had taken a few hundred practice laps, but had an immediate feel for it after just a few dozen circuits around the track. Politus, his newly acquired horse handler, marveled at his natural ability. "You have a talent for this," the old man said. Ulster agreed. It felt good to hold the reins and steer the horses around the figure-eight track. It felt right. He had always been good with horses his entire life, but this took that skill to the next level. He would participate in a few races, get the craving for excitement out of his blood, then worry about finding the extractor and his team. Yes, that's what he would do, or so he had thought at the time of buying the chariot.

But it had only taken two races for the crowd to start to chant his name. "Ulster! Ulster!" It happened so quickly. He had killed four men in those two races, three of them in his second, so perhaps that was why he was so popular so quickly. The crowd obviously liked the bloodshed. He smiled darkly. He would give them plenty of it. Half a dozen more victories and he would already earn back the coin he had paid out to acquire the chariot.

He reveled in the sound of his name being shouted over and over as he finished his victory lap. "Ulster! Ulster!" He had even come up with a possible plan to add to his collection of death gems. He just needed to find a few track workers he could trust and employ them to put death beetles onto any drivers he slew. He grinned at the thought. Not only could he earn coin from winning races, but he could also continue to enrich his flesh with new death gems.

He steered the horse into the tunnel that led to the stables beneath the large coliseum, disappearing from the oval sands. He was hooked. One of these days he would track down the extractor. But not today. There was a victory celebration to be had, and there would be many women eager to celebrate along with him.

"That was quite a show you put on."

Ulster turned to see Farquis standing at the edge of one of his horse's stalls. He studied Farquis for a moment. The man was strong, a good rider. He had dark skin, oily black hair, and a hooked nose that curved down towards his thin lips. He was wearing a loose fitting green tunic and white leggings, his muscles clearly on display in both his upper and lower body. Ulster had seen him in action but had not yet raced against him.

Ulster set the brush back down on its hook, gently patted his horse, and moved towards Farquis. Three men stood behind Farquis, obviously his hard men. Each one wore a dark green leather jerkin; each one had numerous visible daggers stuffed into the green sashes that were tied around their waists, and each had a sword strapped to their sides, the sword handles wrapped in what looked to be the same dark green leather they wore over their chests. Ulster smiled at them all. "Yes, it was, wasn't it?"

"How about you joining the Greens? We'd love to have you on the team," Farquis said.

Ulster was part of the Reds, but not by choice. It had been the team the man was on from whom he had purchased the horses and chariot. He didn't really care what team he was on, but he knew the Races were a team sport. The crowds were known to be insanely passionate about their teams, dressing in their favorite team's colors, constantly getting in brawls over their teams, painting their homes in their team's colors, and even naming their children after their favorite riders. From what he had observed so far, insanely passionate was an understatement. The Greens were the current point champions on the Oval circuit. Farquis obviously had a strong hold on the Green team, a strong leadership position. The Reds had no such strong leader. Until now. Ulster knew he could easily join the Greens and no one on the Reds would have the will to stop him. But where would the thrill be in that?

The look on his face must have been obvious because Farquis spoke again before he even had a chance to reply. "You're staying with the Reds."

"Yes," Ulster said.

"Are you sure you want to do that? We have a very strong team."

"That's why I want to stay with the Reds."

Farquis looked at him. He nodded softly. He reached out for Ulster's hand. Ulster glanced down at it, then took it. "You ride well, but so do I," Farquis said. He released his grip on Ulster's hand. "I have a feeling one of us might not outlive the week."

"I have a feeling it will be you," Ulster told him.

One of the men behind Farquis didn't take kindly to that remark and grunted.

Farquis smiled back at Ulster. "And I have a feeling it will be you." He looked at the death gems covering Ulster's face, stopping his gaze to stare at the blackened gem on his forehead. "Of course, I may have to repeat myself until they all go black."

"That might take some time," Ulster said.

Farquis laughed. "I have plenty of that." He slid back the sleeve of his tunic to reveal half a dozen death gems glittering on his arm. Only one of them was black. Farquis looked at him. "Still want to stay with your Reds? Or do you want to join your real brothers?"

CHAPTER TWENTY-ONE

Sekanna watched the race from high up in the stands. The rows of seats below her were filled to overflowing. Extra guest areas were set up above the last row of seats, standing room only. Each section of the Oval stands was dedicated to one of the four teams participating in the Races. The four teams were the Reds, the Greens, the Yellows, and the Blues.

Sekanna was standing in the Blue section. The Blue team was on the bottom of the rung in the standings this year (and for several years in a row now), so it had been easier, and cheaper, to get a seat in their section, but even their section was crowded. The wooden seats in the higher back rows were all painted blue. Some of the blue coloring was fading on a few seats, but the crews working the Oval usually did a quick job of repairing and repainting them and keeping the colors vibrant. Retractable awnings were often stretched open across the spaces above the seats to provide a makeshift roof to block out any rain that might fall as well as provide relief from the searing sun. For today's races, the awnings, dyed a deep cobalt blue for the Blue section, were deployed and stretched

wide above the crowds, providing protection from
the day's hot and bright sun.

Far below Sekanna, the stone rows that served
as the front rows of seats just above the main track
were all of a grayish hue with a thick horizontal
blue line running across the middle of the seating
area, the blue line extending across the entire length
of the row. Each stone seat in the Blue section was
numbered with a big blue number. Many of the
wealthier patrons who permanently owned those
stone seats brought their own feathered pillows or
some form of soft cushion to sit upon; all of the
seating items they brought with them were dyed
blue or stitched together from some variant of blue
fabric, of course.

Sekanna had purchased a ticket for the top
standing room area. It was an area positioned
behind a blue-dyed rope. It had a slight rising slant
to it so that people could stand three or four rows
deep and the people in the back could still see the
track down below. The oval track was pretty far
away from where she stood, but she could still make
out some of the riders and could easily make out
their colors. The track, as per the name of the
building, was a large oval shape, its surface layered
with fresh sand before each race. The track criss-
crossed in the middle, forming a large figure-eight
shape. The track was bordered by a ten foot high
white stone wall to keep the crowds safely away
from the thundering horses and combating teams as
they roared past during a race; a stray arrow or
thrown dagger would sometimes make its way into
the crowd and several patrons had lost their lives

over the years, but for the most part being in the crowd was safe.

A vendor walked by, hawking warm ale. He was dressed in a plain white tunic with a white belt and white sandals, indicating that he was an Oval worker. A thick rope hung about his neck that held a wooden carrying-container in front of his rotund belly, the flat-bottom box filled with fire-baked clay mugs full of ale. Sekanna ignored him. Another vendor came by from the opposite direction, selling strips of dried salted beef that were attached to a long wooden pole he held, each strip of meat dangling from a tiny wooden hook. She bought one of those and absently chewed on the tough meat as she watched the race play out on the track far below.

The Reds were good. They were damn good. It was a pairs race that she was watching, so one man drove the chariot while another fired short arrows at opponents. Occasionally, a team would throw a surprise into the mix and use a sling or use throwing daggers as weapons, but arrows were used most often in a pairs race. The shooter also had the job of protecting the driver from any opponents' arrows, using a small shield to deflect them away if they threatened the driver. She remembered one race where she saw one Red shooter take out two Blue drivers using only two arrows; both arrows had been expertly aimed to penetrate the Blue drivers straight through their exposed necks. She thought of Irchly and his bow skills, and thought how good he would be if he participated in the Races. She frowned. Where the fuck was he? They had not seen him since he had gone to take care of his ailing grandfather. She pushed the thought away. She couldn't worry about that now.

She focused on the activity happening below her in the Oval. The racers wore no armor whatsoever, not even a helmet. They wore simple, brightly-colored tunics in their respective team colors, with the driver wearing a white belt and the shooter wearing a black cord tied about his waist to give the audience a quick visual indicator of who was who on each team. The belts were more for decoration and in no way indicated the skill set of each racer; if a driver got hit, the shooter could take his place as driver and try to finish the race, and sometimes a driver would take shots at opposing racers with throwing blades or even rocks if the opportunity presented itself.

The horses were well shielded, with thick leather plates colored in their respective team colors adorning their bodies, so it was difficult to take down an opponent in that manner. An arrow could penetrate and stick into the thick leather hides that served as armor, but it was rare that an arrow actually penetrated a horse's flesh because there was a thin layer of metal embedded between the layer of leather hides that comprised the plates, sometimes even two or three layers of metal depending on the skill of the craftsman making them or how much a team's owner was willing to pay. Plus the crowd did not like to see any horses hit with arrows. They would greet such an action with thunderous boos and catcalls. They were okay with seeing men die, not innocent animals.

The crossing was the most dangerous part for the racers, and the most exciting for the crowd. Because the track was in the shape of a figure-eight and the tracks crossed each other in the middle, the intersection was the heart of the race and drew most of the crowd's attention. This is where a team's skill really shone. A driver had to make the split second decision whether to charge forward and try to beat an approaching team through the crossing, or draw back and let the other team pass through the crossing first. Speed wasn't always the answer. Many times the best move was to maneuver the chariot to give the shooter the best angle at his opponent.

It was chaos if a team went down in the middle of the crossing. Sekanna had seen a four chariot pile-up once with men and horses and wheels and chariot frames all smashed and tangled into one blood-soaked mess. But she knew that wasn't going to happen in this race. The Red team was too well trained, too controlled, too smooth to let anything like that happen. They played the crossing smartly, letting the Yellow team cross it first. The Red driver made a slight turn with his chariot, giving his shooter a clean shot at the Yellow driver. The Red shooter fired off three quick arrows, drawing an arrow from the quiver strapped to his leg, knocking the arrow in his bow, aiming and releasing, then repeating that fluid motion two more times all in a matter of a few seconds. The Yellow shooter made an effort to block the incoming projectiles, but he only managed to deflect one of them with his shield. Two of the red arrows sunk into the Yellow driver, one in the side of his midsection and one in his neck. Blood sprayed into the air. The Yellow shooter grabbed at the reins but it was too late. The chariot turned sharply and then flipped over, sending the dead Yellow driver and the Yellow shooter sailing into the air along with an exploding barrage of splintered chariot pieces. The Yellow shooter landed in front of the charging Blue team and was immediately crushed beneath the deadly hooves of the chariot's horses, his body getting punctured and slashed as the hooves ground down into and over him.

The crowd around Sekanna went wild. There was a blood lust in their cries that disturbed her. She never really enjoyed the Races all that much, and this only added to her distaste of the whole sport.

The Reds won the race, crossing the finish line in first place after ten laps around the Oval, well ahead of any of the others. The Greens came in second, and the Blues limped into third as one of their horses had injured itself racing over the fallen Yellow shooter and stumbled on a broken piece of chariot. The Yellows were done when their chariot crashed, so they didn't even cross the finish line. No points were awarded for a non-finish, so the Yellow section of the crowd, who were positioned directly across the Oval from the Blue section, was quiet and glum. The Red section roared triumphantly, some of the Red fans on the edge of the Red section clearly jeering and taunting at the downtrodden Yellow fans who were in the section next to the Reds.

A brief intermission followed as track workers

cleaned up the dead men and broken chariot. They raked in a new layer of sand, preparing for the next race. The crowd milled about, buying refreshments from the flurry of white-tunic vendors who suddenly appeared selling all manner of food and drink. Some of the attendees went to use the public bathrooms. Others simply remained seated or standing, waiting for the next race.

Sekanna scanned the crowd. She wondered how many soul stealers were in attendance. She knew there had to be at least a few. The man standing in the row in front of her could be a soul stealer as far as she knew. Or the woman standing next to him. Most soul stealers were very discrete in their use of the death gems, keeping them well hidden from public view. Only a very few like Ulster brazenly wore them on visible parts of their body. She wasn't sure why he did that. Was it to strut around like some kind of peacock? Was it to counter some deep-seated insecurity? Did he crave the attention? Did he enjoy the shock it brought? She didn't know.

Most people still didn't even know the real truth about the death beetles. They thought the death gems were some kind of tribal decorations, or some kind of cult affiliation. Those who did know of their power either kept it to themselves, or decided to use the death gems for their own selfish purposes. Or both. Only a small select few had decided to join Junto to stop their use.

She wondered how many soul stealers there were in the city. Calkut was on the far western fringe of Moraneesh, so it wasn't the most populous city in Moraneesh, nor was it frequented too often by outside travelers. She wondered how far the soul stealers had spread. How many were in Moraneesh? She stopped trying to figure that out quickly after the question had presented itself. Thinking about the enormity of their challenge just exhausted her. As far as she knew, it might really just be a few dozen. Or it could be thousands upon thousands. They could only deal with one soul stealer at a time. That's how Junto wanted to operate. Considering the potential enormity of their task, that strategy made sense; it kept them all focused and somewhat sane.

But they still needed help. They needed others to join them. But they had to be very careful in who they asked, very careful in who they revealed the truth to. The last man they had revealed the truth to, a young man named Kalandi, had joined the soul stealers. The temptation to counter death had been too great for the young man. He succumbed to the power of the creatures and was now off gods-knew-where, probably adding to his collection of souls.

Trumpets sounded, signaling the drivers of the next race to begin coming out onto the track. Sekanna watched them enter from their respective gates, the horses snorting and pawing at the sand as they entered the arena. The Reds were to her right so she shifted her gaze to get a better look down onto the track. She spotted Ulster immediately. His death gems glittered in the sunlight, visible even from where she was standing. She could hear the crowd in the Red section chanting his name. "Ulster! Ulster!" She turned and headed down the stairs, nervous now but eager to set her plan in motion.

She found a darkly shadowed spot in the stone corridor beneath the stands and quickly removed her tunic, standing naked in the corridor as she turned the fabric inside out, changing it from a deep blue to a deep red. She quickly donned the now-red tunic and moved through the stretch of neutral ground that separated the colors; the neutral sections were clearly designated by their white stone floors and walls comprised of white bricks. She entered the Red section, smiling and nodding at other Red fans as she entered their area.

A hand tapped her shoulder. Sekanna turned to see an Oval worker staring at her, his white tunic clearly marking him as a worker; only men and women employed by the Oval were allowed to wear white tunics inside the track. The man looked questioningly at her. "What are you doing?" the White asked. He was an older man, probably a decade older than Junto, she guessed. If not even older than that. He had short black hair and a strongly aristocratic face. He had a regal bearing about him that silently spoke of former authority.

"I'm sorry?" Sekanna said.

The man in the white tunic pointed back down the corridor in the direction she had come. "I saw you switch your colors. What are you doing?"

Several Red fans nearby stared at her suspiciously.

Sekanna grabbed the White by the wrist and ushered him away from the crowd. "I'm meeting my Red lover. Please don't tell. I don't want my husband to find out."

The White shook his head. "I cannot condone such behavior in my section."

"Please, I must be discrete."

The White shook his head. "You need to return to your section. This is for Red fans only."

"I am a Red fan."

The White stared at her.

"I'm a fan of Ulster," she said. "Isn't he magnificent?" She leaned in closer to the White. "There is no one on Blue that is anywhere near as good as him, am I right?"

"Then why didn't you buy a Red ticket?"

Sekanna looked away sheepishly. "I couldn't afford it. I bought a Blue so I could get in."

"I'm sorry, but you'll have to return to the Blue section."

Sekanna frowned. "Don't make me do that." She sidled up a bit closer to him. "Is there anything I can do to change your mind?" She reached up and touched his chest.

He took her hand and gently eased it away from his chest. "Not that."

The second round of trumpets sounded, signaling the imminent start of the race. The crowd immediately dispersed, everyone hurrying back out towards their seats. In a matter of moments, Sekanna was alone with the White in the dimly lit corridor.

"What are you really doing here?" the White asked.

"I really am here to see Ulster," Sekanna said.

The White looked at her. "I know who you

are."

Sekanna frowned at him. "What?"

"I know who you are," the White repeated.

"And who am I?"

"You are Sekanna. I've seen you with Junto."

Sekanna was speechless for a moment, staring at him with a slack jawed expression. "You know Junto?" she finally asked.

The man in the white tunic nodded. "I know what you want with Ulster."

"Oh, you do, do you?"

White nodded. And then he shook his head. "I can't let that happen."

Sekanna looked curiously at him.

"I bet a year's wages on the Reds this year," the White said.

"I thought you Whites weren't allowed to bet."

He paused before answering. "Not officially, no."

"But you still did."

"Yes," the White said. "The Reds need Ulster."

Sekanna stared at the man. "You know he's a soul stealer, right?"

White shrugged.

"He steals souls," Sekanna said.

"I know what soul stealer means."

Sekanna frowned. "And you don't care?"

White shrugged. "As long as they don't steal mine," he said and smiled.

"What if they steal your family's? Your wife's?"

White shrugged. "I don't have a family. No wife."

"Your friends' souls, then."

White shrugged. "No friends."

The trumpets blared loud and long, signaling the beginning of the race. White looked toward the track. "Go Reds," he muttered forlornly.

The man's presence and his words nagged heavily at Sekanna. How did this man know who they were? How did he know what they were doing? Was such knowledge more widespread than they had realized? If so, that was not a good thing. Not a good thing at all. They needed anonymity to be able to do their work. Not notoriety.

White started to move toward the stands as the sounds of the race and the cheering crowds filtered in.

"Wait," Sekanna said.

White turned to looked at her, a deep frown on his face. "I'm missing the race."

"How do you know of Junto? How do you know what we are doing?"

White shrugged. "I like to know things. I wander the city and I listen. I ask questions." He shrugged again. "I like to know things." He tapped his head. "Knowing things is all I got."

Sekanna studied him more closely for a moment. He was a nice looking man with a decent chin, and a strong bit of cheekbone giving his face some angular strength. His eyebrows were a bit too bushy for her liking, but he had nice brown eyes. And his lips were nice, not too thin, not too thick. Just right for kissing. She pushed that unwanted thought away immediately. She had no idea why that came to the forefront of her thoughts. Probably because you haven't been with a man for months, the voice inside her said. Probably because you are itching to take any man who'll have you right about now. She pushed all that away.

She caught his gaze focused down at her chest. She glanced down to see her nipples nearly bursting out of her tunic. She looked up to see him looking at her curiously with his big brown eyes.

"Been a while?" he asked.

She looked away, cursing herself for a damn fool.

"Trust me. If those are reacting to my presence, then it's definitely been a while for you."

She needed to change the subject, and fast. "You said you like to know things?"

"Yes, yes I did. I do."

"How would you like to be paid for what you know?"

He cocked his head quizzically.

"We need to know things," Sekanna told him.

"You and Junto?"

"Yes."

The crowd suddenly roared with a burst of wild cheering and whistling. White again looked forlornly towards the track. He turned back to Sekanna. "You're making me miss the race."

"Let's go watch it then."

He only hesitated for a brief second, but then nodded. He moved towards the tunnel that led out to the Red section seating area. Sekanna followed.

Junto shook his head softly. This was a mistake. There were too many people. The races were controlled chaos. Fans screamed and yelled and cursed and cheered. The ale flowed heavily. Eyes got redder. Movement got clumsier. Words slurred. Emotions got more and more heated. There was no way to get to Ulster amidst all this madness. Once again, his plans were ill conceived. He derided his continued lack of judgment. Who was he to think he could be a leader? He was a damn idiot, and he kept proving it to himself over and over again.

They would have to just wait until the races were over and follow him. But he knew if the Reds were victorious, there would be a massive celebration at The Fountains. They would replace the water streaming and bubbling out of the fountains with red wine. There would be much more drunkenness and debauchery going on. He didn't attend many Races, but he had attended enough to know about the victory celebrations. Some of the victory parties lasted well into the next day. He often made it a point to avoid the heart of the city for a few days after a race.

He and Sekanna had split up, with her going to the Blue section and he to the Yellow. They thought they could cover more ground if they split up. He wasn't sure why they had even done that. Somehow it had made sense when they were discussing it, but once inside the Oval he realized it had made no sense at all. They should have stayed together. Ulster was racing with the Red team. There was no need to survey the crowd. There was no special advantage to them hiding amidst the throng. They would have to wait until the races were over regardless and then go find Ulster. There was nothing to be done now but watch.

And so Junto watched as Ulster raced. The race he was participating in was a battle of single riders. The man had an obvious talent for handling horses. Four horses were strapped to the single-rider chariot that Ulster stood upon. He gripped the reins with one hand and wielded his whip in the other, using it more to steer the beasts than to strike them. He snapped the whip to the right of the animals to steer them left. The sharp cracking sound of the whip made the animals turn away from it, thus steering them in the direction he wanted them to go.

Ulster was in second place, behind the Green racer. Blue and Yellow battled for third place about ten horse-lengths behind them. Two laps to go. If Ulster was going to make a move, he would have to do it soon, Junto thought.

And then Ulster did make his move, slipping just below the Green chariot, getting an inside edge. It was a brilliant maneuver and Junto was impressed by Ulster's skill despite the loathing he felt for the soul stealer.

But then something happened that set off a chain of events that would change Junto and Sekanna's lives forever.

Ulster died a brutal, body-mangling death.

CHAPTER TWENTY-TWO

Ulster was mangled nearly beyond recognition. Junto had never seen the body of someone trampled by horses and run over by a chariot. It was not a pretty sight. One of Ulster's horses had slipped going into turn three. It was just a slight slip, but it was enough to cause the chariot to flip, sending Ulster straight into the path of the dueling Blue and Yellow chariots. There was no way they could avoid Ulster and both the Blue and Yellow drivers raced right over him. Ulster's body flopped and flipped, twisting this way and that as horse hooves churned and chariot wheels spun over his body. It was over in seconds. Ulster's body lay mangled and twisted and torn in the middle of the sandy track. Splatters of blood stained the sands, forming irregular shapes of spilled fluid. Several men and women in white tunics sped to the dead man and quickly dragged him off the track.

Junto spun and raced toward the tunnel. He knew where they would be taking him and he needed to get there fast.

It was a horribly gruesome sight. Even Sekanna put her hand to her mouth in shock. She turned to see White staring at the track. She couldn't quite tell what expression he had on his face. Was it shock? Horror? Disgust? But then she realized it looked more like fear.

"I'm a dead man," White muttered.

"No," a woman clothed in a red dress next to them said. She pointed to the body of Ulster lying sprawled and mangled on the track. "*He's* a dead man."

Suddenly, White turned and headed back towards the tunnel. Sekanna gave chase. "Wait," she called out to him as they reached the empty tunnel.

He didn't wait.

She quickened her pace. "Wait!"

He kept walking briskly.

Sekanna ran up to him and stepped in front of him, stopping his momentum. "Wait, where are you going?"

"Far from here," he said and made a move to go around her.

Sekanna shuffled sideways, blocking his movement. "Wait, just stop. Where are you going?"

"I need to get out of the city."

"What? Why?"

"Please, get out of my way."

"Not until you tell me what in Hell's Wood is going on."

"It's none of your damn business. Now get out of my way."

She put a hand to his chest. "What's wrong

with you? Haven't you seen someone get crushed in a race before? You look like you've seen a ghost."

"I'm the one who's going to be a ghost if I don't get out of the city."

And then Sekanna realized what was happening. "Your bet," she muttered. "You bet coin you don't actually have, didn't you?"

"Yes. Yes, I did. And now I'm a dead man if I don't get the hell out of Calkut."

Sekanna felt her thoughts spinning. Her mind was awhirl with too many questions, too many decisions to make, too many possible actions to take. Too much was happening. She had to go find Junto and get to Ulster, but she didn't want to just leave White. He looked so desperate and alone. She knew that feeling. She knew that feeling very well and she wouldn't wish that on anyone. "Let me help you," she said.

"You can't help me," White said.

"Yes. Yes, I can. Meet me at Croate's Inn. Meet me there tonight. I can help you."

White looked at her a moment, then brushed past her.

She let him go. She watched him for just a second, then turned and hurried through the stone corridor.

Junto had never seen such a thing before. He hadn't realized it was even possible. He could only watch in anguish as three of the death gems on Ulster's body glowed and shimmered. Three! Three at once. He was absorbing the life-force of three souls at the same time. Junto watched three souls blink out of existence forever as the gems went dark and black.

An infinite sadness welled up in him. He was powerless to stop it. And then a dark rage pushed away the sadness, a bitter anger focused directly on the mangled man who was sprawled grotesquely on a marble slab before him.

Several men and women in white tunics milled about Ulster, fussing over his body. One of the men slowly straightened one of Ulster's legs, and Junto watched the mangled leg heal and reform as the stolen life-force spread through his body. Another white-clad worker gingerly straightened one of Ulster's arms. The men and women in white obviously knew Ulster was a soul stealer and were preparing for his rebirth. Junto felt a sickness tightening his stomach.

One of the men in white finally noticed Junto. "What are you doing here? You are not allowed back here." He turned his attention back to Ulster's arm, gingerly moving it out from beneath the man's torn body.

Junto did not move.

The Oval worker who had just straightened Ulster's leg moved up to Junto. "Leave this area."

Junto pointed to Ulster. "Not without him."

"Leave this area." The man in the white tunic moved his hand down to the dagger at his waist.

"He's a soul stealer," Junto said.

None of the workers made any kind of reply.

Junto looked at Ulster's prone body. "He needs

to come with me."

"No, he doesn't," a voice coming from behind Junto proclaimed.

Junto turned to see a tall man standing in the doorway, flanked by four guards. He wore a short-sleeved red tunic and brown leather leggings. His face was strong, angular, his eyes deep set and menacing. Half a dozen death gems lay embedded in the flesh of his left arm. Five of the death gems scintillated with myriad colors; one was black. The tall man touched an empty spot on his left arm. "I am going to put you right here, Junto of Calkut." The tall man pointed to Junto as he gave the command to his men. "Kill him, then bring me his body. He looks like he has a very tasty soul."

Sekanna wasted no time in striking. She heard the tall man's threat as she approached the room from outside of it and she did not hesitate. She slashed her blade across the hamstrings of the two men closest to her as she entered the room. They both cried out and went down nearly in unison, both clutching at their spurting legs. Sekanna took advantage of their startled cries and struck at the third guard, thrusting her blade across his side, meaning to give him a painful, disabling wound to his flesh. She finished cutting an inch-deep slash into the man, then raised her blade up quickly and swung the hilt, bringing the hard metal edge down on the head of the fourth man, cracking it hard against his skull, cutting skin, sending a torrent of blood pouring from his head wound into his eyes. He dropped his sword and clutched at his face, wiping at his eyes.

By the time the tall man recovered from his surprise at Sekanna's sudden and violent attack, Junto had a dagger pressed tightly against his throat.

"You won't kill me," the tall man said softly to Junto, his voice full of scorn, his words clearly deriding Junto's actions as those of a weak and desperate man.

"Help!" one of the men in a white tunic shouted, clearly calling for reinforcements. "Help!" he screamed at the top of his lungs. The other Oval workers cowered near the far wall, doing their best to stay out of the way, fear filling their faces.

One of the fallen guards swiped at Sekanna's leg with his sword and she had to leap out of the way of the stroke to avoid getting her calf slashed. "We need to get out of here, Junto," she said. "Now."

Junto grimaced. He spun the tall man around and shoved him deeper into the room. The tall man hit the marble slab and bent over from the force of the push, the force of the impact putting his face right over Ulster's face.

Sekanna kicked a guard in the face who was trying to stand back up, then slammed her sword hilt down on the head of another who was stirring. "Junto, let's go!"

Junto hesitated, staring at Ulster, glaring at the tall man.

The tall man rose up away from Ulster and turned back to face Junto and Sekanna with his darkly malevolent eyes. "See you soon," the tall man said.

Footsteps approached quickly from down the stone corridor, closing in fast. Junto and Sekanna had no choice but to flee.

CHAPTER TWENTY-THREE

"Well, that was an epic fail," Sekanna said.

They were back in their manor home, sitting at the kitchen table. Each one of them nursed an ale. Sekanna was on her third. Junto was slowly drinking his first.

"He used three at once," Junto said. "Three. I didn't even know that was possible."

"He was really mangled up. It makes sense in a weird way." Sekanna took a drink of her ale.

Junto frowned. "It makes sense in a weird way?"

Sekanna nodded.

"None of this makes sense!" Junto scowled, deep creases forming around his eyes. "The very nature of the death beetles makes no fucking sense!"

"Okay, okay, calm down."

"Calm down? Calm down? I just saw three souls blink out of existence forever. And you probably took care of a few more by killing some of those men."

Sekanna shook her head. "I didn't kill any of them." She shrugged and took another drink of ale. "I was trying not to."

Junto stared at Sekanna. "How are we supposed to win this war, Sekanna? We can't even kill the men we're fighting. But they can certainly kill us. How the fuck are we supposed to win?"

"We can change tactics," Sekanna replied. She was quiet for a moment, and a serious look came over her features. "Maybe we do need to start killing them."

"And destroy the very souls we are trying to save?"

She leaned forward towards Junto. "Yes, some souls may die, but won't we save more by destroying the soul stealers?"

"I don't know. I just don't know any more." Junto rolled his mug between his fingers. He thought about the death gem on his shoulder. He could barely feel it physically, but it mentally lingered just below his conscious thoughts, like a mental itch he wasn't able to scratch.

They nursed their ales in silence.

"Who was that tall man?" Sekanna asked.

Junto shook his head. "I don't know. I've never seen him before." Junto paused. "But he knew who I was."

"He carried himself like a magistrate or something."

Junto was quiet. She was right. "That's all we need. Soul stealers in positions of power."

"I think the hunters have just become the hunted," Sekanna said. She took another drink of ale.

Junto looked up at her.

"I mean us," she said.

"I know what you mean."

"They are going to be looking for us now." She glanced around the room. "How many people know about this place?"

Junto thought about that for a long moment. "You, me, Wushwan, Nadrini and Velit." Junto paused. "And Irchly."

"Irchly," Sekanna muttered. "Where the fuck is that guy?"

Junto said nothing.

"And the soul stealers we captured," Sekanna added. "They obviously know about this place. Sekanna was quiet for a moment. "Elcor, Liesh, and Baisk," she muttered, more to herself than to him, her words coming out slightly slurred. "It would be easier just to burn them," Sekanna said. "I'm sorry about the souls they stole, but it would be easier just to burn them."

Junto frowned at her. "How much have you had to drink?"

Sekanna ignored his question.

"We are not going to just burn them," Junto said.

"I know. I just said it would be easier." She took another drink of ale. "And you can't forget about Zerin, Torek, and Kalandi," Sekanna said.

Junto shook his head. "Zerin won't betray us."

Sekanna pursed her lips. "Hmm. Yeah, but Torek probably would. And Kalandi might."

"I don't think those two are even in Moraneesh anymore, let alone anywhere here in Calkut," Junto said. He thought again of Torek. They had managed to extract all the death gems from Torek's body, but they had fallen for his feigned illness and he had escaped from the manor home. He was one of their first extractions, so they really had no idea what was going to happen. It was still no excuse for allowing him to escape, but it was at least some sort of explanation they could console themselves with.

He thought of Kalandi. He had completely misread him. He had thought the young man would gladly join their cause, but the seductive allure of the death gems, the mystique of their power, had turned Kalandi into the very thing they now hunted: a soul stealer.

Suddenly, Sekanna bolted upright. "Shit!"

"What?"

"I told that White to meet me at Croate's Inn tonight." Sekanna scrambled for her sword.

Junto frowned at her. "White? Who is White?"

"One of the Whites from the Oval. I don't even know his name. He's in trouble and I told him to meet me at Croate's. I can't just leave him there."

"Can you even see straight?"

She ignored his question and headed towards the door, her gait a little unsteady.

He quickly reached out and grabbed her arm as she passed him, stopping her. "Sekanna, wait. You can't go out like that. Put on your cloak, keep your hood up. Who knows how many men the tall man has working for him. You know he's out looking for us."

"Maybe we should go looking for him? Why wait to be surprised? We should be the ones doing the surprising."

Junto looked at her. Despite her slurred words,

she made a helluva lot of sense. The tall man would find them out eventually. It was inevitable. He tightened his jaw. They had enough to deal with just keeping track of Ulster, and now this. He pushed back the despairing shroud that threatened to cloud his clear thinking. He knew this battle wouldn't be easy, but he didn't think it would get so complicated so soon. He released his hold on Sekanna's arm.

Sekanna turned away and moved for her cloak hanging on a wood peg near the door. It wasn't much of a disguise, Junto realized. The cloak was nearly as silver as her hair. She would stand out in a crowd even with the hood covering her face. He rose up and moved after her, grabbing his cloak as she donned hers. She looked up at him, but said nothing.

"Let's go," he said. "Just stay alert."

"Are you kidding me? I feel like I just chewed a dozen khack leaves."

Junto looked at her. "Did you?" he finally asked.

She didn't answer. He didn't push. Her prior khack leaf addiction was a well-known fact between them, but they never discussed it. She had kicked it years ago and he had never suspected her of using it again. He felt sheepish for asking the question. He knew she hadn't. Her eyes were too clear; they didn't hold the tell-tale green veins of a heavy user. "Sorry," he said. "It's been a really long day."

She nodded. "I have a feeling it's going to get a lot longer."

The inn was crowded, as it usually was at this time of night. Tower women, and a few Tower men, worked the floor. Servers brought out food and drink at a steady clip, always on the move with a pleasant smile to keep patrons happy and to keep mugs and pipes full. Plenty of drink was being had as patrons slurped on ale and banged empty mugs down for refilling. Spiraling whirls of smoke drifted up to the ceiling as pipes were puffed on. Junto scanned the room. There was no one dressed in white that he could see. "You see him?"

Sekanna shook her head.

"You really think he's going to come here?"

She shrugged. "I'd give it even odds. He looked pretty scared and pretty desperate when the Reds lost Ulster. He had a lot of coin riding on their victory." She scanned the room, peering into the gloom of the dark corners. She saw a lone man sitting in a booth near the back wall. "There. He's here. Come on."

Sekanna moved towards the man. He looked up at her approach and Sekanna could see something in his eyes. A warning. His gaze shifted to his left. It was only for a second, but it was blatantly obvious. She slowly turned her head in the direction his eyes had indicated. Three men sat at a nearby table. Their mugs were still full, none of them touched. All three men stared directly at her. She quickly looked away. "Junto," she whispered.

"I see them," he whispered back. "It's too late to stop now. They know we are here. Just keep going."

Sekanna hesitated, but then kept going. They reached the booth and stood over it. Sekanna looked down at White. He looked up at her, his nose ruddy, his eyes red and haggard. "I'm sorry," he said. "You were kind to me."

"But?"

"But Heyeger really wants you."

"Heyeger?" Sekanna asked, echoing the name back.

"I heard you met him at the Oval already," White said. "A tall man with an entourage of bodyguards. He's one of the top patrons of the Red team. Very protective of his riders."

"Yeah, we met him."

White looked away from her. "I had no choice."

"You always have a choice," Sekanna said.

He nodded and drank from his mug. "I chose *him*," he said, not looking at Sekanna, keeping his gaze down on his drink. "He cleared my debts."

Sekanna was quiet for a moment. She felt a severe sense of disappointment and rejection. She barely knew the man, and he barely knew her, but it still troubled her that he so quickly turned on her offer of friendship. "How many men does he have in here?" She forced herself to keep her attention on White, fighting back the urge to look around the inn.

"Ten."

"Ten? I feel special."

"He wants both of you alive."

"So he can steal our souls?"

"Yes. He wants them fresh." He paused. "And

he wants to watch you suffer." White held out the mug to her. "Have a drink."

"No thanks."

He thrust out the mug to her. "Have a drink. You won't regret it. Just drink it slow."

She frowned at him, but did not reach for the mug.

He pushed the mug closer to her. "Really, drink." He looked up at her beseechingly. "It's the least I can do."

There was something odd in his eyes that compelled her to do as he asked. She took the mug and drank. Something touched her lips, a small object of some kind, and she took it into her mouth. She swallowed the warm ale, keeping the object off to the side of her mouth. She handed the mug back to White, looking at him curiously.

"Funny thing happens when that burns," he said. "Creates a lot of smoke. Might create lots of confusion." He took a drink from the mug. He looked up at her. "If we both survive this, come find me at The Fountains. I have a friend who lives near there. He'll hide me."

"What did he give you?" Junto asked, keeping his voice low.

"I have no idea," she whispered back, doing her best to speak clearly with the object still in her mouth. "Just be ready."

The three men at the table nearby started to ease out of the booth.

Sekanna turned toward the fire burning in the hearth and spit the object into the flames. The object immediately crackled and exploded, sending wave after wave of thick white smoke billowing out into the room.

Cries of alarm, the scuffling sounds of chairs being overturned, and scared shouts filled the room.

Sekanna ducked down beneath the billowing wall of smoke and grabbed Junto's arm, pulling him down with her. She tugged him towards the kitchen door in the rear of the room. They pushed through the swinging door and moved into the kitchen. The door swung back and forth, allowing the thick white smoke to billow into the kitchen behind them. Kitchen workers eyed them, and the white cloud that appeared to be trailing them, with a mixture of curiosity and fear. A chicken about to be butchered squawked and somehow freed itself from the cook's hand. It fluttered and screeched wildly about the room.

Sekanna and Junto rose up and raced for the rear door that led to the alley outside the inn.

They hurried back to their manor home, back to their sanctuary, but they hesitated as they approached. The sight that greeted them sent chills up their spines, leaving them frozen where they stood. Their sanctuary was no more.

CHAPTER TWENTY-FOUR

Their manor home had been found. The door was battered open, laying askew, barely clinging to the doorframe hinges by one screw.

An immense feeling of dread welled up inside Junto as they moved cautiously inside. Everything was smashed inside the foyer. The marble sculptures Nadrini and Velit had brought from their home country of Ancii lay in shattered pieces on the wood plank floor. They moved deeper into the manor home, entering their main gathering room. Sekanna drew her sword.

Wushwan lay prone on the floor near Nadrini. Junto hurried over to him, while Sekanna rushed over to Nadrini. Junto immediately saw the tell-tale markings where a death beetle had been removed from Wushwan's flesh, the red welts visible on his neck. He ground his teeth and clenched his jaw tight as he stared down at Wushwan's vacant eyes. He gently closed Wushwan's eyelids. His fingers curled into a fist. Wushwan had been a good man. A good friend. He believed in the cause just as strongly as Junto did. The thought of having to continue on without Wushwan sickened him, making his stomach flutter queasily. Wushwan had practically invented the extraction technique on his own; Junto had really only given him encouragement more than any true guidance.

Junto looked over at Sekanna and she met his gaze with a sad stare. She didn't need to utter a word. Junto knew Nadrini's soul had also been stolen.

They continued to move slowly through their manor home, heading towards the cages, passing the shredded remains of their scrolls scattered about the floor. All of their work was destroyed. The evidence accumulated over years of collecting information, gone.

They entered the holding area and immediately saw that the cell doors had been opened. Elcor was gone. He had been freed.

A noise made them start. Junto drew his battering stick and moved cautiously towards the sound. They stepped into the room and froze. A large naked man was atop Velit, thrusting into her with loud grunts. But she wasn't trying to stop him. Velit had her arms around the man, pulling him in deeper. She saw them standing in the doorway and closed her eyes, continuing to pull the man in deeper. Junto could see that the man's back was bedecked with several slightly shimmering death gems; a few other gems had already gone black. Junto felt dizzy and nauseous. Had Velit betrayed them? Junto couldn't believe it. It wasn't possible.

Sekanna stood still next to him, her sword lowered, her face filled with the sickening disbelief that Junto clearly was feeling.

The man turned his head and they both stared

into the smiling face of Elcor. "I was waiting for you two to get here. Give me a minute." He turned back to Velit and continued thrusting, finishing inside her with a tremendous grunt and a heavy sighing groan. He withdrew and turned to face them, his dangling manhood glistening with a slick sheen.

Junto glanced around the area, as if anticipating the arrival of others.

"Don't worry," Elcor said, noticing his roving gaze. "It's just us. I told that Baisk fellow to leave you two to me, but he didn't want to listen. He was rather rude to me." Elcor pointed to a death gem on his left breast. "So now I'm wearing his soul."

"You killed Baisk?"

Elcor nodded. "He was looking for you, but found me instead." Elcor grinned. "He had a living death gem still on him, so I had to lop off his head and smash in his skull so he couldn't get re-born." Elcor glanced around the floor. "His brains are around here somewhere I think." He looked back up at them. "So much quicker that way. Never seen a soul stealer recover from a smashed head, have you?"

"Where's Liesh?" Junto asked. "You kill her, too? How did you get out of your cage?"

"Her family came for her. Couple of nice boys. Said they were her brothers. They graciously let me out of my cage. They were the ones gave me the death gem I used on your friend Baisk." He looked at them. "See, some people don't treat other people like wild fucking animals." His words came out in a vicious snarl.

Junto felt his world crumbling around him. They failed in capturing Ulster and now some wealthy Red patron going by the name of Heyeger wanted their souls. The soul stealers they had captured over the last few months were now freed. Somehow Liesh's brothers had learned of Liesh's capture and had found the manor home and freed their sister. Liesh's brothers were most likely soul stealers as well. Junto didn't even know Liesh had any brothers. So much for their intelligence gathering. Now Baisk was dead and Elcor was free.

All the scrolls they had created that had identified the soul stealers they had intended to capture had been destroyed. Sekanna could probably recreate some of them by memory, but he knew she would never be able to recreate them all. His grand plan of stopping the soul stealers and freeing the souls they stole was a grand failure. Complete and utter failure. Now they had nothing. Only dead friends, empty cages, and a variety of psychotic soul stealers intent on stealing their souls.

Suddenly, Velit bolted forward from behind the big man and shoved a jagged dagger deep into Elcor's side, slashing and twisting, drawing a thick spray of blood. Elcor swiped at her with a mighty forearm, sending her sprawling across the room. He gripped at the ugly gash in his flesh, blood spilling through his fingers in a red torrent.

"Velit!" Junto shouted. He felt a wild rush of relief and fear all at the same time. Velit had only been trying to distract Elcor, get him to let his guard down, biding her time before she struck, but now she was clearly putting herself in grave danger.

Velit ignored Junto's cry and charged at Elcor again, swinging the blade. Elcor grabbed her arm, stopping her mid-swing. He pulled her to him, putting a crushing forearm grip around her throat as he held her against him.

Junto and Sekanna made motions to step towards Elcor, gripping their weapons tightly as they moved nearer, but Elcor immediately tightened the pressure on Velit's throat and they had no choice but to pause in their tracks.

And then Elcor died. They could see it in his eyes. They just went blank for a brief moment, emptying out of life. One of the death gems on his chest shimmered, glowing hotly before it went black. His eyelids fluttered, and then he was back. The emptiness in his eyes was replaced by a vibrant eruption of alertness. The wound in his side was already nearly gone, only a slight scar remaining visible where Velit had slashed at him.

Junto was amazed at the rapidity of the healing. He didn't realize the re-birthing and healing could happen so fast. He wondered if Elcor's body was acclimated to the process because he had died so many times before. That would make Elcor even more dangerous than Junto already knew he was.

Elcor looked at them and smiled; his eyes had an actual twinkle of mirth glinting in them. "That never gets old." Somehow he had not even lost any of the tight grip he had on Velit's throat. He still clutched her tightly against him. "That's one soul you couldn't save," he said to Junto, a mocking tone distinctly present in his words. Elcor licked his lips. "It's funny how you can taste it on your lips when you use it. Tastes like — that boy I killed last month." He nodded to himself, obscenely smacking his lips. "Yes, that was him all right." He paused. "I'm only going to take young ones from now on. They have so much vitality."

Junto and Sekanna hesitated, but kept their weapons at the ready.

"What do you want, Elcor?" Junto asked.

"I want you all to die and stop hunting me."

"That's not going to happen," Junto said.

"Says you." Elcor snapped Velit's neck with a vicious yank and released his grip, opening his big fingers to let her body fall unceremoniously to the floor. The bloodied dagger rolled out of her hand.

Junto felt a scream of despair welling up in his throat, but he forced it back down. He narrowed his eyes, keeping his gaze focused on Elcor. The big man was in a murderously foul mood and he couldn't afford to take his attention away from him for even one second.

"Too bad I don't have a death beetle on me to use on her," Elcor said, glancing down at Velit's prone body. "She probably would have been extremely tasty." He shrugged. "At least I got to fuck her first. Don't think she had many men." He looked at Junto. "You ever have her?" He looked down at Velit's broken body again. "I might even have her again after I take care of the two of you."

Junto and Sekanna slowly approached him, their weapons ready. They eased apart, forcing Elcor to move his gaze from one to the other as they widened the distance between themselves but moved ever closer to the huge man.

Elcor bent down and picked up the dagger that lay at his feet. It was laced with red streaks, his own blood still wet on the blade. He turned the blade over, casually studying both bloodied sides. Then Elcor suddenly lunged towards Sekanna, moving with surprising speed and agility for such a big man.

"No!" Junto shouted as he surged forward, moving his body protectively towards Sekanna. Elcor whirled quickly on Junto, turning his weapon towards him. The blade went into Junto's gut, slicing deep. Elcor twisted the blade and cut deeper. Junto gasped, then gurgled blood from his lips. He lost his grip on his battering stick and dropped to his knees, staring blankly at nothing as his life faded from his eyes. Elcor withdrew the blade, its steel surface now coated a deep red with Junto's blood. Junto grunted a final gasp, "Sekanna…" then keeled over to lie still. It happened that quickly. One moment Junto was alive and breathing, the next moment he was still and lifeless.

Elcor stared down at Junto's body, clearly quite pleased with himself. He turned to Sekanna, waiting for her scream, waiting for her charge. But she did not scream. She did not charge at him with a wildly waving weapon.

Sekanna lowered her blade as she looked at Junto's fallen body. A stream of blood wet the floor near his slashed abdomen. She turned away to look at Elcor. "He never understood." She looked back to Junto's fallen body.

Elcor just stared at her with curious eyes.

Sekanna set her blade down on the table nearby. She reached for her belt and slowly undid it, tossing the cord to the table near her sword. She slowly pulled down her breeches, revealing the silver curls of her womanhood, and the death gem on the inside of her thigh. She looked up at Elcor. "I understand," she said.

Surprise, and a hungry delight, filled Elcor's eyes.

Sekanna turned around and bent over the table, thrusting her naked buttocks in his direction. She looked at him over her shoulder with a sultry gaze. "Now are you going to give me what you were giving Velit?" She gave her ass a tiny wiggle.

Elcor just stared at her.

She reached behind herself and spread her butt cheeks.

Elcor threw the blade down and approached her, his manhood stiffening as he neared.

CHAPTER TWENTY-FIVE

It was the most exhilarating feeling Junto had ever felt. It was like being drunk, high on leaf, and orgasming all at the same time. It was absolutely incredible. His entire body floated and tingled and hummed. He felt it through every part of his being, as if something was in his blood enriching him, empowering him. His vision started to return. Everything was a hazy blur at first, but then quickly came back into focus. He was lying on the ground, on his side. A pool of some dark liquid was spread out before him. He could see two blurry bodies, but then they quickly came into focus. Sekanna was bent over a table, her breeches pulled down, and Elcor was approaching her, his intentions clear by the grotesque stiffness of his erect member.

Junto felt strength returning to his limbs, then to his hands, then his fingers. He felt incredibly alive. His senses seemed to be augmented with great clarity. Sight, sounds, smells; all of them were heightened. He could see the facets in each of the death gems that were embedded in Elcor's flesh, see the different shadings of color on each gem; the blackened death gems seemed blacker than a starless night and the gems that still held a life-force within them seemed to blaze as bright as the midday sun. He could hear Elcor's coarse, grunting breath as he approached Sekanna. The big brute of a man was clearly excited by the prospect of what was being offered to him; in contrast, Sekanna's breathing seemed calm and even. He could smell the remains of Velit; the smell of death permeated the air. He could even smell the coppery scent of what he now realized was his own spilled blood.

Then Junto saw Sekanna snatch her blade from the table near her. She swung with a strong stroke, lopping Elcor's head off with one mighty strike. His head hit the ground with a dull thud. Dozens of death gem tendrils suddenly extended out of his severed head, the thin rope-like appendages weaving about frantically, looking like thin stalks of wheat thrashing about in a storm wind.

Junto tried to cry out but no words came out. He wasn't fully re-birthed yet. And his mouth was incredibly dry, his throat parched, his body still recovering from the sudden loss of a large amount of liquid. He watched as Sekanna shoved at the headless body of Elcor with her shoulder, knocking Elcor's body away from her. The headless body released all manner of vile fluids as it crashed to the ground. Dozens more death gem tendrils extended out of Elcor's neck, the thin appendages weaving about frantically. Somehow, they must have sensed Elcor's severed head because all the tendrils started to turn in that direction, all of them straining to reach the severed head. In turn, the severed strips of tendrils extending out of Elcor's severed head reached towards the body, clearly wanting to reunite.

Sekanna quickly pulled up her breeches and re-gripped her sword, staring down at Elcor's corpse.

One of the death gems on Elcor's body immediately started to glow hotly, then another and another. The souls were being absorbed into a headless body. They were being destroyed! Forever. Junto knew he had to do something. He finally felt himself able to move and he pushed himself to a sitting position. He glanced over at Elcor's severed head. A death gem glowed hotly on his forehead, then another. More souls were being lost forever. The gems that had just glowed turned a deeply disturbing black. "Sekanna, grab his head."

She looked numbly at him, then brightened at the sight of him, clearly relieved that he was alive.

"Grab his head! Hurry!" Junto exclaimed. He felt fully returned now, able to control his movements, his muscles feeling thick and strong. Junto gripped the headless body by an arm and started to drag Elcor's corpse across the floor. He struggled with the weight of the big man, even with the power he felt surging through him, but the blood slick on the ground helped him ease the body along the floor. Some of the tendrils jutting out of Elcor's neck area turned towards Junto, as if sniffing at him, but then turned back in the direction of the fallen head. He pulled Elcor's headless body out of the room, dragging him toward the cages. He looked up to see that Sekanna had not moved. "Sekanna, grab his head! We're losing souls."

Sekanna moved, lurching towards the severed head.

He pulled Elcor into a cage, then hurried back to the approaching Sekanna and took the severed head from her, gripping it with two hands. The tendrils emanating down out of Elcor's head weaved about madly, thrashing in the air; Junto held the severed head away from his body, not wanting the tendrils to get too close to him. He moved back to Elcor's body and put the head near his neck, touching the two parts together. The tendrils intertwined like family members embracing at a reunion and started to re-attach themselves. More death gems glowed hotly on Elcor's body. Four of them had already gone black. Another death gem glowed on Elcor's face.

Junto and Sekanna could only watch, rapt with fascination. Neither one of them had ever seen anything like this.

Elcor's head fused back onto his body, the flesh joining as if being welded back together from the inside. Two more death gems went black during this process. And then the death gems stopped glowing hotly.

Junto grabbed Sekanna's arm and pulled her out of the cage with him. He quickly shut the door and latched it closed. He grabbed a large padlock nearby and locked the cage door with it. He backed away from the cage slowly, keeping his gaze riveted on Elcor.

"You should have just let him stay dead," Sekanna said.

Junto shook his head. "Look at all those souls. I just can't let them all be destroyed."

"Sacrifices have to be made for the greater

good."

"And we decide whose souls get sacrificed or not?"

Sekanna nodded. "Yes, Junto, we do."

Junto said nothing to that. He looked at Elcor. There were too many souls trapped inside him. He couldn't let them all perish. There were just too many. He looked at the five blackened gems on Elcor's skin and felt his heart wrench and his stomach turn. Was one of those Wushwan?

Elcor opened his eyes and sat up. He blinked at them. Then he rose to his feet and charged at them, his large naked body streaked with blood and other body fluids. He rammed into the heavy metal bars, thrusting his arms between them, desperately clutching at them. Junto and Sekanna backed away out of his reach. They had forgotten to chain him to the wall!

"I will eat your fucking souls!" Elcor snarled.

"Not today," Junto said.

"What are we going to do with him?" Sekanna asked.

In the distance, they could hear Elcor rattling the cage bars, cursing and yelling at them. He hadn't stopped yelling for hours.

Junto replayed the image of the tendrils jutting out of Elcor's severed head, seeing the thin strands weaving about madly in the air in his mind. Those things were in him now. And in Sekanna. Those tendrils were in anyone who had a death gem on them. And now his death gem was black. Did that mean the tendrils would just stay in his body? Would they decay over time? He didn't know the answers to those questions and he dreaded to realize that he was very likely going to find out firsthand.

"Wushwan is gone," Sekanna said. "And the girls. They were the experts with the extractions."

Junto was quiet for a moment. Sekanna's voice brought him back to the present. He thought of Wushwan and his girls. They had burned their bodies on the funeral pyre, all three of them together. He was certain Wushwan would have wanted it that way. The lingering smell of their burning flesh still tainted the air. He knew their bodies had just been empty husks of flesh, but part of him still hoped some semblance of their souls still had resided in their bodies. He just couldn't dwell for long on the fact that their souls might have been destroyed forever. He knew he would go mad if he kept thinking about it. Elcor still had numerous glimmering gems on his body, the life-forces contained within still glowing with whatever energy they contained. Maybe one of those held Wushwan's life-force. Maybe one of them held Nadrini's. Maybe both of their life-forces were still savable.

But then he paused. Wait. No, not Elcor. Elcor hadn't stolen their souls. He didn't have enough death gems on him. Elcor had stolen Baisk's life-force, but he had made no mention of Wushwan or Nadrini. Had Liesh stolen Wushwan's life-force? And Nadrini's? Or perhaps these so-called brothers of Liesh had done it. He felt a glimmering of hope rise in his chest. Maybe Wushwan and Nadrini could still be saved after all. If their life-forces resided in Liesh or her brothers, then there was still a chance to save their souls.

At least he knew Velit had made it into the Everlasting with her soul intact. It was a very small comfort, but it was at least something to hold onto. But she would be forever attached to Elcor because he had murdered her, so that thought chilled him and quickly negated any positive thoughts, any hope, he might have had for Velit. Unless you destroy Elcor's soul, then Velit won't be attached to him, a voice inside him whispered. How could she be attached to him for all eternity if Elcor's soul was destroyed? Would that truly free Velit? Would he have to destroy Elcor to truly save her now? The thoughts were leading him to a dangerous place so he forced himself to stop thinking about the possibilities. "We'll have to do the extractions," he finally said to Sekanna.

"He's a monster, Junto. How are we even going to get him onto an extraction table? The straps probably wouldn't even hold him."

"We'll have to give him blackroot."

Sekanna shook her head. "We don't have any anymore."

"We'll have to get some."

"And then what?" Sekanna asked. "Force it down his throat? Just making him sniff it probably won't knock him out like it did—" She cut herself off, looking guiltily away from Junto.

Junto was quiet for a moment. "As far as we know, there still could be another child's soul in one of those gems on Elcor," Junto said. "Or several. We don't know for sure. Do you really want to let a child's soul be destroyed forever if you could stop it from happening?"

Sekanna was quiet. She looked away from him.

Junto was again quiet for a long moment. There was only a slight twinge of discomfort in his side where Elcor had stabbed him. He was convinced in a matter of days there would be no more pain and only a faint scar would remain to remind him of what had happened.

Elcor continued to curse and rattle the bars of his cage, the angry sounds echoing through the manor house.

Sekanna looked back to Junto. "Are you... okay?"

Junto was quiet for a moment longer, then looked at his hands, turning them over to study them. "It was... strange," he said.

She waited for him to elaborate.

"I understand now why the soul stealers want more and more," Junto said.

She looked curiously at him.

"It was... intoxicating," he said. "It's faded now, but it was—" His voice trailed off.

She reached out and touched his arm. "I'm sorry I did that to you. But I'm glad you're not dead." She smiled at him, trying to be playful.

Junto looked up sharply at her. "You'll never do that again, do you understand? You will not put any more death gems on me."

Her smile vanished. She nodded and pulled her hand away from him slowly. She looked down at her own hands, sitting quietly for a moment before she looked back over to Junto. "What did it... feel like?"

He was quiet.

"Where did you go?" she asked.

He squinted at her.

"When you... died. Where did you go?"

"I didn't go anywhere," he said. "Everything just went black, then everything slowly came back into focus. I could hear and see and smell things I've never felt before. It was... strange." The words thrilling, exciting, and exhilarating came to mind but he left them unspoken.

"Do you... feel her?"

He cocked his head slightly at her question.

"Tallie. Do you feel her? Did you... feel her?" She paused. "Did you... taste her?" The question was repugnant, but she felt compelled to ask it because of what Elcor had said about tasting the soul of the boy he had killed and used.

He shook his head. "No. It was just... it was like a raw surge of pure energy. I didn't feel her at all." He scowled. "And I certainly didn't taste her." But then he paused. He remembered a sound he had heard as the blackness started to withdraw, when things started to come back into focus. He had heard a scream, a shrill scream as if coming from a very far distance. He now realized what that sound was. It was the sound of a soul being extinguished forever. It was the sound of a soul being devoured within him. He kept silent. It was something he didn't feel like sharing with her right now. It was a sound he feared he would hear in his dreams for a long time to come.

He reached up behind him and felt the edges of the death gem on his shoulder. It was cold to the touch now. It was just an empty gem. Oddly enough, it had great value on the black market. It sickened him, but he knew he was going to eventually have to sell it. They desperately needed coin to keep themselves going, to keep their mission alive. Mission? A voice inside him immediately scoffed. What mission? You have nothing. He pushed the doubting voice aside, continuing to run his fingers over the edges of the cold and blackened gem. The blackened gem would fetch a few full bags of coin. And besides, it would rid him of the physical reminder of what he had done, of what Sekanna had done to him. But he also knew he couldn't extract the black gem until they recreated Wushwan's formula. The extraction of a blackened death gem was still life-threatening to its host if the proper precautions and preparations were not made.

Then, a knock sounded in the direction of their battered door and they both froze.

CHAPTER TWENTY-SIX

It was White at their door. He had come to warn them. "Heyeger is coming here for you. I heard them talking. You have to leave this place."

Junto shook his head. "We can't leave. We have a prisoner."

White's head shake was more vigorous. "You can't defend this place. Not just the two of you. There are too many of them. At least six, seven men will be coming. If not more."

Junto tightened his jaw. White was probably right. They had no chance of defending their manor home, especially not with the front door in shambles. He tightened his fingers into a fist. Once again, he had been careless. They should have taken much greater pains to protect the whereabouts of their manor home. They were much too close to the city. They needed to find some remote place, somewhere at the foot of the mountains perhaps. Somewhere that people just didn't stumble onto. Somewhere even treacherous to reach. Maybe they could find somewhere to re-establish their base just past the Roaring River at the foot of Nazarete Mountain. If they survived long enough to even reach it. And even then they needed to post guards who would patrol the grounds all hours of the day and night.

"They are perhaps an hour behind me. Probably less. You must leave." White became silent after his last exhortation.

Sekanna looked at White expectantly. He clearly had something else on his mind. "What? What else?"

"They are after me as well," White finally said. "They know I helped you escape from Croate's Inn."

No one spoke for a moment. Junto looked at the man. Every one he had ever trusted in his life had let him down, or outright betrayed him. Even Sekanna had betrayed his trust. He didn't trust this White. And then he mentally scoffed at himself. He should react opposite to what his supposed instincts told him to do. His instincts didn't seem very reliable. They were always leading him astray.

"Come with us," Sekanna said at the same time Junto spoke those very words himself. He and Sekanna exchanged glances and laughed tiny laughs.

White's face remained sad and distraught. "I — I have nowhere else to go," he said.

Sekanna put her hand on his shoulder. "Turns out neither do we. We can go nowhere together."

White looked up at Sekanna, with a feeling of relief pushing away some of his apprehension. "Thank you," he said. "My name's Calin," he said. "Calin Quintal."

"I was just going to call you White, but Calin will work," Sekanna said.

"CQ for short," Calin said.

Sekanna shook her head. "Okay, umm, no. That doesn't work. You can call me Mistress Sekanna." She leaned in conspiratorially and whispered, "But not in front of everyone else."

Calin looked at her curiously, not quite sure how to react to that.

Sekanna smiled mysteriously and looked away.

Junto studied the man named Calin Quintal for a moment. "Do you have any death gems on you?"

Calin shook his head.

"You speak the truth?" Junto asked.

"Yes. I do not have any death gems on me."

"Do you want one?" Junto asked. "Do you wish you had a death gem?"

Calin did not answer right away. He frowned, squinting curiously at Junto. "Should I? Should I want one?"

Junto did not reply.

Calin looked to Sekanna.

"We all have to figure that one out for ourselves," she said.

Calin looked to both of them, glancing back and forth between them. "Do you have death gems on you?"

"I do," Sekanna said. "I have one." She motioned to Junto. "He did, but it's gone black."

Calin frowned. "Isn't that what you are fighting to stop?"

Neither Sekanna nor Junto answered his question.

"We need to move. We need to gather up supplies and weapons and get the Hell's Wood out of here," Junto said.

"What about Elcor?" Sekanna asked.

"He has to die," Junto said. "We can't let him live. He'll just steal more souls."

Sekanna looked at Junto with surprise. "All of those souls in him will die."

"You think I don't know that?" The question was biting and bitter. "What other choice do we have?"

"I'll do it," Sekanna said.

Junto shook his head. "We'll both do it. Get two crossbows."

"Get three," Calin said.

Junto and Sekanna turned to look at him.

"Get three," Calin said, confirming his words.

"We need a death beetle," Junto said.

Sekanna started to speak, hesitated, but then continued on anyway despite her misgivings. "I have one," she said.

Junto looked at her with a wry expression. "And why does that not surprise me?"

Sekanna shrugged. "I used my last one on you. A girl's gotta protect her interests."

"Where did you get it?" Junto asked.

"From the merchant on the edge of the market," Sekanna replied. "When I was looking for Ulster."

Junto wanted to hear more details about that, but he knew now wasn't the time.

"What are you thinking?" Sekanna asked.

"I'm thinking we need to kill Elcor and — steal his soul. I don't think it's fair to let Velit be attached to him for all eternity because he murdered her. Or Wushwan or Nadrini."

"Who's going to... wear the death gem?" Sekanna asked. "Once we take his life-force we have to put the death beetle on someone."

Calin was listening intently to their conversation and he interjected with a question. "Why?"

Sekanna turned to him. "If we don't, and the death beetle dies, then his life-force will be freed and he'll go into the Everlasting." She looked back to Junto. "Which defeats the whole purpose."

Junto was quiet.

"Someone needs to take the death beetle," Sekanna said. "Someone needs to do that, Junto."

Calin shook his head without either of them even looking at him. "Don't look at me."

"Hey, guys, umm... what did I miss?"

Junto turned to see Irchly standing in the doorway. He froze for a moment, then hurried over to his friend and embraced him in a huge bear hug.

Irchly was startled for a moment and kept his body still, then returned Junto's embrace and patted him heartily on the back. "Good to see you, too, Junto." Irchly glanced around the room, at the destruction. "Looks like I missed a lot."

"You have no idea," Sekanna said.

"I didn't mean to be gone for so long," Irchly said. "My grandfather died and I had to bring his body back to Berjon to bury him. And you know those Berjon funerals. Damn things last for days. I couldn't just leave in the middle of the ceremony."

"I am sorry about your grandfather," Sekanna said. "I liked that old cuss. Of course, he kept trying to get me in his bed, but that was kind of cute."

Junto glanced sidelong at her. Sekanna shrugged. Calin sat quietly next to Sekanna, just watching and listening. Irchly was sitting across from Calin at the kitchen table, Junto and Sekanna flanking him. They all had mugs of ale in front of them, most of them already empty.

Irchly glanced at Sekanna. "You really put a death gem on Junto?"

Sekanna looked sheepish and turned away from his inquisitive stare.

Irchly looked at Junto. "And you already had to use it?"

Junto said nothing.

"So you found that Ulster soul stealer but now he's a champion rider for the Reds? You pissed off some magistrate named Heyeger and he's after you. Liesh's brothers tore this place up and freed her. Baisk is dead. Wushwan and his girls are dead. You've got some insane soul stealer named Elcor locked up in a cage." Irchly looked from Junto to Sekanna and then back to Junto. "Anything else?"

Junto frowned at his seemingly casual mention of Wushwan's death. A sudden feeling of dread filled him. There was more to Irchly's disappearance than he was letting on.

"You need more?" Sekanna asked.

Irchly didn't respond to that. "Well, since we're all being so open," Irchly said and finished off his mug of ale with a hearty swallow. "Then I might as well get my secret off my chest."

Junto and Sekanna waited for him to continue.

"I'm getting out of the soul saving business," Irchly said.

Junto stared slack jawed at him.

Sekanna frowned at him. "What?"

"I met a woman at my grandfather's funeral. I'm moving back to Berjon." Irchly paused. "Well, I didn't really meet her. I already knew her. I grew up with her in Berjon. We just hit it off again and everything sort of rekindled from there." He paused. "I just felt like I needed to come back and tell you. I felt like I owed you that much. I'll be heading back today."

Junto and Sekanna were speechless.

"You're not going to like the next part," Irchly said. He lifted his cup to take another drink, but realized the mug was already empty so he set it back down.

"I already don't like the first part," Junto said.

"She's a mystic." Irchly paused. "And she's a soul stealer."

Junto stared at him. It took him a moment to absorb what Irchly had just told them. "You're moving back to Berjon to be with a soul stealer?"

"I'm in love with her," Irchly said.

"Are you?" Sekanna asked. "Or did she make you think you are?" She paused. "There's a big difference."

"You fucking cowards!" Elcor shouted from his cage. The sound of metal bars violently rattling filled the air.

"Didn't you chain him up?" Irchly asked. "Sounds like he's gotten out of the manacles."

Junto threw up his hands. "I can't deal with all of this right now. We need to — take care of Elcor and get the Hell's Wood out of here before that Heyeger fuck shows up." He looked at Irchly. "Go do what you need to do."

"Wait," Calin suddenly said and grabbed Sekanna's arm as she started to rise up from the table.

She turned to see Calin staring hard at Irchly. She followed his gaze, then turned back to look at Calin.

Calin kept his gaze firmly on Irchly. "You came here to warn them, didn't you?"

Irchly said nothing.

"What?" Junto said.

Calin looked askance at Junto, but quickly returned his gaze to Irchly. "He came here to warn you. To stay away from Berjon."

Irchly took an empty drink from his empty mug.

Junto stared hard at Irchly. "Is that true?"

"I told you I love her," Irchly said.

"You'd better leave right now, Irchly, before I throw you in that cage with Elcor," Junto warned.

Irchly slowly set his mug down on the table. "Stay away from Berjon," he said, then turned and walked out of the room.

"You fucking cowards," Elcor snarled. He stood at the bars of the cage, gripping them with his meaty hands.

A crossbow bolt whistled through the air and struck Elcor in the chest. His body twisted to the left as the arrow struck him, but he still retained his grip on the bars. "Come in here and fight me!" He shook the bars.

Another crossbow bolt raced through the air, striking Elcor in the right breast, knocking his body in the opposite direction from the first bolt strike.

A third bolt missed, soaring past his head.

A fourth, fifth, and sixth bolt did not miss. Two sunk deep into his chest, one in his gut. Elcor died standing up, clutching at the bars.

Junto looked on as a death gem glowed hotly on Elcor's midsection, right above a crossbow bolt that was sunk into his flesh. The life-force contained within the death gem went to work, releasing its energy into Elcor, pushing the crossbow bolts out of his flesh from within, healing the wounds the penetrating sharp tips had caused. Then another death gem on his right arm glowed brightly as it too released its energy into Elcor. The big man's eyelids fluttered, then stayed open. Elcor savagely tugged on the bars, shaking the entire cage. "I will rip your fucking hearts out of your chests, you fucking cunts!"

"This is going to take too long," Sekanna said, lowering her crossbow. "Look at him. He must have at least twenty more death gems still on him. Maybe more. We never really counted them. He was probably lying about how many he had."

Elcor rattled the cage with ferocious intensity. "I will hunt you down and rip off your heads and shit down your fucking throats!"

"Get the oil," Junto finally said.

Sekanna nodded. "Calin, come with me." Sekanna led Calin out of the holding room. They both set their crossbows down on the table as they exited the room.

Junto loaded another bolt into the crossbow and aimed it at Elcor.

"Shoot, you worm. Shoot!" Elcor glared at Junto. "I will relish feasting on your soul. Then I'll feed your body piece by piece to the dogs."

Junto fired, the bolt striking Elcor in the forehead with a bone-crunching sound. The crossbow bolt penetrated his skull, sending rivulets of blood streaming down his face. He released his grip on the metal bars and fell backwards to the cell floor.

Junto's expression remained flat as he loaded another bolt.

A death gem on Elcor's body glowed hot and bright, then went black. The crossbow bolt clattered to the ground and Elcor sat up.

Junto fired another bolt into the big man's head. The force of the striking bolt forced his body back down flat against the floor. A death gem on his thigh glowed and went black. After a moment, Elcor sat back up. He grinned at Junto and smacked his lips. "That was a tasty one. Do it again."

Junto no longer saw him as human. He stared at a rabid animal that had no hope of being cured. He stared at a savage beast that needed to be put down. He loaded another bolt into the crossbow.

Sekanna returned with Calin. She pushed a small wooden cart before her, the cart laden with a dozen large jugs of lamp oil. Calin trailed her, holding a burning torch in his hand.

For the first time, a hint of fear touched Elcor's eyes. He backed up from the bars, moving as far back as he could in the cage, scuttling backwards on the bloodied floor like a crab scurrying away from a predator, slipping as he moved. "You can't do that," he said. He looked at Junto with an almost pleading look in his eyes. "You can't do that. You are not that cruel." He rose up to a standing position, pressing his back firmly against the far stone wall of the cell.

"I wasn't until I met you," Junto said. He set his crossbow down on the cart. He grabbed one of the jugs and threw the liquid towards Elcor.

Most of the oil hit the floor near Elcor's feet, but some of it splashed onto his legs. Elcor frantically wiped at the liquid, trying to brush the slimy fluid from his flesh. As he was bent down, more oil splashed near his feet, then some hit his back and his head. He wiped crazily at the liquid, spasmodically writhing as he desperately tried to get the oil off his body. More liquid splashed over him and soon he was drenched in oil.

Junto splashed a stream of oil on the floor, making a trail leading from the bars up to Elcor. He took the torch from Calin and held it up for a moment, staring at Elcor. "Forgive me," Junto said.

"Fuck you!" Elcor growled.

"I wasn't speaking to you," Junto said. He lowered the flame to the floor and the fire leaped to the oil, then raced towards Elcor, engulfing him in flames. His skin crackled and charred. The smell of burning flesh immediately filled the room. A wave of heat washed over them as the flames brightened and intensified, the fire hungrily feasting on the oil, and on Elcor's flesh.

Even through the bright glare of the fire, they could still see a death gem glowing and flesh beginning to reform on Elcor's body, but then the pinkish layer of new skin quickly burned away. Elcor's eyes opened for a brief second and he screamed before death took him again. Another death gem glowed and flesh again reformed. Elcor opened his eyes and screamed again.

Calin turned away, unable to watch.

Junto and Sekanna did not turn away. They watched Elcor die and live, die and live, over and over again. Soon, five more death gems had gone black. The acrid smell of burnt flesh filled the room.

Then the flames started to die away. Junto and Sekanna did not hesitate and they both threw more oil into the cage, reigniting the flames. Elcor continued to scream and die, scream and die. Five more death gems went black.

"The sun is almost gone. Heyeger and his men will be here any moment. We must leave," Calin said.

Junto grabbed another jug of oil and tossed it on Elcor. The flames burned hotter and brighter. Elcor screamed and died. The whole thing sickened Junto, but he knew he couldn't stop now. He turned to Sekanna. "Grab the coin bags. Let's get ready to get out of here. We'll need those."

Sekanna nodded and hurried from the holding room.

"What can I do?" Calin asked.

Junto pointed down the hallway. "There's some food stores in there. Some dried meat. Grab as much as you can carry. And bring some for me to carry."

Calin started out of the room.

"And grab yourself some weapons," Junto called after him. "The armory is just past the food stores."

Calin nodded and moved out of the room.

Junto turned back to watch Elcor burn.

Sekanna suddenly burst back into the holding area, clutching a single bag of coin in one hand and a shield in the other. "They're coming, Junto. They're just up the hill. We need to go! There are a dozen men at least."

Junto looked back to Elcor. He grabbed the last jug of oil and tossed it on the burning man.

"We need to go!" Sekanna exclaimed.

Junto grabbed his crossbow and loaded a bolt. His face was grim, his expression cold. He fired the bolt square into Elcor's chest.

"Junto, we need to go!" Sekanna clutched at his arm. "Now!"

CHAPTER TWENTY-SEVEN

Heyeger stared down at the charred body of Elcor. They had wrapped him in a few blankets, doing their best to suffocate the flames. The man's body was charred black. But then Heyeger watched in amazement as new flesh started to form. A death gem, what appeared to be the charred man's last non-blackened death gem, shimmered, then went dark.

Elcor opened his eyes, but this time he did not scream. He looked up at Heyeger and he smiled a cracked-lipped smile.

The tall man named Heyeger smiled back.

"Now what?" Sekanna asked.

"We start over," Junto said.

They continued moving quickly through the woods, constantly glancing over their shoulders for any signs of pursuers, but they had yet to see any. They had managed to take two bags of dried meat, and the one bag of coin that Sekanna had grabbed. Sekanna had her shield and her sword. Junto had his battering stick lodged in his belt. Calin had never made it to the armory, so he had no extra weapons beyond the small dagger he always carried with him.

Sekanna sighed. "Where are we going to find another Wushwan?" she asked. She brushed a branch out of her way as she walked quickly through the trees.

"I don't know. Maybe we won't."

"What is a Wushwan?" Calin asked.

"Not what. Who," Sekanna said. "He was our healer. And our extractor."

"Extractor?"

Sekanna nodded at Calin. "He knew how to extract the death gems so we could free the souls trapped within." She looked at Calin. "I thought you knew all this already."

"I know some things about you and Junto. I don't know everything." Calin was quiet, absorbing these new pieces of information. "I know a healer," he said after a moment.

"We know lots of healers," Sekanna said. "But we don't know of any other extractors."

"Rocter may want to help," Calin said.

"Rocter?"

Calin nodded at Sekanna. "He's the healer I use. For my headaches. He's very good."

"Why would this Rocter want to get involved with us?" Sekanna asked.

Calin shrugged. "I don't know if he would. He's the only healer I know."

"The first thing we need to do is find a place to live," Junto said. "We can worry about everything else later. There's an old cabin out this way that my grandmother said she grew up in. I don't even know if it's still there, but we can at least go see."

The others followed, trailing Junto through the dense woods.

Junto, Sekanna, and Calin stared at the Roaring River, standing on the bank about a dozen feet from the water's edge. The sound was deafening. The water swirled and exploded through the narrow paths between the massive rocks that dotted the interior of the quickly flowing river. The bridge that crossed the wide gap leading to the other side of the river was in a serious state of disrepair. More than half the planks were missing and the rope walls of the bridge were frayed to nearly the point of breaking in two. It rocked back and forth in the wind, looking as if it could potentially collapse at any moment.

Calin looked at the bridge with disbelieving eyes. "We're going to cross that?"

"The cabin is in the woods just beyond that little rise over there." Junto pointed to a small hill on the other side of the river, then lowered his hand as he paused. "At least there used to be a cabin over there. I don't know if it still stands."

"Who the hell built this bridge?" Calin asked. "And how?" He stared at the churning waters.

"The waters weren't always this — violent," Junto said. "The warmer summers over the last few years have made the mountain snows melt faster."

Just then, a massive sea snake rose up out of

the river. Its tiny forelegs pressed against a large rock, keeping the force of the current from propelling it further downstream. Its long black body glistened in the afternoon sunlight, its sleek scales shimmering hotly. It stared over at them with hungry eyes. It opened its wide mouth, revealing several layered rows of very sharp teeth.

Calin took several very quick steps back away from the shoreline. Junto and Sekanna joined him, and then they all took several more steps away from the creature, moving in unison.

The sea snake hissed at them, then disappeared back under the water.

Calin turned away from the river, but Sekanna grabbed his arm, stopping him. Calin looked at her with disbelief. He looked at the river, then back to Sekanna. "What? We're still going to cross it?" He pointed at the area the sea snake had just occupied. "After you saw that?"

"We have nowhere else to go." Sekanna released her grip on Calin's arm.

"Umm, yes, we do. How about the complete opposite direction for starters?" Calin pointed in the direction they had come.

"It's already gone," Junto said. "It's moved downstream."

"And you know this how?" Calin asked.

Junto didn't answer.

"And there aren't any more of those in the river?" Calin asked. "That was the only one?"

"Let's go," Sekanna said. "I'm tired. I need a nap." She moved towards the decrepit rope bridge.

"You need a nap?" Calin frowned. "We're

going to cross this damn roaring river because you need a nap?"

Sekanna smiled demurely at him. "I was going to let you snuggle with me, but your tone of voice is destroying your chances."

Calin pointed to the ground. "Nap right here." Then he sat down and crossed his legs. "Here, put your head right here," he said, motioning to his lap. "I'll rub your hair and you can take a nap."

Sekanna ignored him and stepped onto the bridge. Her sword was secured in its scabbard and her shield was secured in place over her back. She moved out a few steps above the madly churning water below. The bridge swayed ever so slightly as she took another few steps forward, but it held. She grabbed onto the fraying rope railing and continued forward, testing each plank with her foot before putting all her weight on it.

Junto followed her.

Calin watched them. He glanced around the area, then cursed silently before rising up off the ground and following behind Junto.

They moved slowly across the bridge, stepping gingerly with very cautious steps. The water splashed against the rocks below, sending up sprays of white foam and cold river water over the bridge planks; an occasional upthrown burst of water even reached far above their heads. They were all thoroughly drenched and shivering with cold by the time they reached the halfway point across the bridge.

Calin looked down into the river and immediately wished he hadn't. A long sleek black sea snake swam directly below the bridge. But this one seemed to have no interest in them and just kept on swimming past.

Calin looked behind them, in the direction from which they had come, and his body froze.

Heyeger and a dozen men were standing at the edge of the bridge. One of the men had a weird blackened texture to his skin. "We have company!" Calin shouted to be heard above the din of the roaring river.

Junto turned at Calin's cry. His eyes filled with disbelief. It was Elcor. The man was still alive! Even from this distance, he knew it was him. An arrow whistled past Junto's head, missing him by a few feet. "Sekanna!" he shouted.

Sekanna turned back to see the men on the shore behind them. She immediately knew what she had to do. She was the only one with a shield strapped to her back. She moved back towards Junto and Calin, moving carefully but quickly to the rear of their little group. She turned her back to the men on the far shore, the small shield on her back at least offering them some protection from the arrows being fired at them. The wild winds above the river sent most of the arrows widely astray, but she knew the archers would soon figure out a trajectory to bring their arrows closer to their marks.

"Let's go," she yelled up to Junto.

He turned back and began moving along the bridge, testing each plank but not as firmly as he would have liked to. He stepped on a cracked plank and the board splintered in two, plunging into the river below. Junto nearly followed the broken plank, but he grabbed the rope railing and held on. He quickly re-found his balance and moved forward.

What he didn't see was the black sea snake wriggling and writhing in the waters below.

But Calin saw it. He saw the long black sea snake just moments before it rose up out of the water right at his side. The black snake struggled to hold its position in the thrashing water, bracing its tiny forelegs on some large rocks. Its upper body weaved ever so slightly back and forth as its dark eyes stared intently at Calin.

And then it struck, darting towards Calin, its head moving with the velocity of an arrow fired from a bow. Its mouth widened and clamped down around Calin's waist. Calin shouted and pounded his fists against the sea snake's head as it clamped down around his waist. Blood seeped out of the sea snake's mouth as a few of its sharp teeth punctured Calin's flesh.

Sekanna reacted quickly, slashing at the sea snake's body with her sword, cutting through its scales, drawing blood from the creature. She slashed again, cutting deep.

The sea snake opened its mouth to hiss at her and Calin dropped out of its jaws, plunging into the madly churning waters of the river below the bridge. Calin was quickly engulfed by the roiling white water, he just disappeared into the chaos of the tumbling river.

"Calin!" Sekanna cried.

The sea snake turned from Sekanna and plunged back down into the river, giving chase to

Calin.

Junto watched Calin flounder in the water as he suddenly popped back up into view. The man batted and slapped at the water with his hands as he struggled to stay afloat, fighting to keep his head above the rolling waves. He watched Calin disappear around a bend in the river. The hulking body of the sea snake followed from beneath the waves. Junto looked away, his gaze moving back to the bridge and their pursuers.

Five of Heyeger's soldiers were already on the bridge, starting to cross. The archers remained on the far side of the shore, continuing to send deadly arrows in their direction.

An arrow zipped past Junto's head. He saw that two arrows were already sunk into Sekanna's shield. She was gripping the shield in her hand now, holding it in front of her; she raised it higher to block another arrow from striking her in the head.

An arrow sped through the air for Junto. He had no time to react. The arrow sped through his legs just below his crotch. He could feel the fabric of his breeches ripping. He even thought he heard it ripping, but that was nearly impossible above the thunderous sound of the madly thrashing river water below. He reached his hand down to his crotch, then raised it up. No blood. He breathed a quick sigh of relief.

Sekanna continued across the bridge, reaching him. She motioned urgently for him to keep going. "Go, go!" He turned and continued across the bridge. Sekanna kept her back tight against him, facing the other way, keeping her gaze glued on the approaching men, using the shield to block the arrows that kept coming at them.

Junto moved forward as quickly as he could, testing the planks with his weight before stepping on them. Sekanna kept glancing down at the planks as she moved behind him, watching where he stepped before following him.

The lead man in pursuit behind them was in too much of a hurry. He stepped on a weak plank and it cracked under his weight. He plunged into the churning water below and was swept away. The four men behind him slowed their pace.

Junto finally reached the other end of the rope bridge and stepped onto firm ground. Sekanna quickly joined him.

"I never want to do that again," Sekanna said.

Junto nodded. "We need to go after Calin. The river is narrower downstream. He might be able to make it to shore." He started to head towards the edge of the woods a few yards away, towards a path that ran near the river's edge, but Sekanna grabbed his arm. "No," she said. "The bridge."

Junto looked at her, then looked at the bridge. The four men were about three quarters of the way across. "They probably have death gems on them."

Sekanna said nothing to that. She moved to the left side of the rope bridge and started to hack at the rope railing.

The four men on the bridge started to move faster.

Sekanna continued to chop and hack at the rope bridge. "If they have death gems on them, then we won't be killing them, will we?" She motioned to the other side of the bridge with a toss of her head.

Another pursuer hit a bad plank and the wood cracked under his weight, but he immediately jumped off the cracking plank onto a more sturdy slat.

Junto moved to the other side of the bridge and started to pound at the rope with a sharp rock he picked up from the ground. More souls would be lost, but what choice did they have? His anger grew and his swing became more violent, more wild as he hacked angrily at the rope bridge with the rock. He would never be able to stop them all. What was the damn point? He should just give up. He should just disappear into the woods and let the world go to Hell's Wood. No one would miss him. No one would care. He hacked and pounded and cut and chopped.

The men on the bridge moved ever closer. One man managed to outpace the rest. He got very close to the edge of the bridge. He paused as he came within a few yards of Sekanna. He looked at her. She looked at him. And then she brought her sword down with a mighty swing, severing the last strand. The rope bridge twisted violently as the left end of its support was now cut away. The man near her dropped into the river below, cracking his head on a large rock, and then he was gone, swept away by the current.

Two of the pursuers were unceremoniously dumped into the river water and immediately vanished into the roiling whiteness.

The last man lost his sword as he clung desperately to the rope support. The bridge swayed sharply back and forth and his body twisted and dangled. A sea snake erupted out of the river and engulfed him whole.

Junto finished with his end of the rope bridge and the severed bridge dropped to the water below. He looked across to the far side of the river to see Heyeger and Elcor watching them. "Go upstream," he told Sekanna.

"Why? We have to go after Calin."

"They're watching us. Just go upstream, then we'll double back once we're in the woods."

Sekanna nodded. She quickly turned upstream and headed towards the woods a few yards away. Junto followed. After a few paces, he paused and turned to look back at Heyeger and Elcor on the other side of the river.

After a moment, Heyeger and Elcor abruptly turned and headed away.

CHAPTER TWENTY-EIGHT

"Anything?" Junto asked.

Sekanna shook her head. They were racing along the riverbank, moving quickly downstream, following the path of the water. The water was much calmer now; it still moved quickly, but there were no whitecaps and very few large rocks. "Oh, shit," Sekanna said.

"What?"

"Look." Sekanna pointed to the middle of the river just ahead of them.

Junto followed her gaze and saw two of their pursuers who had fallen off the bridge, both men resting on a large flat rock in the middle of the river. One man still had a sword. He sat upright, tending to the prone man lying on the rock next to him. The man looked up and locked gazes with Junto. Then the man looked back down at his fellow soldier and shook his shoulder.

"Oh, shit," Junto said, echoing her sentiment.

"Hell's Wood, there's Calin," Sekanna said. She raced downstream towards a body lying half in, half out of the river.

Junto followed closely on her heels. They reached Calin and saw that he was still alive, his chest rising and falling with his coarse breathing. His body was battered and bruised and laced with cuts from the river rocks he must have collided with, but he was still alive. Junto quickly surmised that the sea snake's teeth must not have penetrated him too deeply, or they had missed puncturing his body, because there wasn't much blood near his torso, nor did there seem to be any gaping wounds.

Junto looked over to the rock in the middle of the river and momentarily froze. Both men were gone. He quickly scanned the river, but didn't see them. He turned back to help Sekanna pull Calin out of the river. They moved him well away from the shore line, easing him down to a soft patch of grass near the edge of the woods. "Stay alert," Junto told Sekanna. "Those men are around somewhere."

Sekanna looked up towards the river to see that the rock was vacant, the men gone. She nodded to Junto.

Calin opened his eyes and looked up at Sekanna. He sighed and smiled weakly. "Am I in the Everlasting with you? Because if I am, I'm going to fuck you for days."

"Shut up, you idiot," Sekanna said.

Calin groaned. "I'm still alive."

Sekanna eased him to a sitting position, Calin grunting and groaning the whole time she moved him. "Can you walk?"

"I think so." Calin grimaced. "My side hurts like hell, though."

Sekanna raised his tunic to see a massive bruise and severely abraded skin running along his entire right side, but did not see any severe puncture wounds.

"How's it look?" Calin asked.

Sekanna let his wet tunic drop. "You're not going to die today."

"Where are those men who were following us? And Heyeger? How did you get away?"

"We chopped the bridge down."

Just then, the two pursuers rose up out of the river, right near the shoreline, water dripping off their bodies as they surged towards Junto and the others. One of the men immediately pulled out a throwing dagger from his belt and hurled it at them. Junto reacted instinctively, stepping protectively in front of Sekanna and Calin, but the blade whipped past him. The blade sunk into Calin's left breast and Calin exclaimed with a loud piercing shout.

Junto lunged at the man who had thrown the dagger, striking his shoulder fiercely with his battering stick, stopping the man from hurling a second dagger. The man growled and grabbed at his wounded shoulder. Junto could see the edge of a death gem beneath his tunic. The man most likely had more than one death gem implanted on his body. Junto struck again, delivering a solid blow to the side of the man's head. The man collapsed to the sandy ground near the shoreline, unconscious.

Suddenly, a piercing cry filled with pain exploded into the air near Junto. He whirled to see the second man with his sword raised just over his head, about to deliver what might very well have been a death strike. But the attack never reached its conclusion because the man had a different sword thrust into his side. Sekanna's sword. Sekanna yanked her sword out of the man's side, twisting the blade slightly as she withdrew its bloodied steel length from the man's abdomen. The man lowered his sword, gurgling as blood spilled forth from his lips. The man dropped to his knees, still clutching his sword. His eyelids closed but then seemed to flutter.

Junto could see a bright point of light flare up beneath the man's tunic. "He's got a death gem," Junto said in warning to Sekanna. Junto reached out and snatched at the man's tunic, sharply yanking on it, ripping the fabric down away from his shoulder. Four death gems glistened on the man's upper chest, one of them glowing hotter than the others until the shimmering faded to a deep black.

The man opened his eyes and smiled at Junto through his bloodied teeth.

Junto saw the scintillating flash of the blade, but he was too late to do anything about it. "No!" he cried out, his futile protest doing nothing to stop the sharp edge of the sword slicing cleanly through the man's head because his cry came too late.

The man's severed head dropped to the sand and blood erupted out of the huge gaping maw where his neck had once been connected to his body. The man's body trembled and shook and keeled over to the ground, plopping into the soft sand. Another death gem on the man's chest flared hotly, then turned black.

Junto looked up to see Sekanna gripping her sword tightly, her face flushed, her eyes a little bit too wide. He had no words. She had just killed the man. He would be forever attached to her now in the Everlasting. And she had done it to save his own miserable life. Junto stared down at the head she had just severed, then looked away to the man's headless torso. He pushed the man's tunic down further with the edge of his battering stick, revealing three more death gems embedded in the man's chest. One of them pulsed and glowed, then went black.

The man's hands suddenly moved, as if reaching for his severed head. Junto started, jumping back.

Sekanna kicked the man's severed head away from his body, her boot connecting solidly with its nose. She grabbed the severed head by the hair and tossed it out into the river, hurtling it out as far into the current as she could. The head bobbed a few times as it floated away downstream. She stared out into the river, her breathing a little raspy, a little wild.

The man's hands continued to grasp futilely at the empty air and empty ground. Another death gem turned black and the hands fell to the ground. Another death gem started to glow and the hands moved again, clawing and grasping at nothing.

Junto watched the severed head bob up and down in the river, then turned to see that Sekanna had returned to the decapitated body. She hacked at the moving hands, chopping angrily down at the dead man's fingers, chopping several of them off his right hand. Junto put a hand to her arm, stopping her.

"A little help here," a voice said from behind them.

They both turned in unison to see Calin sitting on the ground, the throwing dagger still lodged in his chest. Blood seeped down from the wound.

They sat on stones near the wood's edge. Calin sat near them, his tunic off, drying on a nearby rock in the hot sun. A make-shift bandage of cloth covered his left breast.

The headless corpse of the man lay on the ground a few dozen yards away, the man now finally truly dead. All of the death gems on his body had now turned black. The souls had nowhere to go and were now extinguished forever, used up uselessly by a body that had no use for their life-force energy. The man who Junto had knocked out was still unconscious. For a moment, Junto feared that he had killed the man but he was still breathing. They had tied him up with his tunic, hooking it around his arm and his legs, bundling him up tight for when he did wake back up.

"I'll be back," Sekanna said, rising up off the rock she had been sitting on.

Junto squinted at her. "Are you okay?" he asked quietly.

"Nature calls," she said.

He nodded. Sekanna moved off towards an outcropping of tall rocks near the river downstream.

"So where is this cabin?" Calin asked.

Junto watched Sekanna for a moment, then turned to Calin. "Back upstream," Junto said. "You okay to travel?"

"Well, I certainly don't want to just keep sitting here."

Junto nodded. "Sekanna will be back in a minute. Let's put some weight on those legs and see how you hold up." He helped Calin get to his feet.

And then they both froze as a low growling sound caused them to turn towards the woods.

It was a wulv. It was a dog-like beast, but larger than any dogs that roamed the streets of Calkut. It had six legs, a long snout, and a body about five feet long, covered in thick fur. The fur had a mottled look to it, with brown and green strands of hair interwoven along its entire length, forming a camouflage pattern to its fur that helped it lurk through the woods unseen.

"Are you kidding me?" Calin said, exhausted disbelief in his questioning words.

Junto looked at the bloodied bandage on Calin's chest, then to the headless body on the ground nearby. "It must have smelled all the blood."

"Oh, great. And I'm covered with wulv sauce," Calin said. "I probably look like a fatted calf to it."

Junto said nothing. Calin was right. "Just don't make any sudden moves."

"I will refrain from dancing, thank you."

The wulv inched closer, sniffing and snorting at the air.

"He look hungry to you?" Calin asked. "Maybe he's just curious about us."

Junto remained quiet. He slowly moved his hand to the hilt of his battering stick, wishing oh so much that he had decided to carry a steel sword like Sekanna instead of a length of wood.

"Do they even like to eat humans?" Calin asked.

Just then, a hand came down on Calin's shoulder and he started sharply, letting out a frightened cry.

"Can't I leave you two alone for a second?" Sekanna asked as she re-joined the two men.

A wet stream stained the front of Calin's almost-dry pants.

The disturbance unsettled the wulv and the beast charged, snorting madly as he raced towards them.

"Stay still!" Junto shouted, but Calin paid him no heed. Calin turned away from the fast-approaching wulv, and ran.

The beast zeroed in on the fleeing Calin, striking him in the back with the brunt force of a battering ram. Calin's body went flying high into the air, landing in the river a few yards from the shoreline. The beast stopped at the water's edge, glared at the sputtering Calin, but it did not cross over the water's threshold. The wulv turned back to Junto and Sekanna, snorting and puffing. It charged at them.

Sekanna grabbed her sword and charged right back at the beast, raising her weapon high, screaming and yelling threateningly at the charging wulv as she did so.

"Sekanna!" Junto shouted.

The wulv stopped its charge and stared at the wild creature racing towards it. Then it turned and bounded away, moving downstream, then darted towards the woods to disappear into the dark depths of the trees.

Sekanna slowed her charge, then stopped, letting her sword dip towards the ground. She watched the wulv vanish into the woods. She turned back to see Junto just staring at her.

They pulled a freshly soaked Calin out of the river. Calin grunted and groaned, grabbing at his back as they helped him out of the water. "Did you break anything?" Sekanna asked.

Calin shook his head. "Just any measure of bravery I thought I might have had left." Calin glanced down and was relieved to see there was no embarrassing stain around his crotch. His breeches were entirely soaked, masking any of his yellow patch of shame. "Can we go find this cabin now? I think I need to sleep for a few days."

Sekanna laughed and patted his shoulder. "I've never seen anyone get so beat up by some many different things in one day."

Calin smiled weakly. "At least I'm still here, right?"

Sekanna nodded. "At least you are still here." She reached out and gave his shoulder a reassuring gentle squeeze.

"Hey," Junto's voice called out from a near distance.

Sekanna and Calin looked over to Junto. He was staring at something near the edge of the woods. "You need to come and see this."

CHAPTER TWENTY-NINE

They all stared down at the trampled body of a death beetle.

"The wulv must have stomped it to death," Junto said.

Calin stared down at the flattened creature. "What are we looking at?"

"It's a death beetle."

"I see that," Calin said. "So what's it doing out here?"

"Maybe someone dropped it," Sekanna said.

Junto shook his head. "I bet there's a nest nearby."

"A nest?" Calin asked.

Junto nodded. "And we need to find it."

"Is that before or after I sleep for days in this cabin were supposed to be going to?" Calin asked wearily.

"Before."

Calin groaned. "I knew you were going to say that."

Sekanna handed a khack leaf to Calin. It was a five-bladed green leaf laced with yellow veins; the top blade portion of the leaf was longer and thinner than the two wider blades on each side of the leaf. A thick yellow vein ran straight up the middle of the leaf, nearly reaching the top of the middle blade, and branching out into many thinner, shorter yellow veins that filled the four wider blades of the leaf. "Here, this will help with the pain for a little while. Chew it a lot before you swallow it. It works better that way."

Junto looked at the leaf, then at Sekanna, but she did not meet his gaze. Now was not the time to discuss her past abuse of the leaf.

Calin took the leaf and sniffed it. He put it into his mouth and immediately made a sour face. He pulled the leaf back out, scrunching up his face and wiping at his tongue.

"It tastes foul, but it works," Sekanna told him. "Just do what I tell you."

Calin looked at Sekanna for a moment, then put the leaf back into his mouth and slowly started to chew, making sour faces the entire time he ground the leaf between his teeth.

Junto pointed to a nearby spot of ground. "There," he said. He moved over to the patch of ground and crouched down over it, studying it. There were clear marks visible in the soft earth, leading back into the woods. They weren't the marks left by any wulv. These were smaller marks, trails left by a much, much smaller creature.

Sekanna looked back towards their bound prisoner. "What about him?"

Junto looked back at the man. He hadn't moved and appeared to still be unconscious. "We'll come back for him. Just leave him."

Sekanna looked away from the bound man. She

glanced down at the crushed death beetle. She quickly jerked her head back up, looking towards the corpse of the dead man, eying the headless man she had just killed. If she had a death beetle on her she could have taken his life-force; she could have prevented him from following her into the Everlasting. Several crab-like creatures were already picking at the corpse. A few scavenger birds were also already hovering about the corpse, some of them intent on plucking some flesh off the dead man's body, while other birds were more interested in trying to snatch up one of the crab-creatures in their pointed beaks. Sekanna's shoulders sagged. It was too late for him now anyway. His life-force was gone. His soul had journeyed into the Everlasting — and would now be waiting for her upon her own journey into the life beyond this one. She forced that thought out of her head; there was no time to dwell on that now. She would have plenty of time to worry about that every single day for the rest of her mortal life. She turned away from the dead man.

Calin was chewing noisily on the leaf now, a stupid grin widening his mouth as he stared with what could almost be called a leering grin at Sekanna. Sekanna sighed at him and grabbed at his elbow, tugging him along. "Come on."

Junto, Sekanna, and Calin followed the tiny trail, moving deeper into the woods. Calin moved a little more clumsily than normal, his steps unsure, his gait a little wobbly as the effects of the khack leaf began to take hold on him.

"You ever see a nest before?" Sekanna asked.

Junto shook his head.

They stared down at the creatures. There were about two dozen of the death beetles, all of them very much alive, all of them busy scurrying about, building their burrow, excavating dirt as they dug their hole deeper and deeper into the earth. They were about two inches long with a rounded head, each covered with a hardened exoskeleton of various different colors. They appeared to have six legs, but their tendrils weren't easily visible as they were mostly hidden beneath their shells.

"They just look like fat bugs," Calin said. He was finished chewing the leaf and had swallowed any bits and pieces that had been remaining in his mouth.

"I wish that's all they were," Junto said.

"Do they fly?" Calin asked.

Junto looked curiously at Calin. He didn't know the answer to that question, and hadn't really thought about it.

Calin shrugged at Junto's curious look. "If they're really beetles maybe they can fly. Some beetles can fly."

"I don't know," Junto finally said. "I've never seen one fly, but I've never seen them in the wild before either. Maybe some of them can fly."

"They really have the power to transfer a life-force from one person to another?" Calin asked. "To absorb someone's soul?"

"Yes. They really do," Junto said.

Calin shook his head. "That's unbelievable."

The motion of moving his head so quickly made him stumble slightly and Sekanna grabbed at his elbow, helping him stay upright.

"Yes, but it's still true," Sekanna said.

"Where did they come from?" Calin asked.

Junto gave a slight shrug. "I wish I knew."

"This is just one nest in one tiny little part of a tiny patch of woods," Calin said. "Do you realize how many nests might be just in these woods, let alone the rest of the world?"

"I try not to think about that," Junto said.

Calin stared at the scurrying death beetles. He looked somewhat transfixed, his eyes glazing over. He cocked his head at the beetles, staring curiously at them, as if straining to hear something he wasn't quite able to hear. "You can't stop them all."

Junto gritted his teeth. "And so I should just quit? I should let every soul ever stolen just perish forever? I should just walk away and not give a damn? I should let the soul stealers have free reign over the world?"

"There are too many of them," Calin said.

Junto frowned. "I should just let the death beetles breed and spread? Hell's Wood, maybe we should just breed them ourselves," he spat out contemptuously. "We can be death beetle farmers. We'd probably make some damn good coin, too."

Calin was quiet.

"I'm not forcing you to stay," Junto said.

Calin stayed quiet. "I have nowhere else to go."

"And I have no choice but to keep trying to stop them."

Calin stared at the death beetles, watching them

work on their burrow. "We need more help."

"Yes, we do," Junto said.

"We *had* more help," Sekanna said.

Junto said nothing to that. "Let's get started." Junto walked calmly over to the nearest death beetle and brought his boot down on the creature. It crunched loudly as guts and blood seeped out from beneath his boot.

All of the other death beetles stopped what they were doing. All of them. They all turned to face the intruders in their midst as if noticing them for the first time. They made chattering, chittering noises.

"They — they are talking to me," Calin said. He put his hand to his head, squeezing at his forehead.

"What?" Sekanna looked curiously at Calin.

"They are begging for mercy."

"What?" Junto looked at the death beetles, then at Calin.

"They are begging for mercy," Calin repeated. He stared intently at the beetles.

"Are you mad?" Junto asked. He looked to Sekanna. "Is he loopy from chewing on the khack leaf."

Sekanna shook her head. "No, he's not. It is the leaf, but it's not making him crazy. I think. It's brought him to another place." She tapped her head.

Junto frowned. "What place?"

Sekanna shook her head slightly. "It's different for everyone." She looked at Calin. "It's brought him to the animal world. Or maybe just the bug world. I don't know."

Junto scowled at Sekanna. "What the Hell's

Wood are you talking about?"

Sekanna looked at Junto. "Have you never chewed the leaf?"

"No."

"Then you'll never be able to understand no matter how many times I try to explain it to you."

"Try."

Sekanna looked at him. "It brings you to other places. Inside your head. The world — changes. But only in here." She tapped her head again.

"And now Calin can talk to death beetles?"

She shook her head. "No, I don't think so. He can't talk to them. He can just hear them."

The creatures continued their chittering.

"Why should I be surprised?" Junto muttered. "The whole world is fucking mad." He looked at Calin. "Now what are they saying?" Junto asked.

"The same thing. They're begging for their lives." Calin stared intently at the death beetles. A tear streamed down his cheek, then another, and another. Soon, his face was soaked with streams of sadness and sorrow.

"If they want to live, tell them to stop stealing souls," Junto said.

Sekanna shook her head. "I told you. He can't talk to them. He can only hear them."

Junto tightened his jaw. What the hell was he doing? Listening to the pleas of bugs? *That* was madness. He stomped on another death beetle, then another and another and another, his rage growing with each forceful stomp of his boot.

Their chattering grew louder and the death beetles started to scatter, racing towards a deep narrow hole situated beneath a bush nearby.

Calin threw his hands to his head, trying to block his ears. "No!" He dropped to his knees, keeping his hands pressed tightly over his ears. "No!"

Junto moved over to the hole, smashing two more death beetles as they attempted to escape into the hole. Junto turned to Sekanna, thrusting out his hand towards her. "Fire up a torch," he ordered.

"I don't have a torch," she said.

"Make one!"

Sekanna opened her mouth to retort to his blustery demand, but then pressed her lips together. She scanned the area, breaking off a branch from a nearby tree. She glanced at her clothes, fingering her tunic. Then, she looked over to Calin. He was still kneeling on the ground, whimpering softly. She moved over to him, grabbed his ripped tunic and tore off a chunk of fabric. But she quickly saw that the cloth was still wet from his recent encounter with the river and tossed the fabric aside. She ripped at the edge of her tunic and managed to tear off a piece of fabric. She wrapped it tightly around the branch, then set it down on an angle on a rock so the cloth-wrapped end was angling upwards. She pulled two flints out of her pocket and started to strike them together, immediately making sparks. Within moments, she had a freshly burning torch. She moved over to Junto and handed it to him. He took it and immediately thrust it into the hole.

Chittering and clicking sounds erupted from the hole, the noises loud and grating.

Calin lifted his head skyward and wailed.

Junto moved the torch around, changing the angle, thrusting it deeper into the hole, turning it this way and that, aggressively trying to cover as much area as he could with the hot flames.

A movement on the ground caught Sekanna's gaze. She glanced down to see a death beetle moving away from the flames. She looked over to Junto, but he didn't see it. He was too intent on shoving the torch into the hole. She looked back down at the creature, then reached down for it. The death beetle must have felt the presence of her approaching hand because it curled up into its dormant position, rolling itself up into a ball, its hard shell completely encompassing it. She picked up the creature, glancing at Junto while she did so. He was still focused on his attack of the death beetle nest. She rose up and stared at the dormant creature in her palm. Then, she curled her fingers closed over it and stuck it into her pocket.

She scanned the surrounding area, looking for more.

CHAPTER THIRTY

Elcor stared down at the dead bodies. The death beetles were doing their work, absorbing the souls of those he had just killed. The death gem on the young infant boy glowed the brightest. Elcor stared at it. He had never used a death gem on someone so young before. Did their souls really have more energy because they were so young? Because their souls were still fresh? He had no idea, but from what he was seeing that certainly seemed to be the case.

They had come across the small manor home in their search for another bridge to cross the river and continue their pursuit of the accursed extractors. The occupants of the home had quickly become unfortunate victims of Elcor's need for replenishment.

The death gem on the infant boy pulsed once, then grew faint. The life-force had been absorbed. He bent down and put his fingers around the hard shell of the creature, then pulled. The tendrils released their grip, sliding out of the boy's neck as Elcor pulled it away from his tiny body. The tendrils wiggled and danced beneath the death beetle's body.

Elcor glanced down at his own body. The flesh covering Elcor's body was now shriveled and pink, looking like the combined skin of a burn victim and a newborn. Even he would be likely to admit that he was quite unpleasant to look at. There was an open spot of pink flesh near three blackened gems on his right side, near his belly button. He lowered the creature towards his skin. The tendrils touched his flesh, then slid into his body.

He closed his eyes, enjoying the rush of warmth that filled him as the tendrils moved deeper into his body. Their grip took hold and he pressed the death gem flat against his skin and released his hold. The death gem remained in place, lodged firmly against his flesh. The creature had taken root inside him and would so remain. A dose of life-force was trapped within the gem now, waiting to be released if, or when, he needed it. The intoxicating rush of delight crashed through his body in wave after wave as the tendrils spread deep and wide throughout his entire body. He could only imagine what the inside of his body looked like now, interwoven with dozens, if not hundreds of tendrils.

He looked over to the woman lying in the corner. She seemed like an elegant lady, dressed in fine clothes. She had a pretty face; her long black hair ended in soft curls that ran down the full length of her back. She was bent over a couch, with her buttocks up in the air. He thought about hiking up her black dress and fucking her, but decided against it. Putting his dick into her corpse held no appeal for him, at least not for the immediate moment.

The death gem on the back of her neck pulsed, then faded. She was ready. He removed the creature from her, then placed it on his left forearm, setting the death beetle down between two blackened death gems. He was running out of clear areas on his body to put them. His left arm was nearly fully covered with death gems now, but unfortunately all of them were black but for the fresh gem he had just placed there.

He had tried to remove one of the blackened death gems before, but the tendrils were so woven into his body, so intertwined with every organ, that he nearly killed himself doing it. That blackened gem still remained in his left arm, still dangling somewhat loosely. He had cut one of the tendrils in his attempt to remove it, but the pain had been so excruciating the act of cutting it had actually knocked him unconscious. He had never tried to cut another tendril again, nor did he even consider doing so. It was a pain like he had never experienced before in his life. It was a pain greater than being stabbed to death. It was a pain greater than being burned alive. No, the blackened gems would stay where they were.

He thought of the man they were pursuing, the man who called himself Junto. They had supposedly perfected a technique to safely extract death gems from a body. Perhaps before he killed them and stole their souls, he would get them to tell him how it was done.

He still felt flush from the two new death gems working their way through his body. He felt good. He felt alive. He now had five functional death gems on his body. He felt a sense of relief. Some of the tension left his body. Not having enough death gems on his body made him feel very anxious. He didn't like feeling anxious. Feeling anxious made him angry.

A whimpering sound made him look up. The girl was still huddled in the corner, clutching at her doll. She wasn't anything more than something he needed to use. She was just replenishment for his life-force. Food for the soul. He pulled out a dormant creature from his pocket. The death beetle was still curled up tightly in its shell, forming a small hard ball in his hand. He looked up at the whimpering girl and moved towards her.

Elcor stepped outside of the manor home to see Heyeger and his men waiting patiently.

"Feeling better?" Heyeger asked.

"Much," Elcor replied.

"Have you made your decision?" Heyeger asked.

"I don't need your men," Elcor said. "I can handle them myself."

"Just as you handled them yourself before they burned through two dozen of your souls?"

Elcor glowered at him.

Heyeger's face remained calm. "I offer you a position with me, and now you refuse?"

"I serve no one," Elcor said.

"I am not asking you to serve. I am asking you to work for me. I will pay you handsomely."

"I don't work for anyone but myself."

Heyeger nodded. "I thought as much. But I did save your life after all."

"And for that I owe you a debt. I will repay it by eating their cursed souls," Elcor said, his tone lethal, his eyes narrowed and dark.

"And what if that is not what I want? What if I would ask something else of you?"

Elcor's face was firm with resolve. "This is something I must do first. Those extractors must die."

Heyeger studied him. "Yes, you do seem a man of single purpose."

"I am who I am."

CHAPTER THIRTY-ONE

"Are you finished?" Sekanna asked.

Junto looked up at her. Sweat dripped into his eyes and he wiped it away with an angry swipe of the back of his hand. He was on his hands and knees now, his face muddied with dirt, his hands and arms caked with mud. He was over the nest entrance, clawing and scratching at the hole, making it bigger, digging deeper down into it. He had been at it for hours, desperately trying to reach the bottom of the nest and slaughter any death beetles he could find. But the nest just kept going. He realized with a growing dread that the burrow was probably connected to a series of deep tunnels. For all he knew, the tunnels were spread out throughout the entire woods. He would never be able to destroy them all. He would have to uproot every tree and dig up the ground for miles all around.

He sat back on his haunches and let out an anguished cry of frustration. He would never be able to stop them all. This was just one nest in one small part of a secluded section of woods, just as Calin had so obviously pointed out. How many nests were in this area alone? How many in the entire woods? How many all over the world? There had to be a better way to stop them. But he had no idea how.

Sekanna moved over to him and squatted down next to him, putting her arm around his shoulder. "It's all right, Junto. You're tired. We're all tired. Let's find that cabin and get some sleep."

Junto nodded.

"But first we need to figure out what to do with our prisoner," Sekanna said. "Do we take him with us?"

"Just let him go," Junto said, his exhaustion obvious in his voice.

"I am not just letting him go so he can keep chasing us," Sekanna said.

Junto stared at his filthy, dirt-streaked hands. He was tired. So tired. "Do what you want with him."

"Yeah, right. I already have one soul attached to me for all eternity. Why not make it another, right? I should just kill him and lop off his head." Sekanna feigned a brightened expression. "Hey, I could be the killer you've always wished our team had. I could be the one who does all the dirty work. At least that way you can keep your precious soul clean and unencumbered."

Junto looked up at her, her comment catching him by surprise, the bitterness in her words coming across very strongly. "I don't want you to kill him, Sekanna. I don't want you to kill anybody. I'm sorry you... had to do what you did. I know you did it to save me." He reached out for her, but then stopped short of touching her. "I'm sorry you had to do that."

Sekanna looked down at his reaching hand. She was quiet for a moment. "I have another idea," she said. She looked at Junto. "But you are *really* not going to like it."

Junto waited for her to continue.

Sekanna reached into her pocket, then hesitated. "Ah, the hell with it. You said you'd never trust me again anyway, so what does it matter?" She pulled out a death beetle from her pocket, holding up the dormant creature in her open palm.

Junto stared at the death beetle in Sekanna's hand, the sunlight glinting off its hardened shell.

"We take his soul," Sekanna said. "Then he can't follow any of us into the Everlasting."

Calin stared at Sekanna. "You want to kill him and take his soul? Isn't that—"

Sekanna cut his words off with an impatient chopping motion of her other hand. "Go check on him," Sekanna said to Calin.

Calin hesitated.

"Go," Sekanna ordered.

Calin still lingered, but only for a brief moment, then headed off back towards the river.

She looked at Junto, waiting for his reaction. "Well?" she prompted. "Yours is black. You could use another one."

Junto shook his head. He rose up to his feet, wiping his hands on his breeches. "We can't do this, Sekanna. We can't keep going down this road. This is the exact thing we are fighting against. The exact thing." He started to move back towards the river.

Sekanna followed him, walking alongside him.

"You have to look at the bigger picture, Junto. We're trying to do good. We're trying to save people."

"By murdering them and stealing their souls?"

"Okay, innocent people, then. If you want to make that distinction. We're trying to save innocent people. The people hunting us, the people trying to kill us, the people trying to kill you and me, are not innocent, Junto. They've made their choice. And they've chosen to be our enemies. We cannot be weak towards our enemies. We can't."

"It doesn't matter," Calin said as they neared his side. He had overheard the last part of their conversation as they approached him. He was standing on the edge of the woods, staring out towards the river. "He's gone."

Junto and Sekanna quickly move to Calin's side and saw that Calin was right. The man was gone, their makeshift bindings laying in a pile on the sand.

CHAPTER THIRTY-TWO

"Don't move!" Junto cautioned Calin, his voice sharp and curt. "Calin, stop!"

Calin froze, afraid to even turn his head to look at Junto who was on the overgrown trail behind him. "Why? What's going on?"

They had been walking briskly, but calmly and quietly, through the woods for about an hour on their way to the cabin before Junto's urgent warning rang out.

"You see it?" Junto asked.

"See what? What's going on?" Calin's eyes were wide, alarmed.

"Shut up, Calin," Junto snapped at him. "Sekanna, do you see it?"

"Yes," Sekanna said.

"See what?" Calin jerked his head about, darting it this way and that, but kept the rest of his body rigid.

"You stepped on a trap," Sekanna said.

"I did?"

"Yes. Now don't fucking move," she said.

"Not moving," Calin confirmed.

Junto circled around Calin slowly, studying the ground around him. Then he looked up towards some nearby brush growth. He cautiously moved towards the bushes, taking one careful step after the next. He reached the bushes and found the crossbow that had been hidden within them. It should have fired when Calin stepped on the string, but it hadn't. And then Junto saw why. The string had been chewed through, probably by some forest animal, its action disarming the trap. "It's okay," Junto said from the bushes. "You can move now."

Calin breathed a sigh of relief, but didn't move.

"It's a crossbow," Junto said. "Some animal must have chewed through the string." He looked up at Calin as he came back out through the bushes. "Lucky for you or that bolt would probably be stuck in your belly right about now."

"We must be getting close to the cabin," Sekanna said.

Junto joined them, nodding. "And there's a pretty good chance someone else is living there now. I don't know how long this trap's been here. It could be years old." Junto studied the trail, the thick trees all around them, then looked at the bush where the crossbow lay hidden. It wasn't a very well-conceived trap. Perhaps it had been laid in haste, or was just an afterthought.

"Maybe we should get off the trail," Sekanna said. "Just move alongside it."

"I'm all for that," Calin said. He moved off the trail, stepping into the low growth of brush that flanked the old trail.

"Wait!" Junto shouted at Calin.

But it was too late. The next step Calin took placed his foot square in the middle of a metal trap.

The trap clamped shut around his boot, the pointed metal teeth of the trap penetrating the tough leather, sinking into the flesh of his foot. Calin howled in shock and pain. He clutched at his foot, falling to the ground to land with a thud on his buttocks. "Hell's fucking Wood! Get it off me. Get it off me!"

Junto grabbed his arm and tugged him onto the trail, pulling him into an area clear of any brush. Sekanna dropped to her knees at Calin's feet, immediately grabbing at the trap, struggling to separate its metal jaws. Calin groaned and winced and threw his head back, gritting his teeth. Junto quickly moved down next to Sekanna and helped her pry the jaws open. Calin pulled his foot free and they let go of the jaws. The trap clamped violently shut again with a loud metallic clang.

Calin quickly yanked his boot off to get a look at his foot. Two puncture marks were visible in his flesh and blood oozed out of both of them.

"How is it?" Junto asked.

Sekanna grabbed Calin's foot and looked at it. "They don't look too deep." She looked at Calin. "He'll live." She looked back to Junto. "For now."

Junto nodded. "Bandage him up and let's keep moving. Give him more khack leaf if you have to."

Calin frowned at Sekanna. "What do you mean *for now?*"

The cabin was occupied, as Junto had suspected it would be. They had made it through the woods without further incident, avoiding two other traps they had seen on their way along the trail, and reached the cabin to find it inhabited.

The old man was tending to a garden that was situated just outside the rear of the cabin when they came upon him. He was a very old man, near the end of his days. His hair was cut short, his face cleanly shaved. He kept himself looking fit and clean, but his wrinkled leathery skin clearly gave his age away, the color of his skin deeply tanned, the flesh weathered by time. And there was a deepness to his brown eyes that could only come from a lifetime of seeing many things.

The garden appeared to be well-tended, the plants laid out in neat rows; the area surrounding the carrots, tomatoes, and other vegetables he was growing was free of any weeds. The garden was surrounded by rows of stakes with their sharp edges slanted and pointing outwards, obviously set up to keep any wild animals out. He looked up from inspecting one of his plants and his gaze retained that same intent focus as he inspected them. "You are all filthy and you smell," the old man said.

"Umm... hello," Sekanna said in reply.

Manole frowned at them. "You will bring the wulvs down on me."

Sekanna noticed the old man had a small khack leaf plant growing in a rear corner of the garden. Several of the leaves had clearly been plucked. And only just recently; the tips of the stems where the leaves had been taken from were still moist.

"Do you live here, sir?" Junto said. It had been many years since he had last been to the cabin, but it had been unoccupied then.

"Sir? Nobody ever called ol' Manole *sir* in his life. Don't want anybody starting now." The man named Manole squinted at him. "You come to fight my claim?"

"No, no," Junto said quickly, holding up his hands.

"We just need to rest," Sekanna said.

Manole eyed them warily. "First, I need to check you. And then you need to clean yourselves up." He motioned to them with a wave of his fingers. "Come. This way."

"Maybe we should just keep moving," Calin said softly to Sekanna so that only she could hear him. "Find somewhere else to rest."

She shook her head. "I'm too tired. I need—"

"A nap. I know," Calin said.

"And you need to rest that foot. How is it?"

"It's sore. But not too bad. I think my boot took the worst of it." He looked up at her and smiled a soft smile. "I'll live."

They stood near a small waterfall that cascaded down over a small cliff, the stream flowing down from the mountains in the near distance. The woods were sparse around the small pond at the base of the waterfall, but then the trees resumed their thickness as the stream pursued its course towards the river they had crossed miles away.

"Just do as he says and take off your clothes," Junto said.

"Why is he so insistent?" Calin asked.

"I'm pretty sure I know why," Sekanna replied.

Calin looked at Sekanna. "Because he's a freak about being clean and neat?"

Sekanna shook her head. She motioned towards Junto who had his shirt off and was now removing his breeches.

Manole stared at Junto's back. A dark concern and anger filled his eyes. He drew a dagger from its scabbard at his waist and pointed it at Junto. "It's blackened. You used it."

Junto looked curiously at the old man, now standing naked before him, not at all apprehensive of the dagger being pointed at him. "You know of the death gems?"

Sekanna, now topless, moved quickly over to Junto's side. "It wasn't his fault. I put the death gem on him. He didn't want it."

Manole frowned deeply at Sekanna, gravely disturbed by her words. His gaze went down to her bare breasts, but he only lingered there for a brief moment before looking back to Junto. "Is this true?"

Sekanna stepped in front of Junto. "Yes, it's true. I did it."

Manole frowned an even deeper frown at Sekanna. His dagger was still raised, still threatening. "Why would you do such a thing?"

"To keep him alive," Sekanna answered. "We are fighting against the soul stealers. He is the only one who can lead us. He is the only one who can stop them."

Manole pointed his dagger toward Junto. "It

looks to me like you are one of them, not against them."

"They are against them," Calin said. "They saved me from soul stealers and killed several of them."

Calin now stood naked before them. He was a well-muscled, well-endowed man. He did a slow turn, revealing that he had no death gems visible on his body anywhere. The bandages over his knife wound and the sea snake bites were all slightly stained with a smearing of red blood.

Junto glanced at Sekanna and saw her staring at Calin's crotch. He elbowed her gently in the side and she looked away from Calin.

Manole pointed his blade at Sekanna. "Now you."

"I have one," Sekanna said. She reached down and touched the inside of her thigh over her breeches. "It's right here."

"Is it blackened?" Manole asked.

"No."

"Let me see it."

Sekanna hesitated a moment, then slid her breeches down, moving the fabric past the silvery curls of her womanhood, to reveal the shimmering death gem embedded in the flesh on the inside of her thigh.

"Why is the inside of your leg wet?" Manole asked.

Sekanna scowled. "Seriously?" Her face flushed with heated embarrassment. She quickly pulled her pants back up. She looked up to see Calin staring amusedly at her, but then she realized he wasn't staring at her face. He was looking at her breasts. She glanced down to see that her nipples were pointed and erect. She looked over to Calin and he gave her a slight lift of his eyebrows and a wry smile. She frowned and quickly put her top back on.

"We are fighting the soul stealers," Junto said to the old man. "We found a nest of death beetles near the river."

Manole nodded. "There are several more nests in the woods."

"Can you show us where? They need to be destroyed."

"Junto," Sekanna said. "Not now. I need to rest."

Junto looked at her, then nodded.

"Clean yourselves. The wulvs can probably smell your stench from a mile away," Manole said. "And then you can rest. And then we can talk." He turned and walked away, heading back towards the cabin.

Calin looked at Sekanna with the beginnings of a playful leer forming on his face. "Want me to scrub your back?"

Sekanna frowned at him. "I can manage."

Manole kept the cabin clean and well stocked with salted meat and plenty of fresh vegetables. There was only one bed in the cabin, but it was a large sized bed, large enough to sleep three if they squeezed together. They squeezed together.

Sekanna wasn't quite sure what kept poking against her buttocks, but she somehow managed to fall asleep between Junto and Calin.

"We cannot stay," Junto said to Manole. "They will be hunting us and I don't want to put you in danger. This is your cabin now."

Manole, Junto, and Sekanna were all seated around the small table in the main room of the cabin. Sekanna chewed on a strip of salted meat. Calin sat on the wood plank floor nearby, working on replacing a bloodied bandage on his foot.

"Who is hunting you?" Manole asked.

"Soul stealers. One of them has at least two dozen death gems on his body. Probably more." Junto paused. "And more than half of them are now black." Junto relayed most of the story of the last few days to Manole, telling him of Ulster and Tallie, then Elcor. He left out Layna and what had happened to her; it was still too painful for him to dwell on her for too long.

"Elcor is probably really fucking pissed at us right about now," Sekanna said as Junto finished telling Manole the events leading up to them coming to the cabin.

Manole frowned. "Where will you go?" he asked.

Junto shrugged.

"Stay here," Manole said.

Junto shook his head immediately. "No."

"You said this cabin used to be in your family.

I am the trespasser here, not you," Manole said.

Junto shook his head. "No, we abandoned it. It's yours now."

Manole was quiet for a moment, then continued, repeating his desire for them to stay. "They don't know this area like I do, these people hunting you. I can help you," Manole said. "How far behind you are they?"

"They could show up any moment," Junto said.

Sekanna looked at Manole. "Why would you help us?" she asked of the old man.

"This soul stealer sounds like a very dangerous man," Manole said. "He sounds like someone who needs to be stopped." Manole paused for a moment. "Besides, the leaf told me you were coming."

Junto looked curiously at the old man. "The leaf?"

Manole nodded. "Yes, it whispers to me on the wind. The voices told me you were coming."

Junto looked at Sekanna. She shrugged. Junto rolled his eyes and sighed.

CHAPTER THIRTY-THREE

Elcor came across the destroyed remains of the death beetle nest. Heyeger had separated his men into several groups, sending teams out in different directions in their pursuit of Junto and the others. They had to travel quite a distance to find another bridge crossing, so several days had passed since they had lost sight of the extractors.

Elcor came across one of the men who had fallen off the bridge and survived. The man had been captured by the extractors, but they had left him alone after they had tied him up and he had managed to escape. He told Elcor where he had last seen them. It was easy enough to track them. They had made no efforts to hide their footprints.

He stared down at the remains of the nest. Most of the bodies of the slaughtered death beetles were gone, eaten by scavengers, but the destruction around the nest area remained; what little bits of the beetles that remained were shards of their exoskeletons, a few severed legs, and several splattered blotches of blood and internal organs.

Elcor chewed on a khack leaf. Even though he had survived the burning, the pain still lingered. The trapped life-forces within the death beetles he had embedded in his flesh had kept him alive, had kept re-birthing him, but they had not healed his burns. The pain was always with him now. It did not fade unless he chewed the leaf. Only then did the pain dwindle down to a level he could tolerate. He did not like the intoxicating effects of the leaf as it made him feel slower, dim-witted, but he liked the pain even less. The leaf was the only thing that gave him any relief.

And he also didn't like the weird tingling feeling in the tips of his fingers that chewing the leaf seemed to cause. Or the voices. Whenever he touched a tree or some other living thing with the tips of his fingers, he heard creepy, whispery voices. He had heard of others having similarly strange sensations in their bodies, and experiencing weird inexplicable hallucinations when chewing the khack leaf, but he fought to ignore those odd sensations. He did his best not to touch anything living while under the influence of the leaf, and he paid no attention to the voices that tried to whisper things to him when he did inadvertently touch something alive.

He thought of Junto and Sekanna. He had never hated anyone with so much hate in all his life. He wanted those two extractors to suffer before he took their souls, but he knew that would be foolish and offer them a chance to escape. No, he would find them and kill them immediately and eat their souls. That would be the only way to get the bitter taste out of his mouth, the only way he could ever get the savage desire for revenge out of his head.

He moved on from the destroyed nest,

continuing to follow the trail.

The three men who accompanied him followed silently in his wake.

Sekanna scanned the surrounding woods. She and Junto were a few dozen paces from the cabin. She had joined Junto as he made his rounds, both of them studying the nearby trees for any odd movements or anything that appeared to be out of the ordinary. "You sure Elcor will come for us? What if he doesn't? How long will we wait? We've already been here for days with no sign of them."

"I think he will come," Junto said.

"This waiting is really getting to me," Sekanna said. She tapped her fingers on her forearm.

"Go work the garden. That seems to relax you."

"Yeah, it does."

Junto glanced around the area. "Where's Calin?"

Sekanna shrugged. "Probably at the waterfall. He said he was going to wash off."

Junto nodded. "He does like to swim."

"I think he just likes to get naked."

Then, a loud scream erupted from the woods in the distance.

Junto and Sekanna exchanged glances, then raced back towards the cabin.

Elcor and two men extricated the third man from the trap the man had sprung. He had stepped on a booby-trapped patch of ground, sending a sharp spike jerking up from the ground to sink deep into his chest. He screamed an awful scream, then died. The death gem on the man's arm glowed, the energy from the life-force he absorbed healing the wound in his chest. He slowly came to and blinked up at Elcor.

Elcor looked at him, then at the other two men. "We're in for a real fight, boys," he said. "You ready for this?"

The re-birthed man looked nervously at Elcor. "I — I don't have any more death gems left," he finally said.

"Then you'd better be damn careful," Elcor said. *Because if you die, I'm taking your soul*, he thought, but kept that to himself.

Manole whistled, making the sound of a bird's cry. He looked towards the direction of the waterfall, but saw no movement coming out of the trees. He turned to Junto. "Your friend knows the signal, yes?"

Junto nodded. "He knows it. But sound it again."

Manole made the whistling sound again.

"I should go fetch him," Sekanna said.

Junto shook his head. "We don't even know if he's there."

"Where else would he be?" Sekanna asked.

"I don't know," Junto said. "He's probably chewing leaf and talking to forest animals somewhere."

"I told you, he doesn't talk to the animals," Sekanna said. "They talk to him."

"Okay, whatever."

Sekanna stared anxiously along the trail that led to the waterfall. Calin did not appear. "Whistle again," she told Manole.

Manole whistled again.

"I'll watch for him," Sekanna said to Junto. "You take the front."

Junto nodded. He reached up and gave her shoulder a reassuring squeeze. She put her hand over his and squeezed back.

Junto turned to Manole. "Show me where the traps are again."

Manole nodded and led Junto back into the main room of the cabin. He unrolled a parchment that showed the surrounding area, various different markings indicating the traps the old man had devised over the years of living here, plus the new ones they had built over the last few days.

Sekanna double-checked the crossbow secured to the rear window of the cabin, making sure it was cocked and ready to fire. Dozens of crossbow bolts rested in a wooden bin nearby. A loose crossbow rested along the wall next to the bin of bolts. She moved the crossbow on its hinge, shifting it to the left, then to the right, surveying its field of fire. She moved the crossbow back to the left, then stopped as she spotted movement in the distance. Something shifted in the trees. She hoped it was Calin returning from the waterfall, but something inside her told her it was not.

What she saw coming out of the woods set her teeth on edge. Not now! That was the last thing they needed. Her blood ran cold.

Calin stood on a small ledge behind the tumbling waterfall. The water cascaded down a few feet in front of him, churning and bubbling as it struck the pool at the end of the falls. For a moment, he thought he heard something in the distance, like a scream of some sort, and he paused to listen, but the waterfall was too loud for him to make out any distinct sound. He dove through the waterfall into the pool beyond.

He rose up from beneath the water and shook the water from his face. He casually swam to the edge of the pool and rose up out of the water, favoring his wounded foot as he moved towards his clothes that were piled on a nearby rock. His chest wound on the upper part of his left breast was healing nicely and now all that remained was a bright pink scar marking the area where he had been struck by the blade. He still had a few lingering scratches and abrasions from his encounter with the sea snake and his travel through the rough waters of the river. He donned his pants.

He popped another khack leaf into his mouth

and chewed it slowly. The pleasing warmth spread through his body. Behind him, the waterfall continued to tumble into the pool, sending up a white spray as it struck the water, the sound soothing and calming. He felt like he was back in the water even though he was standing on dry land, the floating feeling the leaf caused spreading out through his entire body. He sighed a soft sigh. He reached for his tunic that rested on a nearby rock, but then froze when he saw something move out of the nearby trees.

The wulv stopped as it saw him. And then it snarled a menacing snarl. "I'm going to eat you and shit out your bones," Calin heard the wulv say in his head. For a brief moment, that struck him as funny. Wouldn't that be painful for the wulv?

And then he pissed himself as the beast charged straight at him.

"Wulvs," Sekanna said, her voice loud but tight.

Junto came immediately into the room. "Wulvs?"

"Yeah." Sekanna pointed out the window from her position at the crossbow.

Junto looked out the window to see the beast slowly moving towards the cabin at a slight angle. The wulv was about the length of a man, standing about three feet high. Its fur was a deep brown, threaded with hints of dark green and black, giving it good camouflage against the backdrop of the woods. It had a long snout, ending in a bulbous black nose. Several sharp teeth were visible, curling down out of its jaws. Its paws padded silently against the earth as it moved, its dark eyes focused intently on the cabin. Junto scanned the surrounding woods. He knew the wulvs rarely traveled alone. They always moved in packs, some as large as ten, but never less than four. "Where's Calin?"

Sekanna shook her head. "He's out there somewhere. Damn it, I should have gone to find him!"

Junto shook his head. "He's going to have to save himself this time."

Calin spun and raced back into the pool as the wulv charged at him. He hit the water and dove beneath the surface, swimming hard towards the deeper water near the waterfall. He thought he'd feel the bite of the wulv at any moment, feel its teeth clamping down around his ankles. He swam harder, faster. Finally, he needed to come up for air. He burst up out of the water. He was beneath the waterfall, the water dropping hard and fast atop his head, the droplets plunking savagely down on his body as if he were caught in a torrential downpour. For a moment, he couldn't see the wulv. Where was it? But then he was able to focus past the waterfall and see through the thick sheets of water cascading down around him; the wulv paced along the pool right at the water's edge. It was making no move to follow him into the pool.

Calin shivered in the cool water of the pool, his wet pants clinging heavily to his legs, and kept his gaze on the pacing beast who so wanted to eat him and shit out his bones.

CHAPTER THIRTY-FOUR

Elcor slowed his pace, carefully studying the ground before them before moving forward. They had just avoided another trap, a hole dug into the ground covered in a layer of loose branches coated with leaves. He had removed the leaves to reveal what lay in the hole. Several spikes, with what looked like some kind of substance smeared on their sharp tips, most likely some kind of poison, were sunk into the ground at the bottom of the pit.

One of the men scanned the surrounding trees, looking upwards for any other kinds of traps that may be laying in wait from above.

They came across another trap. Several lengths of very thin rope, more twine than rope, were stretched tight across the path. There were a dozen lengths of string, each one pulled across the path, spaced about a foot apart. Elcor eyed them suspiciously. He supposed they could gingerly walk past them, stepping between the rows of twine, but they were so blatantly obvious, so clearly out in the open that it made him nervous. He scanned the surroundings, looking for the real trap, thinking the rows of twine were just decoys to distract them. They could step off the trail, but he was suspicious about that being the point of the twine stretched across the path. Perhaps it was set out in the open to get them to do that exact thing: step off the trail and trigger some other dastardly trap.

One of the men raised his right boot over the first length of twine blocking the path and gently set it down between the first length of twine and the second. Nothing happened. He raised his left boot and brought it cautiously down between the second length of twine and the third. Nothing happened. The man continued forward, easing his foot over the twine, then bringing it gently down on the ground in between the rows of twine that were stretched tight across their path.

Elcor watched the man move, remaining at the edge of the rows of twine. The man reached the last row of twine without incident and triumphantly stepped over the last strand of thin rope. What the man hadn't seen was an even thinner length of string positioned just a few inches above the last row of twine; it was more of a thread than a string. The thread was colored a mottled mixture of black and brown and green, helping it to blend in with the surrounding earth and foliage.

The response was immediate as the man's motion snapped the thin string. A torrent of razor-sharp objects rained down from the overhanging tree branches above the trail, hurtling down with great velocity. The objects were made of tiny clusters of metal, each piece with five, six, or even seven sharp points projecting out from all different angles. Each tip was coated with a very potent poison.

The first man and Elcor were struck by the projectiles; the other two men, one of them being the man with no active death gems left, were far enough back from the trap not to be hit. The first man was hit in the neck and the shoulder, several of the poison-tipped projections penetrating his flesh. He only screeched in pain once before falling silent. He dropped to his knees and his eyes immediately started rolling into the back of his head, turning nearly completely white.

Elcor was struck in his left arm, his chest, and his neck and shoulder. When one of the objects stung Elcor's neck, he reacted instinctively, swatting at the object as if it were a biting skeeter. One of the sharp projections punctured his palm as he went to smack what he thought was a bug on his neck. The poison went to work quickly.

Elcor and the first man died. Death gems glowed on both men, then turned black.

Junto tied some pieces of salted beef to an arrow. He nicked himself with the sharp tip of the arrow and dripped some of his blood onto the beef. He fired the arrow through the cabin window, aiming in the direction he had heard the screeching wail coming from. He instinctively knew it was Elcor or Heyeger and his men. He would give them a lovely welcome greeting in the form of a pack of wulvs eager for their company.

The wulv who been pacing near the cabin raced after the arrow, smelling the beef and the blood.

Junto fired off two more arrows, their tips also festooned with blood-smeared pieces of salted meat.

The wulv following Junto's blood-scented arrows came across Elcor and the other men. The beast did not hesitate, immediately lunging at the first man it came across, going for the man's throat. The man barely had time to even gurgle before he died. One of the death gems on his arms brightened, then went black. His eyes opened to see the wulv's open jaws about to take another bite out of his neck. He shrieked and the wulv bit.

A second wulv suddenly appeared, leaping into the fray, attacking the second man before he had a chance to draw his sword, clawing and biting ferociously at his mid-section. The man screamed an agonizing scream.

Elcor and the man with no death gems left crept quietly away.

The wulv pacing back and forth before the waterfall pool stopped pacing and looked off into the distance as screams filtered through the trees. The beast bounded off towards the sound.

Calin only waited for a brief moment before scrambling towards the shore. He grabbed his shirt as he raced past the rock where it lay and hurried towards the cabin.

"Tell them I just want to talk to them. Tell them I want a truce."

Elcor and the man with no death gem huddled behind a thick grouping of trees. The tree they hid behind had a large trunk, wide enough to keep them both hidden from the view of the cabin in the distance. The man with no death gem gripped his sword, a nervous sheen of sweat coating his face. Elcor crouched near him, his pink shriveled flesh brushing up against the man.

The man with no death gem looked at him. "No you don't."

"Of course I don't, you damn fool. But that's what you are going to tell them. I just need to get close to them."

"No."

Elcor glared at him.

"I'm not doing that," the man said.

Elcor pulled a blade and put it to the man's throat. "Yes, you are, or I will eat your fucking soul right here, right now."

The man with no death gem put his hand up to the blade and pushed it away from his throat. "Don't threaten me. I'm not a slave for you to command."

Elcor snarled and slashed at the man. The man leaped away from the cutting blade. His leap brought him out into the open.

Sekanna wasted no time in putting a crossbow bolt into the man's chest, then another. She had seen the two men from her vantage point in the cabin, but hadn't been able to get a clear shot at them. She was pretty certain one of them was Elcor because she had gotten a glimpse of a man with weirdly pink, wrinkled flesh.

The man she just shot fell to the ground, his body lying sprawled out in the open, the two bolts jutting out of his chest. His body shuddered for a brief moment, then was still.

Sekanna wasn't sure if he was truly dead, or just lying still as he absorbed another life-force. If he was dead, was he another soul now attached to her forever? Would he be waiting for her in the Everlasting? She didn't even know his name, or have any idea who in the Hell's Wood the man was. She gritted her teeth and cursed the man. *That's what you get for tracking us down. That's what you get for trying to kill us.*

Elcor cursed. He pulled out a dormant death beetle from his pocket and glanced at it. He looked at the dying man. He had only moments to put the creature on his body before his life-force escaped into the Everlasting, but he couldn't reach the body from here, not without exposing himself to arrow fire.

He knew he only had eight death gems left on his body. Eight souls who could replenish his life. He wasn't sure that was enough to take the cabin, especially by himself. He realized it should have been plenty but the bastard Junto and the cunt Sekanna were proving much harder to put down than he had anticipated. And now all the men who had accompanied him were gone.

And who knew when the cursed wulvs would make another appearance.

The man with no death gem choked and sputtered, wheezing heavily. Elcor knew he had only moments left. He again looked at the dormant creature in his hand; the death beetle was curled up tightly into a ball, its hard shell protectively formed into a tight circle. The man wheezed a final wheeze and then his chest was still. Elcor tossed the death beetle at the man, aiming for his chest. His aim was true and the death beetle hit the man in the chest. But then bounced off. It rolled through the dirt for a few feet, then was still.

Elcor frowned.

Then the death beetle unfurled itself, its legs sprouting out. It remained in the same spot for a moment, as if getting its bearings, and then it scurried off into the nearby brush.

Elcor cursed.

He didn't hear Manole creeping up behind him. He didn't hear the old man swinging the heavy mallet down towards his head until it was too late. He felt it, though. He felt the heavy dull thud before the world went dark.

CHAPTER THIRTY-FIVE

"No!" Sekanna shouted. "Not again, Junto! Just cut him the fuck up. Cut him into little pieces and feed him to the fucking wulvs!"

Junto abruptly stood up, moving off the chair he had been sitting on. "He has seven gems still in him! Seven souls." He had eight when they had captured him, but Sekanna had slit his throat in a blind uncontrollable rage when he had started to return to consciousness, so now he had seven.

Sekanna stood near the table that was situated in the middle of the small kitchen area within the cabin. Elcor was strapped down tightly on the table with thick strands of leather wrapped around his body, pinning him down to the table. His arms and legs were trussed up, tied together with lengths of rope. She put her hands down forcefully on the table, leaning towards Junto. "So what? He needs to die. Now and forever!"

"Isn't that what we are fighting for? To save those souls?" Junto looked at Sekanna. "Why do I feel like I have to keep reminding you of that?"

"You don't have to remind me," Sekanna said. She lifted her hands up off the table. "Yes, we are fighting to save as many souls as we can, but we can't always save them all. We can't win every battle. It's a bigger war, Junto. Sacrifices have to be made. They will always have to be made. It's a rotten, horrible fucking thing, but that's how it is. That's how it will always be. We won't be able to save everyone. We can't save everyone."

"Don't we have to try?"

"We are trying!" She looked at Junto, clearly exasperated. "Elcor needs to be destroyed. Forever. We should use his life-force for our cause. He doesn't deserve a second chance in the Everlasting. He doesn't!"

Junto said nothing.

"Harden your fucking heart, Junto. You need to. We can't let him live. We can't let him keep taking souls like he's been doing." She thrust her hand towards Elcor, indicating his prone body. "Look at him. Look at how many fucking death gems he has on him. We have to stop him here and now, once and forever."

"I don't want his black soul anywhere near me," Junto said.

"I figured you would say that." Sekanna drew the death beetle from her pocket that she had collected at the death beetle nest earlier. "I'll take it. My heart's already feeling pretty fucking hard right about now."

Elcor started to come around back to consciousness, making low groaning noises. Sekanna drew her dagger and slashed his throat, making another thin line in his neck right above the thin line she had made moments earlier with her dagger.

"Stop! Sekanna, stop!" Junto exclaimed, throwing his hands up in urgent protest.

Elcor gurgled as blood pooled out of the gash, then he became silent. A death gem on his left arm glowed hotly and pulsed. Elcor's neck wound slowly began to heal as tiny segments of skin expanded outward from the edges of the cut to close the gap in his flesh.

Sekanna wiped her bloodied blade on an already bloodied cloth and dropped the red-soaked rag back down to the table. "Now there are six."

Junto stared at the glowing gem on Elcor's left arm as it flared brightly, then went black. "I'm sorry," he muttered.

"We didn't start this war, Junto," Sekanna said. "But we can fight to stop it."

Junto was quiet for a moment, continuing to stare at the blackened death gem. "Don't destroy them, Sekanna. I'm begging you, please. Don't do it." He looked at several of the vibrant death gems embedded in Elcor's flesh with eyes filled with both fear and with great sorrow. "One of those could be Wushwan."

Sekanna looked at the absolute misery on Junto's face. She sheathed her dagger in the scabbard at her waist. "Then extract them. Right now. We have nothing to lose." Sekanna pointed to a vibrant death gem in Elcor's right forearm. "You watched Wushwan do it a dozen times, didn't you?"

Junto looked up at her.

"You'd better hurry before he comes round again," Sekanna said. "It'll probably be much easier to do an extraction when he's… dead."

Junto looked to Manole. "Do you have any blackout root in that garden of yours?"

Manole shook his head. "I do not."

Junto looked at Sekanna. "We don't have any of the herbs. We can't make the mixture. Wushwan used it to loosen the death beetle's grip. It made it easier to extract the tendrils."

Sekanna was unfazed. "Then we'll just have to rip them out."

Junto stood motionless, but only for a brief moment. He held out his hand and Sekanna pulled out her dagger from its sheath and handed it to Junto. He crouched near Elcor's forearm. He put the blade to the death gem and started to pry at it. He managed to lift one corner of the death gem and get the blade behind one of the tendrils. He lifted the gem higher, then reached under it and pinched the tendril between his fingers. He started to pull at the tendril, tugging on it. There was some firm resistance at first, but then he tugged harder and felt it come free from wherever it had its hold inside Elcor, accompanied by a faint popping noise. He continued to pull firmly on the tendril and it slowly started to come out of Elcor's body. "Calin, help me."

Calin came over to his side.

"Grab the tendril and just keep pulling it until its all the way out," Junto told Calin.

Calin hesitated.

"Just do it," Sekanna commanded.

Calin grabbed the wet, bloody tendril and started to pull. "This is just plain nasty."

Junto went to work on the next tendril, pulling

at it.

Manole came over and grabbed the second bloody tendril from Junto's fingers once he had the tendril out several inches. Manole continued to pull the tendril out of Elcor's flesh, tugging hard on the tendril every time he felt it snag.

Junto went to work on the third tendril.

Elcor's body started to shudder.

"He's coming back," Sekanna warned.

All three men hesitated in what they were doing, staring down at the big man's bound body, but then quickly resumed their work, moving with an even greater sense of urgency now.

Calin finally pulled out the full length of the first tendril from Elcor. It was about six feet long. Calin stared at it in wonder. "Are you serious?"

"Come on," Junto urged, motioning to the third tendril he was working on.

Calin let go of the first tendril unceremoniously and grabbed the third tendril and started to pull. The first tendril wiggled and squirmed like a tentacle gone wild.

"Watch that first one," Junto warned. "Don't let it penetrate your skin."

Calin eyed the first wriggling tendril with unease and a little fear as he tugged at the third tendril with his blood-stained fingers. He looked at the bloody third tendril with a sour face as he tugged on it.

Elcor came to and started to writhe and scream, bucking wildly beneath his restraints. Sekanna slashed his throat again with her dagger, creating a new line in his neck. Elcor's body went still.

"Sekanna, stop!" Junto said. "Please. Please stop."

"No," Sekanna said. "You need to hurry." This time, Sekanna didn't even bother to wipe the blood off of her dagger. She just lowered the weapon to her side; small droplets of blood dripped off the tip of the blade and splattered against the wood floor.

Another death gem on Elcor's body pulsed with light, then went black. Junto looked at it for only a brief moment, then returned to the task at hand, tugging and yanking and pulling on the fourth tendril he had just extricated from Elcor's flesh.

They finished pulling out all the tendrils and Junto lifted the death beetle away from Elcor's body. They all stared at the death gem, at the extracted death beetle Junto held by the edges between his thumb and middle finger. The long tendrils weaved and snaked through the air. A few of the tendrils were long enough to reach the cabin floor; they dragged bloody trails across the wood planks as they writhed.

One of the tendrils seemed to lunge towards Calin and he quickly backpedaled away from it. He tripped over a chair and fell hard onto his buttocks with a heavy grunt.

"Now what happens?" Manole asked.

"Now the soul goes free," Junto said.

"Are you sure?" Manole asked. "How do you know?"

"We just know," Sekanna snapped.

Junto said nothing.

"How do you know?" Manole asked again.

"I have to believe," Junto said. "I have to

believe."

The death beetle pulsed, then a soft light flared, moving up and out of the creature. The death beetle's shell darkened and the tendrils stopped moving to hang limply down from the underbelly of the creature. "There," Junto said. "Did you see it?" He looked to Manole. "Did you see it?"

Manole nodded. "But what does it mean?"

"It means we freed the soul. We freed it to go into the Everlasting." Sekanna looked at Manole as if he were a feeble old fool who could no longer comprehend the obvious.

"Did you?" Manole asked. "Did you really?"

"Yes, we did," Sekanna said.

Junto looked at Manole curiously. "What do you think just happened?"

Manole shrugged. "I don't know."

Junto shook his head. "No. I don't accept that answer. You need to tell me what you think just happened."

Manole shook his head. "I really don't know." He looked at Junto. "How can I know?"

Junto frowned. "Is that what we should do? Walk around shrugging our shoulders and shaking our heads? Saying *'I don't know?'*"

Manole was about to shrug, but then stopped himself. "What would you like me to say? That you just saved that soul? That you just freed it so it can go bask in the glory of some afterlife? Is that what you want me to say?"

"It's what we just did, so yes, say it," Sekanna snapped.

Manole looked at the death beetle that Junto

still clutched. "What happens to... that?"

Junto followed the old man's gaze to look at the death beetle he still held by the edges of its shell. "It's dead."

"So an extraction kills it?" Manole asked.

"Yes," Junto said.

"So you killed that creature to free a human soul."

It wasn't a question, but Junto responded with, "Yes." Junto waited for Manole to continue, but the old man remained silent.

"It's just a cursed fucking bug," Sekanna said.

"Is it?" Manole asked.

Elcor made a violent move, struggling at his bonds, taking a huge, exaggerated breath. He was back to consciousness, all the way back.

They all jumped away from him, startled by his sharp movement. But he was very securely bound so the limited wild thrashing and bucking motions he made was the extent of the movement he was capable of.

"I will fucking kill you all!" Elcor ranted. "I will eat your fucking souls and fuck your corpses!" His eyes glared with hate.

Sekanna raised her dormant death beetle before his eyes. "I'm going to eat *your* fucking soul, you son of a bitch."

For the first time in his life, real fear entered Elcor's eyes. The threat of his eternal decimation hit him quickly and it hit him hard.

"Not so tough anymore, are you?" Sekanna said, blatantly taunting him.

"Sekanna," Junto said, his tone cautioning.

Sekanna curled her hand into a fist, gripping the death beetle tightly. She looked down at Elcor and licked her lips.

"No," Elcor said, the word barely coming out of his mouth. "Just kill me," he said. "Just kill me and send me into the Everlasting. Just kill me."

"I've already killed you three times in the last hour," Sekanna said. "But you won't stay fucking dead."

Elcor violently thrashed around, moving so wildly that they all took another instinctive step away from him. He was very tightly bound, the leather straps and ropes holding firm, but his violent spasms had started to move them, to loosen them.

Sekanna stepped forward towards him and raised her dagger above his chest. Elcor stopped moving as he saw the droplets of blood dripping off the end of the blade. Sekanna glanced down at a death gem on an exposed part of Elcor's stomach; the death gem shimmered with a soft yellow light. She looked over at Junto, a sudden exhaustion clearly lining her eyes and lacing her words. "How many more?"

"Four."

Sekanna groaned. "Let's just chop off his fucking head and be done with it."

"What if one of the four was your sister? Would you tell me to just fucking cut his head off then?" Junto said.

Sekanna was quiet. She lowered her bloodied dagger back to her side.

"What if one of them was me?" Junto continued. "Would you cut his head off then?"

Sekanna had no reply. She looked at Junto. She was quiet for a long moment, watching him. "That's how you do it. That's how you keep going, isn't it? That's how you keep caring. Each one of them is someone you know. In your head, I mean. You turn them all into someone you know."

It was Junto's turn to be quiet. He slowly shook his head.

Sekanna looked at him.

"They're all you, Sekanna," he said in a soft whisper. "Every one of them is you. That's how I make it through. That's why I can't stop."

Sekanna just stared at him. "I'm right here, Junto," she said. "You don't have to do that to yourself."

Junto grabbed her and pulled her into an embrace. Tears dripped out of his eyes as he clutched her to his chest. "I'm afraid for you," he whispered. "You need to stop killing." She pulled back from him and he quickly wiped away his tears before she could fully see them. "We need to stop killing. We need to save their souls. We need to stop killing them."

Calin and Manole watched quietly, neither man saying anything.

"That was so fucking touching!" Elcor snarled. "I'm going to fucking cry and drip my fucking tears into the holes in your necks where your fucking heads used to be."

They worked on extracting the next of the four

remaining death gems embedded in Elcor's body, but this time Elcor was conscious during the process. He screamed the screams of a tortured man, but he stayed conscious the entire time. He bucked and writhed and his face contorted into the most pain-filled grimaces any of them had ever seen. Each pull on the tendril seemed to send paroxysms of pain searing through Elcor and he writhed madly and sweated profusely; spittle flew from his lips as he wailed in agony. Curses flooded from his mouth.

"We could give him some leaf," Calin suggested.

"No!" Sekanna countered angrily, her response immediate. "Let him suffer."

"Don't stop," Junto said to Calin and Manole as they tugged at the tendrils.

Elcor only stopped screaming and cursing to catch his breath.

Finally, the second extraction was completed and the extracted death beetle pulsed as the soul contained inside it was released. And then the extracted beetle became deathly still.

There were now three more death gems to extract.

Elcor panted heavily. His body was completely coated in a thick layer of sweat. He looked to be on the verge of death.

"I don't think he can take another extraction without dying," Manole said.

"Give him some leaf," Calin said, repeating his earlier suggestion. "That might dull his pain." He looked at them. "It certainly dulls mine."

Sekanna hesitated, but then reluctantly nodded. "Do you have any on you?" Sekanna asked of Calin.

"No, but Manole is growing it in his garden," Calin said. "I'll show you."

"I know. I saw it," Sekanna said.

"Grab some leaves from that khack plant in the back corner," Manole said. "Over on the left. It's been growing the longest, so it's the most potent."

"I'll go with you," Calin said.

Sekanna nodded.

Sekanna and Calin stepped outside and moved quickly towards the garden that grew near the back of the cabin. Calin favored his wounded foot, walking with a slight limp.

Sekanna suddenly grabbed at Calin's arm, stopping him.

Calin looked at her. "What?"

Sekanna raised her hand and pointed into the distance.

Heyeger stood there, flanked by two dozen men.

CHAPTER THIRTY-SIX

Sekanna burst back into the cabin, with Calin close on her heels. "Heyeger is here!"

Junto jerked his head towards her. "What?"

Elcor looked at them from where he was strapped to the table and laughed. He laughed so hard tears started pouring out of his eyes. His face was a mangled mash of expressions, a twisted grimace of physical pain caused by the extraction mingled with lips upturned in anticipatory joy at their predicament. "You are all fucking dead."

"He's got at least two dozen men, probably more," Sekanna said. Then she turned on Elcor and delivered a vicious blow to his laughing mouth, punching her clenched fist straight into his teeth.

Undeterred, delirious by the amount of pain wracking his body, Elcor just continued to laugh even harder as Sekanna shook out the pain in her hand caused by the blow to his face.

"Man the windows," Junto said. He grabbed for a bow, but Manole put a hand on his arm, stopping him. The old man shook his head at Junto. "That is too many men. You cannot win this battle."

Junto was crestfallen. He dropped his hand to his side, leaving the bow untouched.

"So now we run away to fight another day," Manole said.

"Run away?"

Manole nodded to Junto. "I knew this day would come. I never thought I would be surrounded by men, though. I thought it would be the wulvs who would finally corner me." He shrugged. "No matter. The outcome is the same."

"Give us Calin," a voice shouted from outside. "Give us Calin and we will go."

"They're lying," Calin hissed. "They'll kill you all."

Junto looked to Calin. "Don't worry. We're not turning you over. You're with us now." Junto turned to Manole. "So now what?"

"Now we heat things up," Manole said. The old man grabbed a torch from a nearby bin and touched the tip into the hearth, setting the torch alight. He moved to a nearby wall and dipped the flame towards a tiny gutter in the floor. The narrow gutter was filled with oil. For the first time, Junto noticed the gutter ran around the entire perimeter of the cabin. The flame touched the oil and immediately the oil caught fire, the flames speeding along the gutter, igniting a rim of fire. The fire even started to move up the wall, following paths that Manole had laid down in the past. "I set this up long ago to destroy any evidence that could be used against me when I was smuggling khack leaf."

Some of the flames spread outside the cabin, creating a much larger ring of fire around the entire cabin. The flames grew quickly, flaring up to a man's height, some flickering tips of the fire reaching even higher than six or seven feet.

One of Heyeger's men suddenly burst through the flames, charging towards the cabin, his clothes ablaze, his sword raised. Sekanna took him down with a crossbow bolt, firing through an open window near the front door of the cabin.

"This way," Manole said. He led them to a back room, throwing open a door cut into the ground. A dark hole led into the blackness below. Manole climbed down into the tunnel.

"I'll find you!" Elcor shouted from the main cabin. He writhed and squirmed on the table. "I'll find all of you and kill you all!"

Sekanna pushed Calin towards the hole in the floor. She grabbed a torch, lit it, and shoved it in his hand. "Go."

Calin hesitated.

Sekanna pushed at his shoulder. "Go! Do as I tell you." Her hair shimmered with an angry silver glow.

Calin descended into the tunnel.

Sekanna raced back into the main room of the cabin.

"Sekanna!" Junto shouted after her.

"Just go. I'm right behind you."

Junto looked back towards the main room of the cabin. The walls were ablaze and thick black smoke started to fill the area, obscuring the main room of the cabin. He lost sight of Sekanna. "Sekanna!" he shouted.

A figure emerged out of the black smoke and Junto quickly realized it wasn't Sekanna. It was another attacker. He had somehow managed to get into the cabin, perhaps through one of the windows. But the man suddenly came up short as a blade erupted out of his stomach, the bloodied tip of the weapon pointing at Junto. The blade withdrew and the man collapsed to the side, revealing Sekanna standing behind him. She clutched Elcor's severed head in her other hand, gripping the head by its black hair. "Go!" she shouted at Junto as she charged towards him.

Junto turned and moved quickly down into the tunnel; Calin was right in front of him. Sekanna followed them down. When she reached the tunnel floor, she set the severed head down, pulled the tunnel door closed above her, and then snatched the head back into her hand, clutching Elcor's head again by its hair.

Manole brushed by her. He reached up to the tunnel door and slid a heavy bolt into place, locking it firmly. He turned away and started back down the tunnel.

They came out of the tunnel near the Roaring River.

Junto looked back behind them and could see a plume of black smoke rising up in the far distance. "We need to keep moving," Junto said. He looked at Sekanna.

Sekanna still clutched Elcor's severed head in her hand, her fingers gripping his hair.

"You keeping that as a pet?" Calin asked.

"Get rid of that," Junto said.

Sekanna looked at Elcor's head. "I wish I could have stolen your soul, you sorry son of a bitch." She looked over at Junto. "There's no way I was giving him another chance to live, Junto. No way. I'm sorry about those last souls I destroyed."

Junto said nothing.

"I think you did the right thing," Calin said.

"Yes, I did," Sekanna said, her voice resolute and unwavering. "Except he doesn't deserve a new life in the Everlasting," she said, her words bitter. "It's not fair he gets a second chance." Her hair shimmered with the anger she made no effort to hide. She spit in his dead face. And then hurled the severed head into the Roaring River.

They all watched the head bob up and down in the churning water, and then the head was gone, swallowed up by the river.

"I should leave you," Calin said.

The others turned to him.

"Heyeger wants me," Calin said. "He won't stop hunting me down. Ever. His pride won't let him stop. No matter what it takes, he won't stop until he finds me and steals my soul."

Junto shook his head. "No. You need to stay with us. We need to watch out for each other. Now more than ever."

Calin shook his head. "No. You have your — mission. You have a purpose to your life. I don't."

Sekanna shook her head. "No, you are wrong. You do have a purpose now. You fight with us."

Calin looked at her.

"Besides," Sekanna said. She bent down and showed him a healthy view of cleavage. "There's a chance you might get some of this if you play your cards right." She straightened back up. "That's enough reason to keep on living, isn't it?"

Calin looked curiously at her, then at Junto, then back to her. "But you two— I thought—"

Sekanna looked at Calin's confused face and burst out laughing with a beautiful laugh. Junto smiled. "We are soul mates," she said to Calin, referring to herself and Junto. "You, I just want to fuck."

"I— but—" Calin sputtered. He could find no words.

Sekanna patted Calin affectionately on the shoulder. "You'll never understand, so don't even try."

"What about me?" Manole asked.

Sekanna looked at him dubiously. "Umm, I don't think so. I mean thanks and all for saving our lives, but what kind of a girl do you think I am?"

Manole shrugged. "Can't blame a lonely old man for trying."

Sekanna laughed. "No, I can't." She reached over and kissed Manole on the cheek.

"We need to keep moving," Junto said again. And they moved, quickly hurrying along an old trail that ran near the river.

"We should get off the trail," Sekanna called up to Junto as he jogged forward.

Junto nodded. He turned right and moved into the thin woods that flanked the river. The others followed and they just kept moving, twisting this way and that through the woods, moving past thick brush, then hurrying through a small open field. The woods thickened around them. Finally, they paused, feeling confident they had put enough distance between themselves and their pursuers. They waited quietly for a long moment, listening for any sound of pursuit from the distance. They heard nothing but the normal animal cries and sounds of the forest.

"Where to now?" Sekanna asked. She looked to Calin, seeing him wince and rub at his wounded foot, but she said nothing. They were out of khack leaf so she knew he was starting to feel some serious pain. "We need to find a place to rest."

"I don't know. Away from here. Away from Calkut." Junto looked at the others. "Does anyone know much about NewCrag?"

"I've only been there once, but that was about ten years ago," Calin said. "It's on the edge of Mount Moriaki. They were digging into the mountain when I was there, trying to create a better shelter from the wind storms."

"They finished that years ago," Manole said. "It's an interesting place. Some of them never come out from under the stone roof now. They are afraid of the outside."

"Do you think we could find shelter there?" Junto asked.

"Perhaps," Manole said. "But only for a short while. "They are very clannish and outsiders aren't always welcome. News of your presence would travel fast."

"Or we could go the opposite way and reach

Berjon in four or five days," Junto said.

"Does anyone have any coin?" Calin asked.

Sekanna jangled her pouch. "I have some."

"As do I, but not much," Junto said. "Maybe enough for a week or two at an inn, but that's about it."

"There's another games scheduled in NewCrag. More races. But that's not until next month," Calin said.

They looked at him, waiting for him to continue.

"Heyeger will likely be there," Calin explained. "And that Ulster fellow. If he keeps on winning the races the way he is winning, that is."

"We're in no condition to take on Heyeger," Junto said. "We need a lot more men."

Sekanna cleared her throat loudly.

"We need a lot more men and women to help us."

"You need a damn army, is what you need," Manole grumbled.

"No," Sekanna said. "We just need a damn good plan."

"And what exactly would such a plan entail?" Manole asked.

Sekanna had no answer.

"We need a secure location," Junto said. "Somewhere safe where we can rebuild."

"Nowhere is safe from Heyeger," Calin said. "He has men everywhere. Even children will die for him." He paused. "And kill for him."

Sekanna looked at Calin. "Why? Why would children kill for him?"

Calin was quiet for a long moment. "I did."

"You did? Why?"

"He's my father." Calin paused. "He has hundreds of children."

No one spoke for a long moment.

"All of those men at the cabin were probably my half-brothers," Calin said.

"Whoa," Sekanna finally said. "And I thought *my* father was a rotten bastard. Actually, not was. My father *is* still a bastard." She looked at Calin. "But I will have to admit yours is worse."

"He will never stop hunting me," Calin said. "Or you. You have humiliated him and he will never let that stand."

Everyone was quiet.

Junto thought of his own father, and his mother. They still lived in Greywood. He was afraid to go see them, afraid of bringing enemies down upon them, afraid someone might use them against him someday. So he stayed away from them. He wondered if they thought he was dead. He hadn't sent a message to them in months. No, it was going on a year already. Time continued to speed along without a care for anything or anyone. What a terrible son I am, he thought. Tormenting them like that. They thought he was on a fool's errand. His father ranted at him, then begged him to reconsider, then ranted again when Junto refused to bow to his will. The soul stealers had to be stopped. There was no way he could live the life of a cobbler knowing that innocent souls were being devoured and extinguished forever. There was no way that would ever happen.

Still, he knew he should at least get them a message. Let them know he was still alive. Or maybe you shouldn't, he thought. Maybe you should just let them think you are dead and let them move on with their lives. Why continue to torment them with random messages? What you should do is send them a message proclaiming your death. Let them grieve and move on. He seriously considered sending such a message.

He thought of his sister. Tariana was only twelve when he left. Now she would be eighteen. He wondered what she was doing. Had she married? What occupied her days? She was always good at woodworking. Maybe she was a furniture builder. He smiled at that. That would be a good job for her. A peaceful job. Designing and carving beautifully intricate scrollwork on chairs and tables. He envisioned Tariana in a little shop in Greywood Square, proudly displaying her wares in front of her shop. Father would be sitting in one of her rocking chairs, smoking his pipe, a pipe Tariana had carved for him, enticing shoppers to visit Tariana's shop and check out her work. Junto smiled. He knew such a life was probably a figment of his imagination, but he thoroughly enjoyed it all the same. It gave him comfort. He was even afraid to return to Greywood, afraid the illusion would be destroyed forever, afraid he would find his Tariana working as a dung farmer, shoveling shit for some haughty magistrate, her face smeared with feces. He pushed the unpleasant scenario from his mind and brought the wood shop back into the forefront. Yes, that's what she was doing. Even now, she was carving a fresh pipe for Father.

And Mother. She was always so pleasant to him, always there with a smile. She would have a baker's shop right next store to Tariana's wood shop. The smell of fresh bread would mingle with the smell of freshly cut wood. Father would sit in his rocking chair and slowly nibble at the fresh bread Mother just removed from the kiln. He would hawk the bread to would-be customers at the same time he was hawking Tariana's woodworking.

Junto felt his mouth water. He desperately wanted a piece of fresh bread right now. He dug into his pouch and pulled out a wrinkled, gnarly-looking piece of salted beef. He frowned at it and shoved it back into his pouch.

"Junto?"

He looked up to see Sekanna smiling whimsically at him. "Where the hell did you go?"

"What?"

"I've been calling your name for five minutes now. Where did you go?" She looked at him, studying his face. "You went back home, didn't you? Back to Greywood."

Junto gave her the slightest of smiles.

"Your father's cobbler shop again?" Sekanna asked, pretty sure of the answer.

Junto shook his head slightly. "Tariana's wood shop. And Mother's bakery." He looked a bit sheepish with his answer.

Sekanna gave a slight laugh. "I suppose we need to find you some fresh bread now?"

Again, he gave her a slight smile, as well as a slight nod this time.

"And how's the family?" Sekanna asked, playing along.

"They are well. Father is sitting in his rocking chair, smoking his pipe. Tariana just carved him a new one. Mother just brought him a piece of fresh bread."

"With cinnamon sugar?"

Junto nodded. "Yes, with cinnamon sugar."

"Damn it, Junto," Sekanna said. "Now you've got my stomach growling."

"I love cinnamon sugar bread," Calin said.

Sekanna looked at him. "Who doesn't?"

"My father," Calin replied. His face was very serious. "My father doesn't like it at all."

"Now why doesn't that surprise me," Sekanna said.

"Why are we talking about cinnamon sugar bread?" Calin asked.

Sekanna motioned to Junto with a toss of her head. "Junto. Sometimes he wanders." She tapped at her head. "He visits his home. His mother is a baker."

"Not really," Junto said. "Well, maybe she is now. I hope she is. That's always what she wanted to do."

Calin's stomach grumbled. Sekanna looked at him, then at Junto. "Okay, now you did it. Now we're all hungry."

"Sorry about that."

They all stood around in silence.

"We need a new place to live. A new base of operations," Junto said.

"There is a castle near NewCrag," Manole said,

but quickly corrected himself. "Not really near NewCrag, but it's on the way towards NewCrag."

"A castle?" Junto asked.

"Well, not much of a castle, really. More like an outpost, but it's got plenty of room. It's another leftover remnant from the leaf smuggling days."

"Don't tell us," Sekanna said. "It's haunted, right?"

Manole scowled at her. "No, it's not haunted. It's a thieves' den."

"And they'll just let us stay there?" Sekanna asked.

Manole shook his head. "Oh, no. We'd have to take it from them."

Junto shook his head. "We are not taking anything from anyone." He looked around the group. "Any other ideas?"

"Hold on a minute, here," Sekanna said. "Thieves and soul stealers go together. There could very well be a gang of soul stealers holed up there. At the very least we should go check it out."

Junto was quiet for a moment. He looked at Manole. "How many live there?"

Manole shrugged. "I haven't been there for a few years. It could even be empty now for all I know."

"Or it could be crawling with a hundred thieves," Junto said.

"You think a hundred thieves would get along without killing each other?" Sekanna asked.

Junto was silent.

"We should at least go check it out," Sekanna said. "Where else do we have to go?" Sekanna looked at Manole. "How far is it from here?"

"About half a day's walk at a good pace."

Junto glanced up at the sun.

"We can make it by nightfall if we start now," Sekanna said, following Junto's gaze up into the sky.

"The trail was overgrown the last time I took it, but I think we'll still be able to follow it for the most part," Manole said.

"What else is between us and this outpost?" Junto asked.

"Mostly woods," the old man said.

"Mostly?"

Manole nodded. "Mostly."

"Okay, you will not leave it hanging at *mostly*," Sekanna said. "What else is between us and this outpost?"

Manole hesitated.

Calin looked at Manole and frowned. "Okay, this isn't good."

Junto looked intently at Manole. "What else?"

"It's probably gone," Manole said. "Like I said, I haven't been that way for years."

"What is probably gone?" Sekanna said. "Tell us, old man."

He looked at the others. "It was years ago..." he started, then paused.

"You said that already," Sekanna said.

"It was a harling," Manole said. "I saw a harling."

They all looked incredulously at Manole.

"They are not real," Calin said.

Manole nodded. "So you say. Her wings were

clipped, but I saw them. She was definitely a harling."

"I think you were chewing too much khack leaf, old man," Sekanna said.

"So you say."

Sekanna looked to Junto.

Junto was contemplative for a moment. "If death beetles exist, which we know they do, then anything else, myth or legend or monster, could be real." He looked at the group. "We head for the castle."

CHAPTER THIRTY-SEVEN

They didn't reach the outpost that day. Instead, they came across another cabin. Another abandoned leftover building from the khack smuggling days. It had only two rooms, but no furniture.

They decided to rest and let Calin heal, let him grow a bit stronger before they pressed on. They mulled over their current predicament, discussing their options.

Elcor was gone. Truly dead. That was one portrait they could put a big X through. Only dozens more to go. Junto immediately scoffed inwardly at himself. Dozens? Hah. Not even close. There could be dozens of soul stealers in Calkut alone, let alone all of Moraneesh. There could be hundreds in Moraneesh. If not thousands.

Irchly was going to be a future threat, but they knew they couldn't worry about him now. They didn't think he posed any immediate threat as long as they stayed away from Berjon. But one day, they all knew Berjon would be a destination they could no longer avoid.

Heyeger and his men, his children if Calin's tale was true, were clearly a very dangerous threat, one that could strike at them at any moment. They couldn't afford to let their guard down now, not even for a moment. They were now hunted as extractors as much as they were doing their own hunting of soul stealers.

And there was still Ulster. The soul stealer who had set all of this in motion. He was still out there. Junto grabbed a branch that was burning in the hearth and blew out the flame. He looked at the charred blackened tip, watching the smoke swirling up away from it. Then he handed the stick to Sekanna and motioned with his head to the flat wooden floorboards. "You remember what Ulster looks like?"

Sekanna took the offered stick and looked curiously at Junto.

"We have to start again somewhere," Junto said. "Manole needs at least a rough idea of what he looks like."

Sekanna looked at the floor, glanced at the charred end of the stick, then moved to her knees and started to draw.

Junto studied the portrait of the man that Sekanna drew. It was a rough sketch done in charcoal, but the drawing still revealed the dark cruelty in the man's face, the blatant threat of menace in his eyes. Ulster VoGrat. A bad man. A violent killer. A soul stealer. And they still had to stop him.

This was going to be a long war.

Black Woods

The Black Woods contain darkly gnarled trees born from the seeds of sorcery, strange plants given unnatural life from the fertilizing spread of decaying magic, abnormal soil deeply contaminated with the residue of the Alchemy Wars from decades long past. Pockets of Black Woods have sprouted all over the world of Teradynea in isolated growths of midnight-black trees, most of these unexplored parcels of poisoned land still shrouded in secrecy. The tainted flora and fauna that sprout and flourish within these areas of permanent shadow contain mysterious powers that can be harvested and gathered for good. Or for evil.

What secrets do the Black Woods hold? Rin and his friend Joktala will soon discover that the Black Woods contain a hidden danger far more perilous than any they could have ever imagined...

Jack is also the creator and author of the Land of Fright™ series and the Spine-Tinglers™ series. Read on to learn more about these exciting series on the following pages!

LAND OF FRIGHT™

The Land of Fright™ is a place where the dark side of the imagination roams free. It is a mysterious land shrouded in secrecy. It is a massive realm filled with frights from the ancient worlds of yesteryear, a region where modern marvels lurk and run amok, a territory where future fears come into being before their time. It is a world of spine-tingling short stories filled with the strange, the eerie, and the weird. Some of the story realms you visit will intrigue you. Some of them may unsettle you. Some of them may even titillate and amuse you. We hope many of them will give you delicious chills along your journey. The Land of Fright™ encompasses the vast expanse of time and space. You will visit the world of the Past in Ancient Rome, Medieval England, the old West, World War II, and others yet to be explored. You will find many tales that exist right here in the Present, tales filled with modern lives that have taken a turn down a darker path. You will travel into the Future to tour strange new worlds and interact with alien societies, or to just take a peek at what tomorrow may bring.

Illustrated versions of some Land of Fright™ stories, which are called Fright Bites™, are also available.

Land of Fright™ terrorstories contained in Collection I:

#1 - Whirring Blades: A simple late-night trip to the mall for a father and his son turns into a struggle for survival when they are attacked by a deadly swarm of toy helicopters.

#2 - The Big Leagues: A scorned young baseball player shows his teammates he really knows how to play ball with the best of them.

#3 - Snowflakes: In the land of Frawst, special snowflakes are a gift from the gods, capable of transferring the knowledge of the Ancients. A young woman searches the skies with breathless anticipation for her snowflake, but finds something far more dark and dangerous instead.

#4 - End of the Rainbow: In Medieval England, a warrior and his woman find the end of a massive rainbow that has filled the sky and discover the dark secret of its power.

#5 - Trophy Wives: An enigmatic sculptor meets a beautiful woman whom he vows will be his next subject. But things may not turn out the way he plans...

#6 - Die-orama: A petty thief finds out that a WWII model diorama in his local hobby shop holds much more than just plastic vehicles and plastic soldiers.

#7 - Creature in the Creek: A lonely young woman finds her favorite secluded spot inhabited by a monster from her past.

#8 - The Emperor of Fear: In ancient Rome, two coliseum workers encounter a mysterious crate containing an unearthly creature. Just in time for the next gladiator games...

#9 - The Towers That Fell From The Sky: Two analysts race to uncover the secret purpose of the giant alien towers that have thundered down out of the skies.

#10 - God Save The Queen: An exterminator piloting an ant-sized robot faces the queen of a nest he has been assigned to destroy.

Land of Fright™ terrorstories contained in Collection II:

#11 - Special Announcement: A fraud investigator discovers the disturbing truth behind the messages on a community announcement board.

#12 - Poisoned Land: Savage hunters patrol the Poisoned Lands, demanding appeasement from the three survivors trapped in a surrounded building. How far will each one of them go to survive?

#13 - Pool of Light: A mysterious wave of dark energy from space washes over the Earth, trapping a woman and her friends in pools of light. Beyond the edges of the light, deep pockets of darkness hold much more than just empty blackness.

#14 - Ghosts of Pompeii: A woman on a tour of Italy with her son unwittingly awakens the ghosts of Pompeii.

#15 - Sparklers: A child's sparkler opens a doorway to another dimension and a father must enter it to save his family and his neighborhood from the ominous threat that lays beyond.

#16 - The Grid: An interstellar salvage crew activates a mysterious grid on an abandoned vessel floating in space, unleashing a deadly force.

#17 - The Barn: An empty barn beckons an amateur photographer to step through its dark entrance, whispering promises of a once-in-a-lifetime shoot.

#18 - Sands of the Colosseum: A businessman in Rome gets to experience the dream of a lifetime when he visits the great Colosseum — until he finds himself standing on the arena floor.

#19 - Flipbook: A man sees a dark future of his family in jeopardy when he watches the tiny animations of a flipbook play out in his hand.

#20 - Day of the Hoppers: Two boys flee for their lives when their friendly neighborhood grasshoppers turn into deadly projectiles.

Land of Fright™ terrorstories contained in Collection III:

#21 - The Prospector: In the 1800's, a lonely prospector finds the body parts of a woman as he pans for gold in the wilds of California.

#22 - The Boy In The Yearbook: Two middle-aged women are tormented by a mysterious photograph in their high school yearbook.

#23 - Shot Glass: A man discovers the shot glasses in his great-grandfather's collection can do much more than just hold a mouthful of liquor.

#24 - The Champion: An actor in a medieval renaissance re-enactment show becomes the unbeatable champion he has longed to be.

#25 - Hitler's Graveyard: American soldiers in WWII uncover a nefarious Nazi plan to resurrect their dead heroes so they can rejoin the war.

#26 - Out of Ink: Colonists on a remote planet resort to desperate measures to ward off an attack from wild alien animals.

#27 - Dung Beetles: Mutant dung beetles attack a family on a remote Pennsylvania highway. Yes, it's as disgusting as it sounds.

#28 - The Tinies: A beleaguered office worker encounters a strange alien armada in the sub-basement of his office building.

#29 - Hammer of Charon: In ancient Rome, it is the duty of a special man to make sure gravely wounded gladiators are given a quick death after a gladiator fight. He serves his position quietly with honor. Until they try to take his hammer away from him…

#30 - Pharaoh's Cat: In ancient Egypt, the pharaoh is dying. His trusted advisors want his favorite cat to be buried with him. The cat has other plans…

Land of Fright™ terrorstories contained in Collection IV:

#31 - The Throw-Aways: A washed-up writer of action-adventure thrillers is menaced by the ghosts of the characters he has created.

#32 - Everlasting Death: The souls of the newly deceased take on solid form and the Earth fills with immovable statues of death...

#33 - Bite the Bullet: In the Wild West, a desperate outlaw clings to a bullet cursed by a Gypsy... because the bullet has his name on it.

#34 - Road Rage: A senseless accident on a rural highway sets off a frightening chain of events.

#35 - The Controller: A detective investigates a bank robbery that appears to have been carried out by a zombie.

#36 - The Notebook: An enchanted notebook helps a floundering author finish her story. But the unnatural fuel that stokes the power of the mysterious writing journal leads her down a disturbing path...

#37 - The Candy Striper and the Captain: American WWII soldiers in the Philippines scare superstitious enemy soldiers with corpses they dress up to look like vampire victims. The vampire bites might be fake, but what comes out of the jungle is not...

#38 - Clothes Make the Man: A young man steals a magical suit off of a corpse, hoping some of its power will rub off on him.

#39 - Memory Market: The cryptic process of memory storage in the human brain has been decoded and now memories are bought and sold in the memory market. But with every legitimate commercial endeavor there comes a black market, and the memory market is no exception...

#40 - The Demon Who Ate Screams: A young martial artist battles a vicious demon who feeds on the tormented screams and dying whimpers of his victims.

Land of Fright™ terrorstories contained in Collection V:

#41 - The Hatchlings: A peaceful barbecue turns into an afternoon of terror for a suburban man when the charcoal briquets start to hatch!

#42 - Virgin Sacrifice: A professor of archaeology is determined to set the world right again using the ancient power of Aztec sacrifice rituals.

#43 - Smog Monsters: The heavily contaminated air in Beijing turns even deadlier when unearthly creatures form within the dense poison of its thick pollution.

#44 - Benders of Space-Time: A young interstellar traveler discovers the uncomfortable truth about the Benders, the creatures who power starships with their ability to fold space-time.

#45 - The Picture: A young soldier in World War II shows his fellow soldiers a picture of his beautiful fiancé during the lulls in battle. But this seemingly harmless gesture is far from innocent…

#46 - Black Ice: A vicious dragon is offered a great gift — a block of black ice to soothe the fire that burns its throat and roars in its belly. Too bad the dragon has never heard of a Trojan dwarf…

#47 - Artist Alley: At a comic book convention, a seedy comic book publisher sees himself depicted in a disturbing series of artist drawings.

#48 - Dead Zone: A yacht gets caught adrift in the dead zone in the Gulf of Mexico, trapped in an area of the sea that contains no life. What comes aboard the yacht from the depths of this dead zone in search of food cannot really be considered alive…

#49 - Cemetery Dance: A suicidal madman afraid to take his own life attempts to torment a devout Christian man into killing him.

#50 - The King Who Owned the World: A bored barbarian king demands he be brought a new challenger. But who can you find to battle a king who owns the world

Land of Fright™ terrorstories contained in Collection VI:

The Spine-Tinglers™ series
by Jack O'Donnell

I don't know who I am, or where I came from. All I know is that I can see things and hear things. I have no physical presence, yet I am somehow able to travel through space and time and witness untold events happening all around me. I suppose some of you will label me as a ghost, but that's not truly accurate as I have no recollection of ever being alive, no childhood memories, no remembrances of any traumatic life events that might be keeping me trapped in this world. Nor do I feel as if I am a manifestation of a dead person. I leave no shadowy trace. I am shapeless, formless. Don't get me wrong. Ghosts do exist, as I have seen them. I am just not one of them.

For the most part, all I can do is watch and listen and report back to you what I have seen and heard. I can enter a body and experience feelings and emotions, yet the owner of the body never feels my presence; I don't do this very often, as the feeling is unsettling and mostly unpleasant. Which again is odd in that I have no sense of a body, no sense of a brain, yet somehow I can still feel uncomfortable in certain situations. I do not know where this sense of feeling comes from, yet I can't deny it can affect me. I am as perplexed in trying to explain my current state of what could be called existence as I am sure you are in trying to comprehend it.

I seem to be drawn to those events that have a sinister side to them, a darkness. Perhaps it is my mission to shine some light on that darkness, to reveal the truth that is hidden in those dusky shadows. Perhaps I am here to warn you of what really exists in the world around you, make you a little more aware of the mysteries that often hide shrouded in the bliss of ignorance. I don't really know. All I know is that I am compelled to chronicle what I have observed, what I have heard, what I have felt, and share those experiences with you. Here are the latest stories I felt compelled to chronicle...

The Scarecrow - Spine-Tinglers™ #1

Beware what grows in the corn!

Hideous monsters borne of the blood of the Civil War follow the commands of a demonic scarecrow bent on preserving the sanctity of her crop.

Metamorphosis - Spine-Tinglers™ #2

Beware what lurks in Nektala's Tomb!

Archaeologists unearth the tomb of a mysterious Egyptian ruler and unwittingly discover a secret that threatens to transform all of humanity.

ABOUT JACK O'DONNELL

Jack grew up on Jack Kirby comics, Creature Features, Godzilla movies, Stephen King, Andre Norton, Edgar Rice Burroughs, Don Pendleton, and a smorgasbord of science fiction and fantasy books.

He is the co-producer and co-screenwriter of Stephen King's The Night Flier, based on Stephen King's story.

Visit Jack O'Donnell's author page on Amazon to see his other published works at: **www.amazon.com/Jack-ODonnell/e/B00P43NP00**.

Please also visit the ODONNELL BOOKS bookstore on Amazon to see all of the other books published by ODONNELL BOOKS available at: **www.amazon.com/odonnellbooks**.

If you enjoyed this book, or any of his other works, please take the time to leave a review. Your feedback is greatly appreciated!

Thanks for reading!